PHRONSIE AND THE CHILDREN. — *Page 21.*

PHRONSIE PEPPER

THE YOUNGEST OF THE "FIVE LITTLE PEPPERS"

BY

MARGARET SIDNEY

AUTHOR OF "FIVE LITTLE PEPPERS AND HOW THEY GREW," "FIVE LITTLE
PEPPERS MIDWAY," "FIVE LITTLE PEPPERS GROWN-UP"
"OLD CONCORD: HER HIGHWAYS AND BYWAYS"
"THE GOLDEN WEST," ETC., ETC.

ILLUSTRATED BY JESSIE McDERMOTT

BOSTON:

LOTHROP, LEE & SHEPARD CO.

    ❦   **PEPPER**   ❦

TRADE-MARK

Registered in U. S. Patent Office.

Copyright, 1897,

by

Lothrop Publishing Company.

Copyright, 1925, by Margaret M. Lothrop.

────────────

All rights reserved.

One Hundred and First Thousand

PRINTED IN U.S.A.

In Memoriam.

PREFACE.

As Phronsie Pepper was the only one of the "Five Little Peppers" who had not a chance to become "grown-up" in the three books that form the Pepper Library, it seemed (to judge by the expressions of those persons interested in this family) a little unfair not to give her that opportunity.

The author has had so many letters from the elders, as well as the children, presenting this view of the case, that she has been brought over to that opinion herself. And as Phronsie appeared to have something to say on her own account, that the public, ever kind and attentive to the Peppers, desired to hear, it was thought best to let her speak, to make her appearance as "grown-up," and then to draw the curtain over the "little brown house" and the "Five Little Peppers," never more to rise.

Nothing was farther from the mind of the au-

thor of the "Five Little Peppers" than a series
concerning them; for she did not naturally in-
cline to the extension of a book into other vol-
umes.   But the portrayal of the lives of the
Peppers seemed to be a necessity. They were
living, breathing realities to her; and when
pressed by many importunate readers to know
"more and more" about "Mamsie and Polly,
Ben, Joel, David, and Phronsie," it was only like
telling the stories in the twilight hour, of what
was so real and vital to their author, that it was
as if she were not speaking, but only the scribe
to jot it all down as it fell from the lips and
the lives of others.

And here let the author state, in answer to the
question so often asked her, "Did the Peppers
really live ? and *was* there any little brown house ?"
that the whole story is imaginative, existing only
in her mind ; although they always seemed so alive
to her, that she let them talk and move and act
from beginning to end without let or hindrance;
believing that Margaret Sidney's part was to
simply set down what the Peppers did and said,
without trying to make them do or say anything
in particular.

And now the closing volume, that shuts the door of the little brown house forever, takes the whole scene back to dear old Badgertown; and life begins over again in rollicking, merry, and home-y fashion; and the "Five Little Peppers," with their troops of friends old and young, control the book, and say and do and live, just as they like, without the meddlesome intervention of

THE AUTHOR.

CONTENTS.

1

CONTENTS.

LIST OF ILLUSTRATIONS.

5

PHRONSIE PEPPER.

CHAPTER I.

THE LITTLE BROWN HOUSE.

"O CHILDREN!" said Phronsie softly, "what are you doing?"

"They're pulling all the hair out of my mamsie's cushion," shouted King-Fisher, in a tone of anger; and, struggling with the two delinquents on the floor, he bestowed several smart pulls on the chubby shoulders bent over their task.

"Oh, oh!" cried Phronsie, dropping needle and scissors, and the little sheer lawn bit destined to adorn Mamsie's head, the lace trailing off by itself across the old kitchen floor, as she sprang to her feet. "How can you, King?"

"Stop pulling all the hair out of my Mamsie's cushion, Barby," screamed King-Fisher, very red in the face. "Look at that, now! I'll bite you, if you don't stop!"

9

"O King!" Phronsie seized his arm, as he began to set his white teeth on the little fat arm.

Barby sat still in the middle of the floor, both hands grasped tightly around the old calico cushion, which she huddled close to her small bosom. "Go 'way!" she commanded, her blue eyes flashing at him from her tangle of brown hair. "Go right 'way, bad, naughty boy!"

"I'll take care of him. There, now, see if you come biting round here, Mister King!" The other figure deserted the old hair cushion pulled out of the rocking-chair, and, throwing itself on the unsuspecting King, rolled over and over, pommelling and puffing furiously.

"O children, children!" cried Phronsie in great dismay. Just then the door opened, and in walked old Mr. King, bending his handsome white head to clear the doorway.

"Well — well — well! this is beautiful upon my word!" Then he burst out laughing.

"O Grandpapa!" exclaimed Phronsie, clasping her hands in distress, "this is so very dreadful! Do make them stop!"

"Nonsense! Let them alone," said the old gen-

tleman, in the midst of his laugh. "I don't doubt
King-Fisher has been putting on airs, and Polly's
boy is aching to take it out of him. That's right,
Elyot, give it to him! I dare say he deserves
it all, every bit."

"Grandpapa," begged Phronsie, hurrying up
to clasp his arm entreatingly, "do please make
them stop. They're in the little brown house,
Grandpapa; only just think, the little brown
house. *Please* make them stop!"

"To be sure," said old Mr. King, pulling himself out of his amusement, and wiping his face,
"that is a consideration. Come, now, boys, hold
up there; you must finish all this out-of-doors,
if you've got to."

"O Grandpapa!" interposed Phronsie, "please
tell them not to finish at all. Make them stop
always."

"Well, at any rate, you must stop now, this
minute; do you hear?" He stamped his shapely
foot, and the combatants ceased instantly, King,
in the sudden pause, finding himself at last on
top.

"I could have beaten him all to nothing," he
declared, puffing violently; "but he jumped whack

on me, and my arm got twisted under, and —
and " —

" Never mind the rest of it," said Grandpapa
coolly; " of course you'd have beaten if you could.
Well, Elyot, you did pretty good for a boy of
five."

" He was biting my sister," declared Elyot,
squaring up, with flushed cheeks, and clinching
his small fists.

" Oh — oh ! " cried Barby, who had held her
breath in delighted silence while the encounter
was in progress; and running up, her brown hair
flying away from her face, she presented a fat
arm for the old gentleman's inspection.

" I don't see any bite," he said, after a grave
scrutiny of it all over.

" Not yet," said Barby, shaking her brown
head wisely; " but it was coming — it truly was,
Grandpapa."

" Don't worry till your miseries do come, little woman; " he swung her up over his white
head, then put her on his shoulder.

" There Phronsie used to perch," he said, smiling over at the young girl.

" O Grandpapa, she's too big — why, she's

Aunt Phronsie, and she's most dreadful old," said Barby, leaning over to look at him.

"Well, she used to sit just where you are, Miss," repeated the old gentleman. "Now, you be sure you're always number two." He pinched her toes, making her squirm and squeal.

"What's numtwo?" she asked at length, all out of breath from play.

"Lucky you don't know," said the old gentleman, his mouth close to her ear; "well, it's just always after number one, and never gets in front. There, now, jump down, and help Phronsie patch it up with the boys." He put her on the floor, and went over to the corner, to sit down and view operations.

Phronsie, meanwhile, had a boy each side of her, both trying to get into her lap at once.

"It would just kill Mamsie," she said mournfully, "to think of you two boys behaving so, and she's only gone a week!"

There was an awful pause. The old gentleman over in the corner kept perfectly still; and Barby, finding all obstructions removed, placidly engaged in completing the destruction of Mother Fisher's cushion.

"And you promised her, King, you'd be a good boy, and be nice to the children."

"I — forgot," blurted out King, winking very fast, and not looking at Elyot. "I — I — did. Don't look so, Phronsie," he mumbled; and instantly after his head went over in his sister's lap, and he sobbed in her dress, "Don't write her, Phronsie — don't!"

"And to think," said Phronsie, gravely regarding Elyot, "that you should fly at him, when he only wanted to protect Mamsie's dear old cushion. O Elyot! I am so surprised .at you for pulling it to pieces."

"I only wanted to see inside it; you said Mamsie and Uncle Ben made a Santa Claus wig of it once; I was going to put it right back," said Elyot stoutly. Yet he looked at the ceiling diagonally, not trusting himself a glance into Phronsie's brown eyes. "Say, you don't suppose Grandmamsie will know?" he asked suddenly.

"I suppose I must tell Mamsie everything," said Phronsie soberly. "I promised to, you know. And, besides, we always have."

Elyot shivered all over his small frame, while

King howled, and burrowed deeper than ever in
Phronsie's lap.

"But I can tell her how sorry you two boys
are," Phronsie went on, "and that you never,

"There! I got it all out alone by myself," said Barby.

never will do such a naughty thing again; that
is, if you never will, boys."

"Oh, we never will!" they both protested over
and over; and King came up out of his shelter,

and wiped his eyes, and the two put their arms around each other, and made up splendidly; then turned to hear Barby say, "There, I got it all out alone by myself;" and there was the hair out of Mamsie's cushion all sprawled over the floor.

While the children were picking this up, and crowding it back into the big calico cover, Phronsie making Elyot do the best part of the work, as he was older, and had helped Barby along, King working vigorously, as penance, old Mr. King called, "Now, Phronsie, I want you, as those youngsters seem to be straightened out;" and she had gone and sat on his knee, her usual place in a conference.

"Well, I've just done such a good stroke of work, child," he said complacently, pulling softly the golden waves of hair that lay over her cheek.

"What, Grandpapa?" she asked, as he seemed to wait her reply.

"Yes, such a good piece of work," he ran on. Then he chuckled, well pleased. "You must know, Phronsie," for he was determined to tell it in a way to suit himself, "that I was sitting on the back veranda — Polly's gone to town to-day, you know."

" Yes, Grandpapa."

" Well, and the house was quiet, thanks to you and the little brown house, and I had a chance to read the morning paper in peace." This he said, unconscious of the fact that every one knew quite well he courted the presence of the children on any and every occasion. " Well, I had considerable to read; the news, strange to say, is very good, really very good to-day, so it took me quite a long time." He forgot to mention that he had lost himself a half-hour or so in a nap; these occurrences were never to be commented on in the family. " And I was turning the paper — it's abominable that editors mix things up so; it's eternally turning and returning the sheet, to find what you want. It's very hard, Phronsie, when we pay such prices for articles, that we cannot have them to suit us, child."

" Yes, Grandpapa," said Phronsie patiently.

" Well, don't look at those youngsters, Phronsie; they're all right now. They won't fight any more to-day."

"O Grandpapa!"

"I mean it, child. Well, I was turning that contemptible paper for about the fiftieth time, — I wanted to read Brinkerhoff's editorial, — when I caught sight of a figure making around the lawn to the front veranda. Thinks I, 'that looks wonderfully like Roslyn May.'"

The pink glow in Phronsie's round cheek went suddenly out.

"And so it was, as sure as you're here on my knee." He had her hand in both of his, and was affectionately pressing it. "Yes, Phronsie, there was that fellow. So I jumped up, and told Johnson to send him around to me; and he came."

Old Mr. King drew a long breath of pleased reminiscence. Phronsie sat quite still, the afternoon sunlight that streamed through the western window glinting her yellow hair. Her hands lay in Grandpapa's, and her eyes never wavered from his face. But she said nothing.

"You don't ask me anything, Phronsie," said the old gentleman at last. "Hey, child?" pinching her ear.

"No, Grandpapa, because you will tell me yourself."

"And so I will; you are a good girl not to badger me with questions. Well, he came about the same thing, Phronsie, — wanted to see you, and all that. But I couldn't allow it, of course; for, if I did, the next thing, you would be worried to death by his teasing. And that's all out of the question. Besides being decidedly unpleasant for you, it would kill me."

"Would it, Grandpapa?" Phronsie leaned forward suddenly, and held him with her brown eyes.

"Not a shadow of doubt," he answered promptly; "I shouldn't live a month if you went off and got married, Phronsie."

"I wouldn't go off and get married, Grandpapa!" exclaimed Phronsie. "I could stay with you then; didn't Roslyn say we could, and you would always go with us if we went away? O Grandpapa, you didn't think I would ever leave you!" She threw her arms around his neck, and clung to him convulsively.

"Yes, yes, that's right," said the old gentleman, immensely pleased, and patting her on the back as if she were a child of three; "but you see this is nothing to the point, Phronsie, nothing at all." Then he went on testily, "You'd belong to somebody else besides me, and that would be the same as being a thousand miles away. And as long as I'm sure you don't love him, Phronsie," — which he had found out by taking care not to ask her, — "why, I've done just the very best thing for you, to send him away about his business."

"Did he ask to see me?" Phronsie sat up quite straight now, and waited quietly for the answer.

"Why, of course he did; but I knew it would only trouble you to see him."

"O Grandpapa — just one little minute — I wouldn't have let him stay long. Couldn't you have sent him over here just for one minute?"

"Nonsense! You're so tender of his feelings, it would only have been hard for you. No, I thank my stars, Phronsie, I saved you from all this trouble. What you would do, child, if it were not for your old Granddaddy, I'm sure I don't know. Well, he's gone, and I told him never to come back again with that errand in view; and I only hope to goodness it's the last time I shall be so worried by him."

"There, we've got the hair all in," announced King triumphantly, rushing up, followed by the other two, Barby wiping her grimy little hands in great satisfaction over her white apron. "Now please say we've been good boys, and " —

"And a good girl," chimed in Barby, flying after with red cheeks.

"And sew up the old cushion," begged Elyot. This would be almost as good fun as the pulling it open had been, to see Phronsie sewing it tight, and she could tell them stories meanwhile.

"Let the cushion wait," began Mr. King.

"But, Grandpapa, the hair may get spilled out again," said Phronsie gently, and getting off from his knee. "I really think I ought to do it now, Grandpapa dear."

"Yes — yes," cried all the children, hopping up and down; "do it now — do it now, Phronsie."

So Phronsie found her thimble and scissors once more, and got out the coarse brown thread from her little sewing-bag, and sewed the big seam in the old calico cushion fast again, the children taking turns in poking the wisps of hair in the crevice.

"Now tell all what you used to do when you

lived here — just here," demanded Elyot, patting the old floor with his hand, "every single thing, Phronsie;" for the children, except on rare occasions, never called her "Aunt." "Don't leave out anything you did in the little brown house. Now begin."

"O Elyot," said Phronsie, "I couldn't tell it all if I tried ever so hard."

"Polly tells the best stories," said King, pushing and picking the hair into place in the last corner.

"So she does," said Phronsie; "there now, King-Fisher, that's all you can do. Look out; my needle is coming up there," as King with a final pull settled the last little wisp into place.

"Let me — let me," begged Barby, thrusting her little hand in. "I want to do it last. Let me, King."

"No," said King stoutly, hanging to the corner. "I shall; it's my mother's cushion."

"O King," began Phronsie gently, "Mamsie would like it better if you let Barby do it. She's so little."

"She's always pushing, just the same," said King stoutly, "as if she was big folks."

"Well, if you want to please Mamsie, you'll let her do it," went on Phronsie, pausing with needle in mid-air. "Hurry, now, children; I can't wait any longer."

"You may, Barby," declared King, relinquishing with a mighty effort the pinched-up corner. "There, go ahead," and he winked fast at her great satisfaction while she pushed and poked the wisps in with her fat little finger, humming contentedly meanwhile.

Phronsie flashed a smile over at King. "Now, children," she said, "you must know we were very poor in those days, and"—

"What is poor?" asked Barby, stopping singing.

"I know," said Elyot; "it's wearing rags like the ashman. Oh, I wish I could!"

"Oh, no!" cried Phronsie in horror; "that isn't poor; that's shiftless, Mamsie always used to say. Oh, we were just as nice! Well, you can't think, children, how spick and span everything was!"

"What's spick 'n' span?" demanded Barby.

"Make her stop," cried Elyot crossly; "we shall never hear all about it if she keeps asking questions every minute. Now go on, Phronsie."

"Well," said Phronsie, "now that corner's all done beautifully, Barby; take care, or I shall prick your finger. Why, Polly would scrub and scrub the floor and the table, till I used to try to see my face in them, they were so bright."

"They're bright now," declared both the boys, jumping off to investigate. Barby pushed her hair back from her round cheeks, and leaned over. "I don't see my face, Phronsie," she exclaimed.

"No, and I couldn't see mine; but I always tried to, for Polly kept them so bright, and one day I remember I was scrubbing Seraphina, and " —

"Who's Seraphina?" burst in Barby, coming back to crouch at Phronsie's feet.

"Ow! Be still!" cried Elyot, with a small pinch.

"Seraphina was my very first doll, the only child I ever had until Grandpapa gave me all the rest," Phronsie sent a smile over to the old gentleman in the corner, "and she's in Mamsie's big bureau in the bedroom now."

"I'm going to see," declared all three children at once, hopping up.

"Oh, no! you mustn't," said Phronsie; "not till this cushion is done. Then, if you're very good, I'll show her to you."

"We'll be just as good," they all cried, "as we can be," and running back to sit down on the floor again at her feet. "Do go on," said Elyot.

"You see, I wanted Seraphina to be just as nice as Polly kept things; and so I was scrubbing her with soap and water one day, when Polly called out, 'O Phronsie! the big dog's out here that scared the naughty organ-man; and the boy;' and before she could wipe my hands and my face, for you see I'd got the soap all over me too, I ran to see them, and Jasper kissed me, and got the soft soap all in his mouth."

"Ugh!" cried King, with a grimace.

"Yes, that's just the way Japser looked, and that's what he said too!" said Phronsie, going on with the recital.

"Who was Japser?" demanded Barby.

"Why, he was our Popsie," said Elyot, who had heard the story many times. "Now do stop talking, Barby. Well, go on," he begged, turning back to Phronsie,

"And I couldn't say Jasper," said Phronsie, "and then sometimes we called him Jappy."

"How funny!" laughed all three. "Oh, goody! here comes Mr. Tisbett," howled King in a sudden rapture, lifting his head to see the top of the

"Oh, goody! here comes Mr. Tisbett," howled King.

old stage through the window. "Why, he's stopping here! He's stopping here!" and, tumbling over the other two, King found his feet, and pranced off over the big flat doorstone, and down

the path, Elyot and Barby flying after, to see
Mr. Tisbett open the stage door with a, " Here
you be, ma'am, and the boy too."

" Grandpapa," cried Phronsie, taking one look
out of the window, "it's Mrs. Fargo and Johnny!"

"The mercy it is!" exclaimed the old gentleman ruefully. " Well, good-by, Phronsie, to any
sort of peace. now that boy's come!"

CHAPTER II.

A BADGERTOWN EVENING.

"BOOKS ! I've a fine packet for you to-night, Polly." Jasper's eyes glowed. Polly ran up to meet him.

" O Mamsie ! let me take the books — let me ! " Elyot thrust in his small figure between them, and tugged at the parcel.

" You take yourself off, young man," said his father. " Now, Polly, hold your arms."

" Oh, what richness ! " sighed Polly ecstatically, " as Alexia would say ; " and, clasping her parcel closely, she sank into a big chair, and examined her treasure. " O Jasper ! " she cried, isn't it just magnificent to be a publisher's wife ! "

Jasper laughed, and swung his boy up to his broad shoulder.

" I thought you'd like them, Polly," he said with great satisfaction, looking at her.

"Like them!" repeated Polly in a glow. Then she sprang to her feet, tossed the whole pile into the easy-chair, and ran up to her husband, putting her hand within his arm. "But where is the bag, Jasper?" she asked suddenly.

"Oh, what richness!" sighed Polly.

"Well, the fact of it is, Polly," said Jasper slowly, "I left the bag at the office. Just for this night," he added, as he saw her face.

"Why, Jasper?" asked Polly quickly, the color dropping out of her cheek.

"Well, the truth is, I was afraid," began Jasper.

"Oh! go on, and dance me up and down, Daddy," screamed Elyot, beating his heels with all his might.

Polly laid her hand on the small feet. "No, no, dear; Mamsie's going to talk now. Why, Jasper?" she asked again. This time she stood quite still, and looked at him.

Jasper swung his boy lightly to the ground. "Off with you!" he cried with a laugh, and Elyot scuttled away. "Now, Polly," as he put his arm around her, and drew her to a seat, "the fact is, I thought you wouldn't sit down and go over those books to-night if I brought out the bag."

"And so I wouldn't," declared Polly. "Of course not, with the dear old bag waiting. How could I?"

"That's just it," said Jasper; "and it's not fair for me to bring the bag, with those waiting, either;" he nodded over at the untied packet and the new books scattered about. "You ought to

have at least one go at them before being tied
down to business matters."

Polly broke loose from him, and ran over to
the easy-chair. "And did you think I would so
much as look at these once?" she cried, her face
flushing up to the brown waves. "Oh! oh! I
just detest them now." She looked down at the
pile with the same face that she carried in the
little brown house when the old stove burned
Mamsie's birthday cake.

"But, Polly," said Jasper, hurrying over to
comfort her, "you see it's just this way. I'm
tying you down too much to business detail, and
you ought to be enjoying yourself more, dear."

"And don't you suppose, Jasper," cried Polly,
turning on his troubled face a radiant one, "that
lovely old bag is just the dearest dear in all the
world next to you and the children? Oh, say
you will never leave it again! Do say so, Jasper;" she clung to him.

"I am so afraid I'm making your life too full
of care, Polly," said Jasper gravely, "to bring
the bag out every night. And this evening we
might go over the new books, and have a break
in the routine for once."

"And let you work over all your papers alone Jasper," cried Polly, aghast. "O Jasper!"

"Dance me up and down, daddy!" screamed Elyot.

"I can find time to do them, dear; don't worry. And it would be better for you."

"And indeed it would be the worst thing in

all this world, dear," protested Polly, shaking her brown head. "I should be so dismal, Jasper, you can't think, without our lovely time working together after dinner. When the bag is done, then we'll play and read, and do all sorts of things. But that first hour is the best of the whole evening, Jasper; it truly is."

"I'm sure I love it," cried Jasper, with kindling eyes; "I never could do it so well without you, nor in half the time, Polly."

"Well, then you must just promise you'll never leave the bag back in the office," said Polly, laughing. "Promise now, Jasper."

"I suppose I must," said Jasper, laughing too. "Here come Alexia and Pickering," looking down the carriage drive.

"We've come out to dinner, Polly, if you want us," said Alexia, hurrying in, Pickering's tall figure following. "Goodness me! how you can live so far out of town, I don't see!"

"So you say every time I chance to meet you, Alexia" said Jasper.

"Yes, and that's the reason she's decided to try it herself," said Pickering with a drawl.

"O Alexia!" Polly gave her a small hug, as

she helped her off with her things, "are you really coming to Badgertown? Oh, how nice!"

"Pickering is always springing things on me, and telling everything I say," said Alexia, trying to send a cross grimace over at her husband, but ending with a short laugh instead, "and just because I said I wanted to have a house near you, Polly, he's got it into his head I'm coming out here to live."

Pickering indulged in a long laugh.

"And I think it's a shame," declared Alexia, with a very injured face, "to have one's husband go about, and spoil all one's surprise parties — so there!"

"Then you really do mean to come to Badgertown to live, Alexia?" cried Polly with sparkling eyes. "Oh, you dear! how perfectly delightful!"

"I suppose I'll have to, Polly," said Alexia, "as I must be just as near you as I can get. But I do think Badgertown is utterly horrid, and you ought to be ashamed to live out here so far. I'm dying to have that cunning little yellow house on the hill, Polly," she broke off suddenly, "with the barberry bushes in front, and we've

come out here to see it after dinner. Now you
know it all; only I was going to ask you to go
out and take a walk, and then bring you up there
with a flourish, and give you a grand surprise.
And now it's as tame as tame can be." She
shook her finger at Pickering, who bore it like a
veteran.

"How's baby?" asked Polly, when the wraps
were off, and they were all seated on the long
veranda for a talk.

"He's the dearest little rat you ever saw,"
said Alexia, who couldn't forgive her boy for not
being a girl, whom she could call Polly. "He's
two teeth, and four more coming."

"Alexia always counts those teeth that are
coming with so much gusto," said Pickering.

"And why shouldn't I?" cried Alexia. "It
would be perfectly horrid if he stopped with two
teeth; you know it would yourself, Pickering.
And to-day, Polly Pepper, you can't think" —

"I decidedly object to having my wife called
Polly Pepper," said Jasper, trying to get on a
grave look. "Polly Pepper King is all right.
But be sure to put on the King."

"Oh! we girls shall never call her anything

else but Polly Pepper — never in all this world, Jasper," said Alexia carelessly. " Well, you tell what baby did to-day, Pickering. I'm quite tired out with all my trial of getting here, and the disappointment of my surprise spoiled." She leaned back in the rattan chair, and played with her rings.

" Our child," said Pickering solemnly, " developed a most astonishing mental power this morning, and actually uttered two consecutive syllables like this, ' Ar-goo! '"

" So did Elyot at the same tender age," observed Jasper, "and Barby too, I believe."

"Now, you just be quiet, Pickering!" Alexia cried, starting forward; "and aren't you ashamed, Jasper, to help him on? Baby actually said the most beautiful words; he really and truly did. And that's what I wanted to come out for to-night, Polly, as much as to look at the house, to tell you that baby's talking; and he's only eight months old! Think of that, now!"

" I met Roslyn May down town to-day," said Pickering when the laugh had subsided.

" Did you!" exclaimed Jasper.

Polly stopped laughing at one of Alexia's sallies, and met her husband's eyes. His look said, "Strange he did not come out here."

"Yes; he just got in day before yesterday, he told me, from England. I couldn't understand what he came over for."

"He is going to stay some time, I suppose," said Jasper, "now he's here."

"No, he was on the way to the steamer, when we ran across each other on Broadway, — sailed to-day on the Cunarder; that is, he said he was going to."

"He was going right back!" exclaimed Polly; and going over to Jasper's side, she lay her hand on his. "What do you mean, Pickering?"

"It's just so, Polly," said Pickering, feeling awfully that he must make the sad droop in her eyes, and the color go out of her face.

"He probably is coming back soon — he may have been cabled back — a dozen things may have happened," said Jasper. "Don't feel so badly, dear."

"Well, Phronsie must never know he has been over," said Polly. "Promise, Alexia, you never 'll tell her! You won't, dear, will you?" She ran over and put her arms around Alexia.

"Horses won't drag it out of me," declared Alexia. "I won't ever mention Roslyn May to"—

"Hush!—hush! here she comes," warned Polly frantically, pinching Alexia's arm to make her stop.

"Oh, mercy! Well, I didn't say anything," said Alexia.

Phronsie came around the veranda corner in her soft white gown. "We're going to have a candy party to-night," she said.

"And a peanut party," cried the children at her heels, as they scurried over the veranda steps. "Tell it all, Phronsie; tell it all."

"And you're just in time, Alexia and Pickering," said Phronsie, with a smile, "to come over to the little brown house after dinner, to the party."

"And you've got to pull candy with me, Mrs. Dodge," declared Elyot, who just adored her, racing up to possess himself of her long white fingers, glittering with rings.

"Oh, mercy me! I can't. Why, I've on my best dress," she said, to tease him.

"Mamsie will let you have one of her

aprons," he cried, "or my nice Mrs. Higby will.
I'll go and ask her."

"No, I'm going to; Mrs. Higby will let me
have the aprons," shouted Barby, turning her
back on her father, in whose lap she had thrown
herself, and rushing after him.

"We're all in for it, I see," said Pickering.
"Well, King, you're my boy, seeing the others
have got champions. What do you want? I'll
see you through this candy scrape."

"I'd rather have my brother Jasper," said
King, not over politely, "but I'll take you."

"O King!" remonstrated Phronsie gently.

"Let him alone, Phronsie," said Pickering.
"King is delicious when unadulterated. Well,
my boy, so I'll consider myself engaged to you
for this evening at the party."

"All right," said King coolly.

"And Mrs. Higby says we can have all the
aprons we want," announced Elyot, rushing back.

"And she'll boil the candy while we're at
dinner," piped Barby, tumbling after.

"This knocks your pretty plan of gazing at
the yellow house, sky-high, Alexia," whispered
Pickering, under cover of the noise.

"No, it doesn't," she retorted. "We'll go afterward, when the children are abed. It's moonlight, and we can see it just as well."

"Think of choosing a house by moonlight!" laughed Pickering.

"Just as well as to choose it by sunlight, as long as we can see," said Alexia, jingling the house-key they had secured from the agent on the way up. "Yes; we'll have quite time before we take the train home."

"Oh, you can't go home to-night!" cried Polly and Jasper together. "The idea! with a party and house-hunting on your hands. Stay over, Alexia."

"I must be in town at eight in the morning," said Pickering, getting out of his chair to stretch his long legs and look at the hills. "Alexia can stay if she wants to."

"As if I could or would, when my husband can't," she cried. "And there's that blessed child left all alone!"

"But since he's learned to converse," said Pickering, "he can ask for his rations. So he's not to be considered."

"Well, I'm perfectly shocked!" declared Alexia. "And I shall go home with you in the late train."

Oh, the candy frolic of that night! Everybody had such a glorious time that the little old kitchen rang with the jollity that flowed over, taking in all Primrose Lane, and down as far as "Grandma Bascom's" little cottage. "Grandma" now had to lie abed with her rheumatism; but Polly and Jasper found time to slip away a bit in the midst of the festivities and carry her a little dish of the candy before the nuts were put in, for "Grandma" didn't like nuts, and she did like molasses candy. And Polly carried a few other things in a small basket on her arm.

"For I never shall forget, Jasper," she said as they hurried along, "how good Grandma was the day Phronsie hurt her toe. Oh, that horrible old ' receet ' of Mirandy's wedding-cake! I thought it would kill me to wait for it. Dear, dear," laughed Polly, "how we do remember, don't we, Jasper, things we used to do when we were children ? "

"I'm sure I never want to forget what we did in the little brown house," said Jasper. "Well, Grandma was always good, I remember, bringing

raisins and all that. Now, Polly, we must tell
her every single bit of Joel's last letter; for
she'll question us up just as closely, you may be
sure."

"We've come out to dinner, Polly," said Alexia.

"I know it," said Polly, hanging to his arm;
"and Joel thinks as much of Grandma as she
does of him. It's so nice of him, Jappy, isn't
it?"

"Oh, yes, indeed!" said Jasper, nodding briskly;

" for no matter how tired Joe is, — and he must
get awfully used up sometimes, Polly, with that
big parish of his, — he's always doing something
for her. It was fine for him to buy her that big
easy-chair with the first money he had saved up
after he paid father back for his education."

" Dear, beautiful old Joel!" cried Polly, with
shining eyes.

" How upset father was," exclaimed Jasper, in
a reminiscent mood, " when Joe made him take
that money back. I declare, Polly, I never saw
him so upset in all my life!"

" It was right for Joel to make him," said
Polly stoutly.

" Yes, I know it. But Father had so set his
mind on doing it for Joe."

" But Joey couldn't take it to keep," declared
Polly. " You know he really couldn't, Jasper."

" Of course not," said Jasper quickly. " But
what we should have done without Phronsie to
make the peace between them, I don't know.
Well, here we are."

" See here," cried Alexia, Mrs. Higby's red
plaid apron working all up her long figure, as

she had tied it by the strings around her neck, "if somebody doesn't go over and call Polly Pepper home, why I'll just go myself." She brandished the big wooden spoon, a few drops of molasses trailing off over the floor.

"I suppose that is meant for me," said Pickering, placidly eating the big piece he ought to have been pulling, "as I'm the only one she orders round."

"Horrors!" cried Alexia, glancing along the tip of the spoon, "just see the mischief I've done! Now the Peppers won't ever let me in this kitchen again."

"I'll wipe it up," said Elyot, running over to her, with sticky hands, and face streaked with molasses.

"Oh!" exclaimed Alexia with a grimace, and edging away. "Oh, my goodness, me! and see my husband eating candy like a little pig, and me in this dreadful scrape."

"I wish I was your husband," said little Elyot, getting down on his knees; and, seizing the first thing he could find, which proved to be a fine damask napkin, he began to vigorously mop the floor.

"Mercy me! what have you got?" cried Alexia, her sharp eyes peering at him. "Oh! give it to me." She seized it from his hand, and threw down the spoon. "Come along, do," and she hauled him out into the entry. "It's one of Polly Pepper's bestest napkins; we brought it over on the cake-plate. Now we must just douse it into a pail of water; but goodness knows where that is."

"Hoh!" said Elyot, "I know where there's one, just as easy as not. Come on."

It was now his turn to haul Alexia, and he did it so successfully that she was soon over the little steps, and in the "Provision Room."

"If ever I'm thankful," she sighed gratefully, "it is to see that sticky mess come out," when Elyot had delightedly plunged the napkin into a pail of water standing in the corner. "Oh, my goodness me! if it had spoiled that; and it's one of her great big embroidered K's, too! Well, come on; we must run back, or the whole troop of them will be after us. Wring it out and hang it up, do! Now come on."

She picked up her skirts, and skipped over the steps, Elyot scuttling after, in time to hear Pickering say, "Evidently my wife doesn't intend to take the train with me, for she's disappeared."

"Somebody take off this!"

"I haven't disappeared at all; I'm here," cried Alexia at his elbow. "The idea! Why,

I'm going to look at the house on the hill; but 'tisn't time yet," drawing a long breath.

"Going to look at the house on the hill! Well, I guess you won't to-night," said Pickering, taking out his watch; "it's just a quarter of ten, and the train leaves at ten. So, good-by, Alexia; you've got to stay all night."

"Oh, I can't — I won't!" cried Alexia. "Oh, dear! somebody take off this horrible old apron," wildly twisting this way and that.

"I will — I will," cried little Elyot, fumbling at the strings.

"Oh, dear — dear!" wailed Alexia, "my face is all stuck up; somebody — where's Mrs. Higby? Oh, somebody wash it, please!" She was rushing around after her bonnet now, Elyot hanging to the apron-strings valiantly, this process tying them tighter than ever at each step.

"Here, hold on, can't you!" roared Pickering. "You'll never get her undone at that rate."

"Yes, I will, too," cried Elyot, tugging away, and tumbling against Mrs. Higby with a towel, wet at one end, in her hand.

"Oh, dear, dear! and that blessed child at home alone," cried Alexia. "Mercy! here's my

best bonnet down by the coal-scoop. Well, as
long as I've got anything to put on my head I
suppose I should be thankful. Oh, dear! where's
that wet towel? Do cut the strings of this horrible old apron — Oh, dear! what shall I do!"
She whirled around on them all, as the door
opened, and in ran Polly and Jasper, with glowing cheeks.

"For goodness sake, Alexia!" began Polly.

"Whew! Is it a menagerie?" cried Jasper.

"Well, it's bad enough to go visiting, and have
your friends run off to see horrible old women,"
said Alexia, whirling more than ever, "without
coming back to laugh at one's misery. Oh,
that's a dear, Mrs. Higby!" as that good lady's
scissors clicked, and set her free. "I'll bring
you out a new pair of strings next time I come.
Come on, Pickering — good-by, everybody;" and
she was out and running down the path by the
time he found his hat.

"Oh dear!" and back she came again, "I forgot my face; it's all stuck up. Do, somebody,
wash this molasses off." And Polly gave her a
dab with the wet towel, and a little kiss at the
same time.

"You didn't wash it in the right place," grumbled Alexia, running off again; "it was the other cheek. "Oh dear, dear! Come on, Pickering; we shall lose the train."

CHAPTER III.

JOHNNY.

"WHAT a pity that Johnny couldn't come to the candy party," sighed Phronsie the next day, looking over at the little brown house across the lane, which presented the same serene appearance, as if such jovial affairs had not been; "but I suppose Mrs. Fargo knew best, and he really was too tired, as they'd just come."

"Mrs. Fargo surely does know best," said Polly, stopping long enough in her trial of a very difficult passage in the sonata to fling this over her shoulder to Phronsie; "for you know, Phronsie, Johnny is just awful when he's tired out."

"Yes; I know," said Phronsie, with another sigh, "but then he's Johnny, you know, Polly."

"And the dearest dear of a Johnny too!" cried Polly warmly, going on with her practising. "O Phronsie, supposing I *shouldn't* play this —

good!" She stopped suddenly, and leaned both hands on the music-rest at the dreadful thought.

Phronsie stopped looking over the children's books on the table, and, setting them straight, came over to her side.

"You can't make a mistake," she breathed confidently. "Why, Polly, you play it beautifully!"

"But I may," broke in Polly recklessly. "Oh, I may, Phronsie! And then, oh, dear! I could never hold my head up in all this world. It would be so very dreadful for Jasper and the children, for me not to play it as it ought to be."

Phronsie leaned over Polly's shoulder, and put two soft arms around her neck. "You will play it good, Polly," she declared; "and Mamsie would say, — I know she would, — that you're not to think of what you'll do at the time, till the time comes."

"You blessed child!" cried Polly, whirling around on the music-stool. "O Phronsie! you're just such a comfort as you were that day when Grandpapa brought you and put you in my arms, when I broke down practising, and I'd almost made up my mind to go home. Now, then, I'll just stop worrying, and play ahead."

And she sat up straight, and flashed all the brilliant passages over again, Phronsie standing quite still to watch Polly's fingers flying up and down.

But, notwithstanding all Phronsie's comfort, Polly knew that she would have to give hard and constant work to make this, the supreme effort of her life thus far in a musical way, a success. It was the first time that anybody outside of the highest professional lines had been asked to play with the Symphony Orchestra; and when this urgent request had been laid before Polly, she had said, " Oh, no ! I cannot play well enough."

But Mrs. Jasper King's reputation as a pianist had gone farther than Polly knew. A request came, signed by a long list of people whose names were high in an artistic sense, fortified by the best citizens of the good old town of Berton, — itself a guaranty of anything in that line, for was it not the home of the Symphony ? When this came, and Polly saw Jasper's eyes, she gave a little gasp. " I will, dear, if you think best," she said, looking at no one but him.

" It's just as you say, Polly," Jasper had answered. But his eyes shone, and he instinctively straightened up with pride. And when she had said, " O Jasper ! if you think I can, I'll do it," — " I know you can, Polly," Jasper had declared, and Polly had said " Yes," and great delight reigned everywhere ; and Grandpapa had patted her head, and said, " Well done, Polly ! To think of all those hard hours of practice in the old days turning out like this ; " and Mamsie had smiled at her in a way that only Mamsie could smile. And Polly and Jasper had hurried off to Berton the next morning, Jasper swinging the little publishing-bag, on the way to the train, with a jubilant hand ; and in the lapse of the hard working hours, when things eased up a bit, he had said to Mr. Marlowe (for it was Marlowe & King now, in bright gilt letters over the big door), " I am going with my wife to select the music," for Polly was a prime favorite with Mr. Marlowe, and everything was told to him.

And Jasper and Polly went to the music-store, and ransacked the shelves, and tried various selections, for Polly was to play what she liked ;

and after the piece was picked out, then the two went to luncheon at the cunning little restaurant on a side street, nice and quiet, where they could talk it all over.

But sometimes, when Polly was all alone in the big music-room opening on the side veranda, she trembled all over at the terrible responsibility she had taken upon herself. It seemed so very much worse to fail now that she bore Jasper's honored name, than if she were only unknown and simple "Polly Pepper." And to-day she could not help showing this dismay to Phronsie.

"But Mamsie would say so," repeated Polly over and over to herself bravely, "just what Phronsie did." And then at it she would fly harder than ever. And every evening after the "publishing-bag" had been looked over in Jasper's and Polly's little den, and its contents sorted and attended to for the morrow, Jasper would always say, "Now, Polly, for the music;" and Polly would fly to the piano, while he drew up a big easy-chair to her side, to settle into it restfully; and the others would hurry in at the first note, and then Polly's concert would begin. And every night she knew she played it a little

bit better, and her cheeks glowed, and her heart
took comfort.

Phronsie put away the little sewing-bag as
soon as Polly finished practising this morning,

Tying on her big garden hat, Phronsie went across the road.

and hung it on its hook over Grandpapa's newspaper rack, — for she always sat and sewed in
the music-room mornings when Polly practised,
generally making sails for the boys, just as Polly
had done years ago, or clothes for Barby's dolls,

— and tying on her big garden hat, she went over across the road, and down around the corner, to the big house where Mrs. Fargo and Johnny had come to board for the summer, arriving a week earlier than they intended, as it was warm at home, and Mrs. Fargo watched jealously over Johnny's health.

"It does seem so very nice to have you here, dear Mrs. Fargo," she said, coming upon that lady in one of her big square rooms. For Mrs. Fargo had taken the whole upper floor of the house, and was in the depths of the misery of unpacking the huge trunks with which the rooms and hall seemed to be full, the maid busy as a bee in the process, while Johnny was under foot every other minute in a way terrible to behold. "And now I'm going to help." She laid aside her big hat on the bed.

"O Phronsie!" cried Mrs. Fargo, turning a pink, distressed face to her, "it's perfectly lovely to see you; but you're not going to work, dear. It's bad enough for me. Joanna, the nails aren't out of that box of books. You'll have to go down, and tell Mr. Brown to come and draw them."

"I'll draw them," cried Johnny, springing out from behind a trunk he was trying with all his might to move. "I've got my own hammer; yes, sir-ee! Now get out of the way; I'm coming."

"O Johnny! you can't," remonstrated Mrs. Fargo quickly. "You're not big enough; it needs a strong man."

"I'm 'most a man," said Johnny, twitching away from her. "I'm going to do it."

"But your hammer is in the box of your playthings," said Mrs. Fargo, glad to remember this.

"I don't care; I'll get Mr. Brown's, then," declared Johnny, prancing off.

"Oh, dear me! Phronsie, do stop that boy," begged Mrs. Fargo, tired and distressed.

"Johnny," called Phronsie softly. She did not offer to go after him. "Come here, dear."

"Am going for Mr. Brown's hammer," said Johnny, edging off.

"I want you, dear."

"Am going for Mr. Brown's hammer." Yet he came back. "What you want?"

"I'm going to take you over with me, if your mamma says so, to our house; and if you're very good, Johnny, you shall ride on the donkey. May I take him, Mrs. Fargo?"

"Oh, if you only will!" breathed Mrs. Fargo thankfully.

"I don't want any old hammer!" screamed Johnny in a transport; "the donkey's a good deal gooder," scrambling down the stairs.

"And I'll send Mr. Brown up to open the box," said Phronsie, tying on her hat, and going after him.

But she didn't get Johnny over to the donkey, after all; for, just as she had seen Mr. Brown on his way up-stairs to open the box, some one ran up the steps, two at a time, with, "O Phronsie, I've a day off!" most joyfully.

"Why, I don't see how, Dick," said Phronsie, looking at him from under her big hat.

"Never mind. I have it, anyhow; tell you later. Now for some fun! That chap here?" looking suddenly at Johnny, who now began at the bottom of the steps to howl to Phronsie to hurry for the donkey.

"Yes; they came a week sooner than they expected," said Phronsie. "They got here yesterday."

"Botheration! Well, now, Phronsie, let the boy alone. I'm only here for a day, you know. He's all right if turned out in the dirt to play. I want you to go to drive."

"I promised him he should ride on the donkey," said Phronsie. "I had to, for his mother and Joanna have all the unpacking to do. And he must, Dick."

"Hand him over to me, then," said Dick. "I'll give him a donkey-treat, Phronsie."

"Oh, thank you, Dick; and then I can help Mrs. Fargo," turning back to the door.

"See, here," cried Dick; "I'm doing this to help you out of it. Now, you've got to go to drive with me afterward, Phronsie." He stopped with his foot on the upper step, and looked at her. "Grandpapa said I might try the new pair next time I came out. Will you?"

"We can take Johnny," said Phronsie, pausing a bit. "Yes, Dick, I'll go."

"Bother him for a nuisance!" growled Dick.

But as this was all that he could get from Phronsie, he hurried off, and overtook Johnny trying to get on by himself to the donkey's back, where he peacefully browsed in the paddock.

"Hold on there!" roared Dick at him, as only a college boy can roar. But Johnny was in no mind to hold on to anything but the donkey. This he did so effectually, sticking his toes into the sides of the animal, that the donkey at last sent out a hind foot. Away went Johnny, half

"Johnny! open your eyes," cried Dick.

across the field, it seemed to Dick, hurrying up; and then he lay still as a stone.

"Oh, dear!" cried Dick, in the greatest distress. "Here, Johnny, open your eyes," kneeling down beside him on the grass. "Come, get up, and stop shamming;" for there was a dreadful feeling at Dick's heart, that, if he didn't keep joking about it, Johnny would be found to be hurt.

But Johnny wouldn't get up, and he wouldn't open his eyes; so Dick was forced to pick him up, the donkey, finding that he incommoded no one by running away, now trotting up to stare at the little figure on the grass. "Here, give me some of that water," cried Dick hoarsely, to one of the stable boys, who appeared around the paddock with a pail. "Dash it over his face," as the boy came shambling up. "Donkey kicked him — oh, my goodness! he doesn't stir," as the contents of the pail streamed over Johnny's face.

"I'll carry him for you," said the boy, setting down the pail.

"You get out — oh! beg your pardon — I'll carry him myself."

Just then Polly looked out of the window, humming the last bars of her sonata.

"Why, Dick!" as she spied him, "how funny that you're home. Oh, what" — as she caught sight of a little boy's figure in his arms.

"It's Johnny," said Dick, lifting his pale face to the window, as he hurried along. But Polly didn't hear; speeding over the stairs, she ran out to the lawn, and over the walk to the paddock-edge. "O Dick!" she exclaimed again. Then she held herself in check, as she saw his face. "I believe he's all right," she began cheerfully.

"He's dead!" declared Dick hoarsely, and staggering on.

"Oh, no, Dick!—oh, no! protested Polly, hurrying by his side. "Bring him in here," she said, pointing to the side veranda.

Dick still staggered on, up the steps, and into the house.

"Oh, if Papa Fisher were only here!" sighed Polly; then she looked at Dick. "But how nice it is that there's such a good doctor here. You know, Father Fisher told us to send for him if anything was the matter with us. There, lay Johnny on the sofa here, and then run, Dicky, do, and get the doctor. He lives on Porter Road, the third house this way. Take the ponycart. Dr. Phillips is his name," she called after him; then she touched the electric bell at her elbow.

"Tell Mrs. Higby to come here at once," said

Polly to the maid, who popped in her head in obedience to the summons.

"I must get some hartshorn," said Polly; "he won't stir, poor boy. I'll run up to my room

"Oh, he's rolled off," cried Polly, aghast.

and get it." In less time than it takes to tell it, Polly was off and back, to find Mrs. Higby just arrived in the doorway, saying, "Did you want me, Ma'am ?   Jane said as how one of the boys was sick."

"O Mrs. Higby!" gasped Polly, the color beginning to come back to her cheek. "It's Johnny — on the lounge.   Here, I've the hartshorn," holding up the bottle. "He was kicked by the donkey — Dick's gone for the doctor." All this in one breath, as they were going across the room, the good woman in advance.

"I don't see," — began Mrs. Higby.

"And some one must tell Mrs. Fargo," mourned Polly, back of the ample figure. "Why — where" — for the sofa was empty.

"Oh, he's rolled off! though how he could, I don't see," said Polly, aghast, and tumbling down on her knees to peer under the sofa, Mrs. Higby pulling it out from the wall to facilitate matters. "He was just as if he were dead.   O Mrs. Higby! where do you suppose he is ?"

"I'm sure I don't know," declared Mrs. Higby, thoroughly alarmed; "like enough, Mrs. King, it's flew to his head, and he's gone crazy."

At this direful prospect, Polly set up a most diligent search here, there, and everywhere a small boy of eight would be supposed to rest

under such conditions, assisted as well as she
could be by Mrs. Higby, whose ample figure, im-
pelled by her fright, knocked down more articles
than she could well set to rights again, until at
last they were compelled to call in others to the
search.

And in the midst of it all, they heard a shout
out in the direction of the stables; and, running
out to the veranda, they saw Johnny triumphantly
sticking to the donkey's back, while he waved a
small switch the stable-boy had just obligingly cut
for him.

"Pay him up now for your tumble," advised
the boy.

"See, I did get on all by myself!" shouted
Johnny at them. "Runned away when Mrs. King
went up-stairs;" then he turned, and waved his
stick at Dick and Dr. Phillips driving at a furi-
ous pace into the side yard.

CHAPTER IV.

CAN SHE GO TO MRS. KING'S RECEPTION?

" I'LL ask Uncle Carroll. Uncle Carroll, sha'n't Aunt Fay take me? Please say yes."

"No use to ask him, Grace; you're too young."

" *Please*, Uncle Carroll, don't mind what Aunt Fay says. Just *you* say I'm to go."

"Where?" he dropped his paper.

"Out to Mrs. King's reception to-morrow afternoon."

"Nonsense! You're too young."

"Child, I told you so," said Aunt Fay quietly, slipping the cosey on the tea-pot again.

"Too young!" Grace pulled savagely at the girlish hair on her brow, and twisted her long braid hanging down her back, up high on her head.

"I'll do up my hair, and pull down my face — so," lengthening her round cheeks — "anything, to just get the chance of going," she cried. "O

Uncle Carroll! and I'm sixteen. You're positively cruel."

"You're nothing but a school-girl," said Aunt Fay; "the idea of going to a reception."

"Why, those receptions of Mrs. King's are packed; you don't seem to understand, Grace; and you'd take the standing-room of some one else," added Uncle Carroll.

"I'd take my own standing-room," declared Grace positively, "and I wouldn't tread on other people's toes;" seeing a chance for her, since the two guardians of her peace had begun to argue the point. "Just think, I've never seen the King house nor Miss Phronsie."

"Well, she's a raving, tearing beauty," said Uncle Carroll, "and worth going miles to see, I tell you."

"And I want to see Mrs. King again," cried Grace, pursuing her advantage. "I got a peek at her once, when she came to call at the Drysdales. Bella and I heard she was in the drawing-room, and we crept in behind the cabinet. She was just lovely; and the color kept coming and going in her cheeks, and her brown eyes were laughing, and I'll do anything to see her again."

"She's the rage, that's a fact," assented Uncle
Carroll. "Well, Mrs. Atherton, why don't you
take the child for once; I would."

"Carroll Atherton!" exclaimed his wife in
dismay, "how could I ever look her father and
mother in the face, and they've trusted her to
us, while she went to school, to do the right
thing by her. The idea of a sixteen-year-old
girl, and a school-girl, going to a reception!"

"The child won't have a chance to get there
any other way," observed Mr. Atherton. "One
little social break won't matter."

"The worst place to make a social break is
at Mrs. King's," said Mrs. Atherton. "No, Grace,
you can*not* go." She set her lips tightly together.
"Any other thing you might ask, I'd try to in-
dulge you in; but I won't make a *faux pas* at
Mrs. Jasper King's."

"I don't want anything else," cried Grace in
a passion. Just then a young girl ran over the
steps, and plunged without ceremony into the
pretty breakfast-room.

"Oh, joy — joy — joy!" she cried, beating her
hands together, "mamma's going to take me to
Mrs. King's reception to-morrow afternoon."

"The idea of a school-girl going to a reception," said aunt Fay.

"Bella Drysdale!" shrieked Grace, deserting her chair to throw her arms around her friend. "There, Uncle Carroll, now you see what Mrs. Drysdale's going to do for Bella," she flung over her shoulder, not deigning to notice her aunt.

"It's too bad," began Mr. Atherton.

"I shall see that lovely Mrs. King again," cried Bella in a rapture. "Brother Tom's going to get a look at Miss Phronsie; and we've got a cousin from Chicago, and he's going for the express purpose of seeing her. Oh! everybody will be there, Grace. Mamma says you *must* go."

"You're older than Grace," began Mrs. Atherton to gain a little time before the storm should begin again around her head.

"Only one month," said Bella; "what's that?"

"Sixteen days!" cried Grace, "only sixteen days! Just think of that paltry atom of time to keep one away from that glorious reception. Uncle, wouldn't you be ashamed to have every one know that Aunt Fay kept me away for just sixteen days? I should positively die of mortification."

"Well, you cannot go anyway," suddenly and decidedly declared Mrs. Atherton. Mrs. Drysdale or no Mrs. Drysdale, whom she followed when it suited her to do so, she was determined to keep to that decision. "It is of no use to argue and to tease — you can*not* go."

Bella dragged Grace off to her room, and shut the door on their woes.

"I shall go! I shall go!" declared Grace in a white heat, raging up and down the room.

"Oh, mercy! Mrs. King won't have you, if you go on that way. She's awfully nice and particular. Stop it, Grace." Bella shook her arm.

"I'm going — I'm going — I'm going, so there!" declared Grace determinedly. "That's settled. Now, how shall I do it? Help me to think, Bella." She stopped suddenly.

"What's the use of thinking," cried that young lady, throwing herself on the broad window-seat in among its cushions, and stretching restfully, "as long as you can't go?"

"As long as I can go, you mean," corrected Grace, an ugly little gleam in her blue eyes.

"Well, you're a regular Western fury," declared Bella, regarding her. "Gracious, I wouldn't have taken you from the 'wild and woolly plains' as your aunt has for a year!"

"Don't speak to me of Aunt," commanded Grace, frowning heavily. "What has she done? Kept me out of this, the thing I wanted most of all. And besides, the 'wild and woolly West'— why, I haven't been educated there, as you know. It's New England, if any place, that's to blame for me. Oh, oh, I've an idea!"

Bella sat up straight, the transition was so great, to stare, as Grace ran softly to the door, opened it, and looked and listened; then locked it again, and tiptoed back.

"The very thing!" She seized Bella's hands, and dragged her off the window-seat. "I'm going to be your Western friend; you put that idea into my head—don't you see? dressed up. O Bella, you stupid, you owl, I'm going as your visitor; and I'll hire my bonnet and gown, and change my hair, so Aunt won't catch me. And — and — what joy!"

When the luckless Bella, nearly danced out of breath, was released, she made a faint protest. But she was fairly talked off her feet again; and by that time the fun of the thing had entered into her soul and clutched her. So she said "yes," and began to plan as smartly as Grace herself.

"But mother never will take you in all this world," she said, sobering down.

"Did you for an instant suppose I was going to let your mother know who I am?" cried Grace, bursting into a laugh. "Oh, what a sweet owl you are, Bella Drysdale! Of course I'm going to fool her too."

"Well, she won't let me take a stranger," said Bella sharply, tired of being called an owl twice. "I guess I'm as smart as you, Grace Tupper. I should know better than to get up such a silly plan."

"I'm to be Miss Strange from Omaha, Nebraska," said Grace solemnly; "a pupil of Miss Willoughby's boarding- and day-school. All this is true — my name is Grace Strange Tupper. And because I don't happen to board, instead of going to her day-school at Miss Willoughby's, isn't my fault. I would if I could. Now, Owlie, do you see?"

"If you call me an owl again I won't do a single thing about it," cried Bella stubbornly; "that's flat."

"So she was a dear," cried Grace, soothing her, and launching at the same time into an animated

discussion as to ways and means; which milliner
to hire the bonnet from, and which was the most
becoming way to do up her hair, and how to
darken her eyebrows, till Bella looked at her
watch aghast. "And I've a horrible French
letter to write for to-morrow, or Mademoiselle
will kill me, and mamma won't let me go to
the reception."

"Oh, misery! Hurry, do; run every step of
the way home," begged Grace, nearly pushing her
out of the room as she ran off.

And the next afternoon Grace shut herself up
again in her room; and while the French maid
was evolving the usual fine creation out of her
aunt for the reception, Grace was also doing
wonders, — to steal softly down the stairs, and
out and away to Bella's.

"I thought I'd save you the trouble of calling for me," she said, in a sweet little drawl
as far unlike her usual tones as possible, as she
entered the long Drysdale drawing-room. "Oh,
beg pardon, I thought Bella was here!"

"Er — no; allow me to do the honors." A
tall young man with shoulders built for ball-
team work, came slowly into the centre of the

room. "Bella will be down soon. Take a seat,
Miss " —

"Strange," murmured Grace faintly, and won-
dering if her front frizzes had slipped, and if the
pencilling under her eyes looked natural. "I— I
— it isn't any matter. I suppose I'm too early."

She sank into an easy-chair in the darkest
shadow of the room, and covered her feet primly
with her hired gown, regardless of the wasted
elegance of her new little boots. These had been
her one extravagance; but now she was too far
gone to care whether or no they were seen.

"Oh, Bella's the same as she was ten years
ago when I last visited here," observed the young
man, carelessly leaning his elbow on the mantel-
piece, and staring at her. "She was always a
tardy little thing, I remember; kept us waiting
everlastingly when we were going outing."

So this was Bella's cousin from Chicago. Well,
he was perfectly horrid to talk that way of her
dearest friend; and besides, what sharp black
eyes he had, piercing through and through her.
She put her hand up involuntarily to feel of her
frizzes, shivered, and drew in her boots farther
than ever under her chair.

"I don't think it is very nice to speak so of your relatives when you are visiting them," she observed to her own astonishment. Then she would have bitten out her tongue sooner than have spoken.

"Er — oh, beg pardon, did you speak?" exclaimed the young man, starting out of a revery.

Joy! he hadn't heard her. "No — that is — it isn't any matter," said Grace hastily. "I was going to say I think Bella is perfectly splendid. We all do at school."

"You attend Miss Willoughby's boarding-school, I believe," said the black-eyed young man, bending on her a sharper gaze than ever. "It's a delightful school I'm told. Isn't that a fact?"

Grace was saved from replying by his next remark, which he presented without any pause to speak of. "I've two cousins, Jenny and Francina Day, there. I'm going over to call on them this evening after dinner."

Oh, horrors! Why hadn't Bella told her of this before she had taken upon herself such a scrape! Well, there was no help for it now; there was no other way, if she would see Mrs. King, and be part and parcel of Mrs. King's great reception. She tried to recover herself enough to smile; but she felt, as she afterward told Bella, as if her face wobbled all over.

"I'm glad to meet somebody who will give me a sort of a welcome there. Fact is, I don't know my cousins by sight. Never saw but one of them, and she was a kid of three years old. Are they nice girls?"

"Perfectly splendid," said Grace recklessly, glad to think she had made up a long, outstanding fight between Jenny and herself just the day before, and stifling the qualms of conscience when she reflected on Francina's heavy dulness. "Oh, I'm so glad they're your cousins," she said, smiling radiantly.

The sharp-eyed young man showed two rows of even white teeth as he also smiled expansively.

"Miss Willoughby is extremely gracious to allow you to go to a swell reception," he said slowly. "If I'd supposed it would be of any use, I'd have begged my cousins off. I presume it's too late for me to run around now and get them."

"Oh, yes, yes," cried Grace, starting forward, and beating one little boot in terror on the carpet. "Miss Willoughby doesn't like short notice about anything; and — and — it's an awful long way there — and — here comes Bella." To her great relief in came that young lady, resplendent in a new blue hat quite perky, with a grown-up air that was matched by Bella's manners as she drew on a white kid glove.

Grace deserted her shady corner, and flew at her. "O Bella, do hurry," as she threw her arm around her; "it's dreadfully late; do be quick; we ought to go."

"There's oceans of time," said Bella with a drawl, and smoothing out the little finger in a painstaking way. "Mamma isn't half ready yet — at least she hasn't her bonnet on. Oh! do you know my cousin Charley Swan ?" indicating with a nod the sharp-eyed young man.

"We've entertained each other for a good half hour or so," observed Charley, not particular as to exact statements. "Say, Bella, if Aunt Isabel isn't ready, I believe I'll run around to Miss Willoughby's, and get her to let Jenny and Francina off to go with us. Stupid in me not to think of it till I saw Miss Strange come in."

"Er — ow !" Grace gave a sharp nip to Bella's

plump arm. "Stop him," she whispered tragically. Bella pulled out a hairpin from some mys-
terious quarter under her hat, and set it in again,
before she condescended to answer. "No, you
must not, Charley," she said, pursing up her
small mouth, and then falling to on her glove
again. "Button it, will you?" presenting it to
him. "You see, mamma will be very angry; for
she's just as likely to settle her bonnet right
the first attempt. I've known her to. And although Tom's no doubt wrestling in the agonies
of tying his necktie, yet it's just like him to hop
down without the least warning before you could
possibly get back. Then think of me!" She
spread her white gloves dramatically out, as if
words were unequal to the occasion.

Just then Tom whistled his way in. "Whew,
you ready in your togs, Charley! Well, it takes
you Western fellows to be spry. Where's the
mother?" turning to Bella.

"Here's Miss Strange, Tom," said his sister,
clutching Grace's arm; "haven't you any manners? Angela, this is my brother Tom."

Grace started at the word Angela, and forgot
to bow, as Tom doubled up like a jack-knife and

made her his best obeisance. Then it was too
late when she remembered; and she stood there
blushing under the hired bonnet, till Charley remarked in a way that did not help matters any,
"Oh, so I am an older acquaintance of Miss
Strange than you, Tom."

"How did you ever tell such an awful story as
to say my name was Angela," cried Grace in a
whisper as they hurried off to the carriage, Mrs.
Drysdale at last appearing.

"I didn't say so; stop pinching me; I'm black
and blue already," retorted Bella. "I've a right
to call you what I've a mind to. And I'm going
to call you Angela the rest of this blessed afternoon. So mind you act as if you'd heard the
name before. If you don't, I'll tell everybody
who you are."

This had the effect of throwing Grace into such
a panic that she answered Mrs. Drysdale's kind
attempts at conversation with her at random,
and the twenty miles to Badgertown were made
in a whirl of emotions possessing her, till by the
time the train paused at the little station, she had
a confused notion of either telling her whole
story and throwing herself on the mercy of the

chaperone, or of picking up her long skirts, and
fleeing over the country meadows toward home.

Instead, she was saying, "Thank you; yes,
I'd rather walk," to Cousin Charley. Bella and
Tom said the same thing. Mrs. Drysdale was
helped into one of the carriages that always ran
back and forth on Mrs. King's reception days — a
bevy of ladies and gentlemen filling the others;
and off they all set, to meet in the dressing-rooms
at "The Oaks."

CHAPTER V.

MRS. JASPER KING'S RECEPTION.

"WE'RE in an awful hole," gasped Bella, pulling Grace off to the farthest corner of the dressing-room. " Er — do get away from that maid; you don't want her sharp eyes all over you. No, we don't either of us want any help;" over her shoulder at that functionary. "Now, Grace, er — Angela, you've gone and got me into this scrape, and I shall never hold up my head again in all this world."

Poor Grace's head couldn't droop any more than it did, as she mumbled miserably, "I know it. Oh, dear me!"

This was worse than all, and Bella took fresh alarm. "For mercy's sake, hold up your head and look big, as if you were somebody." It was now her turn to pinch Grace.

"I can't; because I'm not somebody," sighed Grace. The frizzes even seemed to droop miser ably on her brow; and she looked like a wilted flower, all her smart hired glory gone suddenly out of her.

"What a horrible scrape!" cried Bella between her teeth. "Oh, dear me, Grace, you *must* behave! Dear, dear!" as some ladies hovered near.

"I think your mother wants to go down now," said one; "she is trying to signal you. Introduce your young friend to me, will you?"

"Oh, I can't go down-stairs!" cried Grace in a spasm of terror, and catching Bella's arm in a way to make her faint, as that young lady looked over to the knot of ladies by the door, one of whom was waving her fan frantically.

The lady who had requested the introduction, extending her hand in a winning way, Bella twitched away from the clutch, and said quickly, "Miss Grace Strange — I mean Miss Angela Tupper. Oh, dear me! I don't feel very well, and mamma wants me. Come on." She fairly hauled Grace out through the ranks of elegant women, regardless of their dismay at her haste. "See what you have done," her black looks said when at last she permitted Grace a glimpse of her face.

"You young ladies must attend to my movements, and not expect me to signal you," said Mrs. Drysdale, her face only sweetly black, like a becoming thunder-cloud, as Miss Willoughby's parlor boarder was one of the offenders. She could scold Bella easier at home. Just then a stout lady trying to get by, with a good deal of jet trimming about her person, sent out one of the octopus threads, and hooked Mrs. Drysdale in the most vulnerable point, — the choice old lace on her sleeves.

"Excuse me," panted the stout lady, pulling at the entanglement. "There, break it, I'm sure I don't care."

"I'll get it out," cried Mrs. Drysdale in a terror, laying a quick hand on it.

"Step out of the doorway, please," said some one. And the stout lady and Mrs. Drysdale edged off as one person, and everybody in the vicinity fell to helping; even Grace was brought out of her misery enough to take her turn. As she bent over her task, some one's elbow gave her French bonnet a knock. Out fell a hair-pin from her frizzes, and she felt rather than saw the curious eyes of the lady next to her upon her hair. So she deserted the jet and

lace, making Mrs. Drysdale say with some as
perity, "I think you have not bettered it any,
Miss Strange." Then she looked up into the face

Grace darted behind a tall fern, and hid her hot, distressed face.

of her next neighbor. She was the lady who had
asked Bella to introduce her.

Grace fled out into the wide upper hall, fragrant
with its wealth of blossoms, and darted behind a

tall fern, where she hid her hot, distressed face,
and tried to stop the throbbing of her heart.

"Well, now get Miss Strange," Mrs. Drysdale
was saying as she emerged into the hall. "It is
the last time I shall ever allow you to ask a friend
to go with you, Bella. Where in the world is
she?" peering about.

Bella flew back into the room. "Grace, Grace,"
she cried in a loud voice.

"Here I am," said Grace miserably, and creeping out from behind the fern. "I was so hot, and
it's cool out here," feeling the necessity for words
with the audience that now hung on the scene,
and the throng of ladies coming and going to
the dressing-room, and whose passage they were
blocking up.

Mrs. Drysdale did not vouchsafe a word, only
gave her one look, stepped back, and called her
daughter in a tone that scared Bella more than all
the rest, and the three sailed down-stairs. That
is, the lady sailed; but Bella went with the tread of
an angry young lion, while the parlor boarder at
Miss Willoughby's slipped after as best she could.

The next thing she knew, she was being introduced to a radiant vision, and feeling the warm

touch of a kind hand, and looking into clear brown eyes, and hearing Mrs. Jasper King say, "I am very glad to see you, Miss Strange." And then, despite the crowd pressing her, and that Bella was picking her by the sleeve, the kind hand retained her trembling one, "I want to see more of you. Come up and speak to me later," said Mrs. King, and she smiled; and that cut deepest of all.

Grace broke away from her friends, and made a dive for oblivion. Anywhere — perhaps behind a sheltering palm, till the Drysdales were ready to go home; she could watch and slip out then. Instead, however, of reaching such a haven, she ran against a tall young man in the hall, and not stopping to beg pardon, rushed on.

"Hello!" exclaimed Mr. Charley Swan startled out of his politeness, and following her after the rebound, "anything I can do for you, Miss Strange?"

The sound of this name only added to Grace's terror, and he had some difficulty in gaining her side.

"If you please, I'd advise you to stop. People don't run about in this way, you know, at receptions; knocking folks down, and all that. Now

what's the trouble ? " He stood squarely in front
of her, and between annihilating with his looks
a curious youth who was taking this all in, and
preserving a calm exterior for the rest of the
throng surging through the hall, he still gave her
a penetrating glance.

" Oh, I'm so wretched ! " gasped Grace, all cau-
tion thrown to the winds, and clasping her hands.

"Not altogether festive," said Charley Swan,
"that's a fact. Well, now that orchestra's going
to play, thank Heaven for that. You just take
my arm — Miss — Miss Strange, and we'll get
out of this mob."

He had to slip Grace's hand himself within
his arm. There it lay, and shook like a leaf.
Charley piloted her into the large conservatory
opening into the library, and somehow she found
herself in a quiet corner with just room enough
for another person on the rattan seat.

"Now, that's what I call comfort," he said,
not looking at her, to give her time to recover
herself. "Mrs. King is a perfect marvel in the
flower line, and her music. Did you know that
all these orchids are given her by Mr. King the
father ? Gracious ! don't I wish some old gentle-

man would take a fancy to me, and pet me with
bank-notes and smother me in orchids.　Look
around a bit, Miss Strange."

"I can't," said Grace in a low voice; "I've
no right to."

"Hush! here comes a perfect old harpy for
news, I know by her pinched-up nose, and the
way she sets her lorgnette.　Hold your tongue,
Miss Strange, — beg your pardon, but it's a des-
perate case, — till she gets away.　Yes, as I
was saying, these orchids are surely the rarest
specimens I've ever seen."

The "old harpy" drew near, and levelled her
glances behind her lorgnette at Grace.　It was
the lady who had asked Bella to introduce her
young friend.

"Are you ill, Miss" — she hesitated, and then
laughed unpleasantly, "Tupper — or — Strange?"
she asked sweetly, and drawing near till she stood
over the two.

Charley Swan surveyed her coolly as Grace
stammered out something.

"Thanks," he drawled.　"Miss Strange was
faint; but as she is a great friend of our family
and came with us, I believe I can take care of

her.   Anything I can do for you, Miss —"
he hesitated, just as she had done, looking her
squarely in the face; so that, without supplying
the name, she murmured something about the
beauty of the flowers, and moved off.

"Are you ill, Miss Tupper—or—Strange?" and she laughed unpleasantly.

"Old reptile," said Charley between his teeth.

"Oh, don't!" protested Grace, with a little
shiver; "she's right. She sees I'm a humbug."

Mr. Swan did not seem to be at all surprised
at this confession, but stood up suddenly.

"Look here," he said; "you keep your seat.
Don't say a word; *she* won't come back, and you

don't know any one else, I'll be bound. Anyway, don't talk. I'm going to get you an ice."

"No, no," cried Grace, the color flooding her face; "not a single thing; I won't take it. I can't. Why, I've come here all dressed up as one of Mrs. Willoughby's parlor boarders. I'm only Grace Tupper — you don't know. It would choke me."

"It's pretty bad, I'll not deny," said Charley, sitting down; "but if everybody told how they got to receptions, you wouldn't be alone in hum-buggery, I'll venture to say."

"But I've disobeyed my Au — Aunt Ath — Ath-erton," said Grace, battling with her sobs, and twisting her fingers to keep from crying like a baby, "and — I — hired this bonnet, and — and " —

"And you've spoiled yourself with those hor-rid eyebrows," finished Charley; "and if I were you, I'd take off that monstrosity of a frizz, and put the thing in your pocket."

"Oh, I can't!" gasped Grace, raising her blue eyes in terror to his face; "why, Aunt will know me then."

"Is she here?" demanded Charley with a

whistle. He couldn't help it; this last was too much even for him.

"Yes — that is, she was coming. Oh, dear me! and I suppose I'll be expelled from Miss Willoughby's school, and I'll go home, and it'll kill father and mother and Jimmy and the baby. I never thought of that."

"At least I believe we'll save Jimmy and the baby," said Charley in a tone of encouragement.

"And Mrs. King smi — smiled at me." Grace broke down, and cried into her handkerchief, so that Charlie jumped up. "See here," he said abruptly, "I want to take you down to see some of the greenhouses; they're wonders." He made her get up, and take his arm again, while he hurried her off over the grounds. But they hadn't gone far, when she saw a lady in advance walking with two gentlemen.

"There's Aunt!" she cried; and before Charley could say anything, she broke away from him, and rushed down a side path.

It was worse than useless to follow her, as the attention thus drawn to her would be disastrous. So Charley sauntered along, first getting a good view of "Aunt" in her lavender bonnet, so he would know her again, and then hastening to the mansion, if perchance he might befriend Grace once more.

"Charley Swan!" exclaimed Bella, running up, "where *is* — er — Angela Strange?"

"Miss Tupper has just left me," said Charley gravely, and pausing abruptly.

"Miss Tupper? Oh, my good gracious!" cried Bella with a little laugh, "you mean Miss Strange."

"She says her name is Tupper," said Charley. "I really suppose she ought to know."

"Oh, dear, dear! then she has told you," said Bella with a long sigh. "Well, I'm glad. Such an afternoon as I've had!"

"See here, Bella," said Charley. "You get her; she's run down that path," nodding in the direction of Grace's flight; "and you and I will take her home. She took fright because she saw her aunt. Be lively now."

"Dear, dear!" cried Bella in vexation and alarm. "Well, I'm sure, precious little comfort I've had at this reception!"

"Hurry up, now. I'll go in and make our excuses to Aunt Isabel."

But when Bella reached a turn in the shrub-bery, she found a little heap on the ground, a group of people bending over it, conspicuous in the front being the lady who had asked her to introduce Grace, now using a lorgnette most vig-orously.

What happened next, Bella never could tell. She only knew that the gardeners lifted Grace, and carried her into one of the back doors, giv-ing her up to the care of the housekeeper, whom they called Mrs. Higby, and that some of the ladies and gentlemen followed, proposing various remedies, the lady with the lorgnette pressing after most assiduously.

"She tripped on her gown and fell just as we were coming along," said this lady sweetly. "She seems somehow unused to a long gown. Let me bathe her face."

"Here comes Miss Phronsie," said Mrs. Higby. "Now that blessed dear has heard of the acci-dent. Make way for Miss Phronsie."

Phronsie came softly up in her beautiful white gown. She laid down her bunch of lilies-of-the-valley on the table, and bent over the young girl, laying a quiet hand on the cold one. "Poor thing," she said, and she dropped a kiss on the white cheek.

To everybody's surprise, two tears gushed out and rolled down the white face. "Leave her to me," said Phronsie gently. "Now, if everybody will please go out, Mrs. Higby and I will take care of her."

"You would better let me stay" the lorgnette lady had the temerity to say.

"We do not need you," said Phronsie, coolly regarding her. "Will you please go out with the others?"

When Charley Swan came stalking in by the back door, it was to see Miss Phronsie Pepper with her arms around Grace as they sat on the lounge in the housekeeper's dining-room, and Bella Drysdale crouched on the floor, with her hands clasped in Phronsie's lap.

CHAPTER VI.

GRACE.

"DON'T cry," Phronsie was saying; "because if you do, I cannot help you."

"She has told everything — just every single thing, Charley," announced Bella, tragically turning around to him.

Charley Swan stood like a statue, with no eyes for any one but Phronsie. She turned a grave face on him. "I'm afraid she's badly hurt," she said. "I think you will have to get Dr. Phillips, Mrs. Higby."

"It's only my foot," said Grace with a little moan.

"Let me go for him," begged Charley, coming out of his frozen state.

"One of the men'll go," said Mrs. Higby. "La! don't you stir a mite." She went to the door, gave the message, and came back with a sigh of relief. "You poor child, you," bending over Grace's foot. "You must have turned it clean over itself. There, there, the cold water'll be the best we can do for it till the doctor gets here. My!" as her glance fell again on the dark circles under the blue eyes, and the elaborate frizzes; then she fell to coughing, and speedily betook herself to the farther end of the room.

"I'll hold her," she said presently, coming back. "Miss Phronsie, you're wanted every single minute in the best room. Let me sit there where you be."

Bella sprang to her feet, and blushed rose red. "I forgot you'd left the reception. Oh, do excuse me! And please, Miss Phronsie Pepper, don't stay here any longer."

"I shall stay," said Phronsie, "till I see that she is better."

"Where's Phronsie? Mrs. Higby, do you know where Miss Phronsie is?" cried old Mr. King, putting his head in the doorway. "Oh, my good gracious!" as his eye caught the group.

Grace hopped off the lounge, and hobbled along on one foot. "Oh, sir! it's my fault," she panted; then she fell flat on the floor.

When she came to herself, she was lying on a

bed whose white hangings she could dimly see as she opened her eyes. Her foot felt heavy and queer.

"I'm sure I cannot apologize enough to you, Mrs. King," said a voice that she was quite familiar with. "This school-girl prank is quite unforgivable, I know, but I hope you won't lay it up against me."

"We ought not to talk here, Mrs. Atherton," said Polly gently; then they went out into the other room.

"I don't think Bella Drysdale is just the right companion for her," said Mrs. Atherton. "I have thought so for some time. Now I shall do my best to break up the intimacy."

"Ugh — O Aunt Fay!" shrieked Grace, trying to raise herself in bed. But she only succeeded in falling back heavily with a groan.

"Dear me, that girl has quite upset me," cried Mrs. Atherton, trembling nervously.

"Do you stay out here, Mrs. Atherton," said Polly brightly, with a gentle hand putting her on the sofa; then she went into the room where Grace lay, closed the door, and stepped softly up to the bed.

"Now, little girl," she said, just as if Grace were six years old instead of sixteen, "you must stop crying, and do not move. If you do, your foot may be injured for life."

"I can't help crying," said poor Grace, covering her face with both hands.

"You can help doing anything that is wrong," said Polly gently. Then she brought a brush and comb, unpinned the frizzes, and laid them on the white toilet-table, and began to brush the soft, straight, shining hair.

"It wasn't Bella at all," sobbed Grace. "She didn't want to do it, but I made her. Oh! I can't give Bella up, Mrs. King."

"You shall tell your Aunt all about it when you are better," said Polly. "Now we must not talk about it. You are going to stay with me until your foot is well enough for you to be moved."

"What, here in this house with you?" cried Grace, almost speechless with astonishment.

"Yes," said Polly; "you see, you've given your poor foot a terrible wrench, and Dr. Phillips isn't willing that you should be moved just yet. And he can come and see you so much easier here, Grace."

"I shall get my Mamsie," cried a small, determined voice.

"O Mrs. King!" Grace rolled her head on the pillow to look at her, "you don't know how wicked I've been. You can't know, or you never'd keep me here in all this world. Why, I disobeyed my aunt to come here."

"Yes, I do know," said Polly gravely. "I know it all. But I said we wouldn't talk about it now." Then Polly sat down on the edge of the bed in her beautiful reception-gown, and Grace felt too wicked to touch it with one finger, although she longed to; and Mrs. King held her hand, and told her stories about her own girl-hood, — how the Peppers lived in the little brown house just around the lane, "where you will go when you are able to walk, dear;" and how Joel was the pastor of a big church in New York, and where Ben and Davie were; and how the dear mother had gone abroad with Father Fisher because he was tired and needed rest, and wanted to visit the hospitals again, and some foreign doctors; and then she told about Johnny, and the railroad accident that took his mother away to heaven, and how good Mrs. Fargo had adopted him for her very own boy, and they were there at Badgertown for the whole summer.

And how Mr. Higby, in whose farmhouse the people were all carried who were hurt, had sold his farm, and was now their head gardener, and good Mrs. Higby was the housekeeper.

"Yes, I think she is quite good," said Grace, snuggling up to the kind hand; "she didn't scold me a bit, but she looked so sorry for me, Mrs. King."

"And Johnny's just the dearest dear," said Polly, who always believed him but little short of a cherub; and then she told how he was thrown from the donkey just the week before, but " it didn't hurt him a bit, and " —

"If you please, Mrs. King, the children are ready to go to bed," said Katrina, putting her white cap in the door.

"And now I must go to my chicks," said Polly, getting off the bed. Then she bent over, and set a kiss on the pale cheek. "Don't you worry about anything," she said. "I shall ask my sister Phronsie to stay with you."

"Mrs. King," cried Grace, nervously clutching the brocade dress, "there is one thing, — if you could keep Aunt Fay from writing this to my mother. Oh, please do, dear Mrs. King!"

"She won't do it," said Mrs. King quietly;
"don't be afraid, Grace."

Grace gave her one look, and relaxed her hold.

"I shall get my Mamsie," cried a small, determined voice; and Elyot rushed in in his nightgown, followed by Barby in hers, hugging a
dilapidated black doll. "Mamsie," cried Barby,
stumbling over to her arms.

"Don't you go in there," commanded King,
coming last, in his nightgown. "Sister Polly, I
couldn't help it, I came to keep them out."

"Oh, dear me," cried Katrina, who had gone
back after delivering her message, now hurrying
in. "Children, how can you!"

"Bad, naughty Katty," said Barby, shaking
her curls at her, "to keep me away from my
mummy. Go 'way, Katty."

"O Barby!" said Polly gently, and nestling
her little girl up to her.

"Oh, what a cunning little thing!" cried Grace
in a rapture. "Oh, do let her stay, Mrs. King!"
as Polly made signs for Katrina to take her.

"What you in my bed for?" cried King sturdily; "say, and who are you?"

"O King!" said Polly; "why, that isn't like
my boy."

"Oh, have I taken his bed?" asked Grace in dismay, and making another effort to rise.

"He calls it his because once when he was

Elyot perched at the foot, where he surveyed Grace at his leisure.

sick he left the nursery and came in here to sleep," said Polly. "Now come, children, say good-night to Miss Grace, and then we must fly to bed." Elyot had one of her hands now; and he clambered up on the bed, where he perched on the foot, and surveyed Grace at his leisure.

"Is that her name because she says grace at the table?" he asked after a pause.

"No, dear, that was her baby name; isn't it a pretty one?"

"Was she ever a baby?" asked Barby, looking with intense interest at Grace's long figure under the bedclothes.

"Yes, indeed; she was once a little baby just like all you children."

"O mamma! not a *little* one," said Elyot incredulously.

"Not a wee, wee, teenty one," said Barby, shaking her head,

"I guess she was as long as that," said King, measuring off a piece on Grace's frame, that he supposed a suitable length, "just about as long as that."

"Take care, dear. You may touch her lame foot," said Polly.

And then the children, who had been in the little brown house when the accident occurred, clamored to know all about it. But Polly was firm; and telling them they should hear how it happened on the morrow, she held Barby down for a good-night kiss, a proceeding all the others imitated, till the three swarmed around Grace's pillow.

"Good-night," said Barby, with a sleepy little hum; "do you say 'Now-I-lay-me-down-to-seep'"?

"No," said Grace. How long ago it seemed since she had felt too old to repeat that prayer!

"Mamsie, she doesn't say 'Now-I-lay-me-down-to-seep,' "said Barby, trying to open wide her eyes.

"Come, dears."

"What *do* you say?" cried Elyot, pulling the bedspread, "say?"

"Elyot!" said his mother. He took one look at her face, and then scuttled off, picking up the nightgown to facilitate progress.

So Polly went off, her baby on her arm. Barby, whose eyes drooped at every step, dropped the black doll out of her sleepy hand; Katrina picked it up, and helped the boys along.

Just then Phronsie came in with a pleased expression on her face to see how cheery everything was.

"Your aunt has gone," she said; "but she is coming out to-morrow to see how you are."

So Polly went off, her baby on her arm.

Grace achieved a sitting posture, impossible as it had seemed before. "Oh, *dear* Mrs. King!"

she screamed, "now I know she will write to mamma this evening."

Polly set Barby in her little crib, then sped back. "No, Grace," she said, "she won't write; you can trust me, dear."

"She always writes evenings when she's anything on her mind," said Grace; "and she'd hurry about this." But upon Mrs. King's assuring her that she would take the care of this upon herself, Grace cuddled down again, and let Phronsie comfort her.

And by and by, while Polly's messenger was speeding to the city with just such a letter as she knew how to write, addressed to Mrs. Carroll Atherton, Mrs. Higby herself came up with Grace's supper; and when she saw how cheery things were, and how everything was beginning to mend, she put her arms akimbo, and said, "My land! but you'll be as spry as a cricket in a week."

"I brought you some flowers," said Phronsie, laying down a little bunch where Grace's fingers could reach them.

Grace looked at them, but did not offer to touch them.

"What is it?" asked Phronsie.

"Might I just have one little sprig of those you held in your hand when you came after I was hurt, Miss Phronsie?"

"Why, yes, you may. Mrs. Higby, will you get them? You may have the whole bunch," she said to Grace.

"Oh, only just one sprig, please," said Grace eagerly.

But the whole bunch of lilies-of-the-valley was brought; and Grace held them in her hands, and buried her face in them, and then she opened her mouth obediently, while Mrs. Higby, after tucking a napkin under her chin, fed her from a generous plate of milk-toast, and everything was getting quite jolly.

"She looks better already, don't she, Miss Phronsie!" exclaimed Mrs. Higby in admiration of the effect of the treatment. "My! but ain't this nice milk-toast, though! I guess I know, for I made it myself. There, take this, poor dear."

"I'm sorry to make you all so much trouble," said Grace penitently, with her mouth half full.

"Don't feed her too fast, please, Mrs. Higby," said Phronsie, looking on with the deepest interest.

" My land ! she ought to eat to keep her strength up," said Mrs Higby, plying the spoon industriously. " Just so much milk-toast such as this is, and every hour you'll see that leg of hers getting well like lightning."

And then old Mr. King had to come and stand in the doorway, and say how glad he was that the foot was hurt no worse, for it had given him a dreadful fright to see her fear of his displeasure. And when Grace saw his handsome face light up with a smile for her, her last fear left her ; and she gave a sigh of relief as he went off, obediently finished the toast, and settled back on her pillow.

" Land, how weak she must be to eat like that ! she feels the need of victuals," said Mrs. Higby. " Now I'll run down and make you another slice," nodding to Grace, " you poor dear, you."

" Oh, don't let her !" begged Grace in alarm. " O Miss Phronsie ! I couldn't eat another morsel.

" She doesn't want any more, Mrs. Higby," said Phronsie ; " truly she doesn't."

" But just s'posin' she should be weak and faint in the night," said Mrs. Higby. " I'd better make just one little thin slice, hadn't I, Miss Phronsie," standing irresolute in the doorway.

"No," said Phronsie firmly. "I don't think you had, Mrs. Higby. There, I'm going to tuck her up now, and then I shall stay with her."

"Will you, Miss Phronsie?" cried Grace in delight.

"Yes," said Phronsie "I shall stay just as long as you want me to."

CHAPTER VII.

POLLY MAKES MATTERS RIGHT.

"POLLY," said Phronsie the next morning, "I do wish Mamsie was here."

It was the first time that Phronsie had said anything to show she wished the mother back; and Polly, who knew so well how all such utterance had been controlled, turned and stared at her.

"I do really wish that Mamsie was home again," said Phronsie, this time with a sigh, shaking her head decidedly.

"How you can, Phronsie," broke in Polly impulsively, "oh, I don't see, when you know how Mamsie needed the change, and how she would never let Papa Doctor go alone! O Phronsie!"

But in spite of that, "O Phronsie!" Phronsie still reiterated, "Yes, I do wish she was here!" And then she told the reason.

"Poor Grace," she said, "is crying, and Mamsie would know what to say to her."

"She shouldn't cry," said Polly vexedly. "Dear me, I think it is the weakest thing after a person has done wrongly to cry over it."

"Ah, but Grace was very wrong," said Phronsie sadly; "and she can't help it, Polly, when it all comes over her again. Just think, she disobeyed her aunt."

"To disobey mother" had always been such a heinous crime in the "Pepper children's" eyes, that Polly's work dropped in her lap, and she sat as still as Phronsie for the space of a moment. Then she said brightly to cheer Phronsie, "But it doesn't help matters any to cry over it. Yet to be sure," very suddenly, "I cried dreadfully when I'd been cross and hateful to Mrs. Chatterton. To be sure, so I did."

Suddenly Polly laid down her work, and went swiftly out of the room. She positively ran into the pretty bed-chamber where, under the white hangings, Grace was sobbing her young heart out.

"Dear child," said Polly, kneeling down by the bed, and laying a steady and gentle hand on the shaking figure, "I know just how you feel; for I cried once, just as miserably as you are crying, because I had been wicked."

"*You* wicked!" cried Grace, backing up so suddenly that Polly was nearly upset, "O Mrs. King, that could never be!"

"Ah, Grace, but it was; and it was much worse

"Dear child," said Polly, "I know just how you feel."

for me to be wicked, for I had had Mamsie all my life, — and you don't know what our Mamsie was, — while you have been away from your mother, you said, ever since you were six years old."

"Yes," said Grace. It was some relief that she did not have to tell that boarding-school life as she had found it in New England schools was ever so many degrees better than those years could have been under the nominal care of a mother given up to her own pursuits.

"And I was rude and hateful to a poor sick old woman," said Polly suddenly, laying her soft, warm hand on Grace's shaking ones; "and I said awfully cruel things to her, Grace; oh, you can't think how it makes me feel now to remember them!"

A tear or two crept out of Polly's eyes as she said this, and dropped on the counterpane.

"Why, you're crying yourself, Mrs. King!" exclaimed Grace, lifting her red, swollen eyelids in astonishment.

"I know it," said Polly, smiling brightly, and dashing off the tears with a quick hand. "You can't think how it makes me feel, Grace, after all these years, to remember what I said to old Mrs. Chatterton."

"She must have been horrid to you to have made you say those things," said Grace stoutly. "I just hate her, to make you feel badly even now."

It was a new thing to comfort any one else, and she pulled away one of her hands from Polly's clasp, and laid it on Mrs. King's shoulder, forgetting her own misery while she did so.

"She didn't make me," corrected Polly, "never mind what she said to me. Mamsie always used to say no one but ourselves could make us do and say things. No, Grace; it was because I lost my temper. Oh, I was so frightfully angry, I remember! And then I went up-stairs as hard as I could run, wishing every step that I could only get back the words I had uttered; and I hid in the trunk-room, and got down on the floor, and cried and cried — oh, how I cried! And then, when I finally came out and went down-stairs, everybody was hurrying about, troubled and anxious, because Mrs. Chatterton was ill; and then I thought that I had killed her."

"Oh, dear me!" said Grace.

"And after that," went on Polly, "I can't tell you how I felt. But I didn't cry any more. I just tried to do something for the poor woman. And after the longest time, Grandpapa told me Mrs. Chatterton had received bad news, — her favorite nephew had been drowned at sea."

"I'm glad of that," said Grace. "I mean, I'm glad that you knew it wasn't anything you had said that made her sick. Well, do please go on, Mrs. King."

"This all happened — the telegram coming, I mean — while I was up in the trunk-room," said Polly; "so of course I did not hear the news, though everybody thought I had. But I felt, oh, so dreadfully, that I had made her unhappy just before that awful blow came. And I shall always remember it."

"Please don't feel badly, dear Mrs. King," begged Grace softly, turning comforter. "Oh! I wish you wouldn't," gently patting Polly's shoulder.

"But I did not cry any more," said Polly. "I remember I used to squeeze the tears back, when they seemed determined to come, as I thought about it; for Mamsie had told us it was very wicked to cry over anything we had done, because it distressed every one about us."

"Did she?" asked Grace with great interest, as a wholly new idea struck her. "Why, I thought one's eyes were one's own, and one could do as she pleased with 'em."

"Ah, but you see, no one of us can do as she pleases, Grace," said Polly, shaking her head. "That you will find out more and more, the older you grow. And besides, Mamsie said it was a great sign of weakness to give yourself up to fits of crying after you had done wrongly. I remember what she used to tell us: 'To set about righting the wrong was better than a million tears.'"

"Mrs. King," exclaimed Grace suddenly, letting her hand fall idle on the bedspread, to peer into Polly's face, "I think your mother must have been just the nicest" — mother, she was going to say, but pulled herself up in time — "person in all this world."

"Oh, you can't guess what she was — what she is," cried Polly warmly, "till you see our Mamsie."

"And I won't cry another single bit," declared Grace, setting her lips tightly together; and doubling up her handkerchief into a little wad, she threw it to the foot of the bed, as a thing for which there could be no further use.

"That's right, dear," said Polly, setting a kiss on the flushed cheek; "because, you see, it troubles

Phronsie dreadfully. She's made almost sick by it, Grace. You can't think " — and Polly's face drooped.

"Oh, dear, dear!" wailed Grace remorsefully, and wriggling about in distress; "what have I done? Oh! please, dear Mrs. King, do tell her I've stopped crying, and that I never will cry again in all this world. Please hurry, and tell her so this very minute."

"So I will," promised Polly cheerily, and going out. "And I will ask her to come in and see for herself how good you are." She gave her a bright smile that seemed to hop right down into the sorry heart, telling her there was still some comfort left for her.

When Polly next looked in, about an hour after, Grace was propped up against the pillows, her fingers busy with one of the sails for the boys' boats, Phronsie sitting by her side, stitching away on the counterpart. A little table was drawn up to the side of the bed, with the work materials on it; and Phronsie had just been telling something gleeful, for Grace broke into a merry little laugh.

"Now, this looks something like," said Polly

approvingly in the doorway. She had her walking things on. "Grace, dear," she said, coming in and standing at the foot of the bed, "I am going to town this morning; and I thought I would go around and see your aunt, Mrs. Atherton, — I wrote her so last night, — and report how well you are getting on. It will save her the trouble of coming out. And now, do you wish me to do anything for you?"

She sent a keen glance out of her clear brown eyes full into the troubled face.

Grace threw down her work. "Mrs. King," she cried, while the hot blood went all over her face, "I told Miss Phronsie I'd like to write to Miss Willoughby, and tell her all about it."

"You cannot write," said Polly, while a gleam of pleasure came into her face, "until Dr. Phillips has been here and said you can. But I will go to Miss Willoughby, and tell her everything you say."

"Will you, Mrs. King?" cried Grace. "But oh, won't it trouble you too much?"

"No," said Polly, "it will not trouble me too much, child."

"Mrs. King," said Grace, brokenly, and clasping her hands, "will you please ask Miss Willoughby to forgive me for the disgrace I've brought on her school; and please tell her I didn't think of that when I began. I thought it was only myself I had to consider. And please tell her I mean to study and do everything I can to please her after this. But perhaps she won't let me ever come back to her day-school;" and Grace's face became suddenly overcast, as if she were going to cry; but she bit her lips, and held her hands tightly together instead. "Then I suppose I must bear it."

"I'll tell her every word," said Polly. "Anything else, dear?"

"If you could see Mrs. Drysdale, and tell her how sorry I am, perhaps some time, in several years, she'll forgive me for disgracing her so. Oh, and do tell dear Bella that she mustn't mind if Aunt Fay should happen to say anything cross to her, because everybody knows now that Bella didn't want to take me here, but I made her."

"Anything else?" asked Polly, after a pause. "How about the hired bonnet and dress at the milliner's?"

"Oh, dear, dear!" cried Grace, with a rush of

dismay at the throng of bad results of her wrong-doing; "you can't do all these things, Mrs. King! Oh, dear me! what shall I do?"

"Grace," said Polly warningly.

Grace looked up and struggled with her tears, but she could not say anything for a minute. Then she broke out, "She said it would be five dollars for the two; and my pocket-book is at home. There's plenty in it," she added hastily, in confusion, "for papa had just sent me on my allowance; but I can't get at it."

"I shall go in and pay Madame Le Farge," said Polly quietly, "and then you can pay me afterward, Grace. And Mrs. Higby is to pack up the dress and bonnet, and send them in by express. And Mrs. Atherton is to send your trunk out to-day. Then, dear, you will be quite comfortable as to clothes. Good-by;" and Polly came around to the side of the bed, and leaned over the back of the little table, and kissed her.

Grace, regardless of the fine walking-dress with its dainty bonnet and lace boa, threw both arms around Polly's neck, and hugged her close.

"Take care," warned Phronsie.

"Never mind," said Polly, taking a rosy face

from the embrace; "no harm is done. That is just the way we all used to fly at Mamsie. All right, Gracie;" going off with a smile.

"And now I've gone and done the wrong thing again," mourned Grace in confusion, huddling down into the bed, and not looking at the discarded sail. "Oh, dear me! I wish I could think in time."

"King wants his boat-sails this afternoon, Grace," said Phronsie gently, "and I promised them."

So Grace picked up the boat-sail, with its needle sticking in it just as she had thrown it aside, and Phronsie gathered up the narrative of some funny mishaps they had in a little German town when they were all last abroad, and presently they were both as merry again as before; and only the Dresden clock on the white mantel interrupted them.

Without a bit of warning, the door that Polly had left ajar was pushed wide open, and a tall figure appeared just about to stalk in. "Oh, beg your pardon!" he exclaimed, beating a retreat.

"O Joel!" cried Phronsie, jumping out of her chair to run across the room and into the tall figure's arms, "when did you come?"

"Just got here," said Joel; "walked from the station; didn't run across anybody but Patsy on the grounds. Anybody sick? and who's that?" nodding into the room, as they had now edged off into the hall.

"That's a friend," said Phronsie, "who only came yesterday, and she fell and hurt her foot. O Joe, it is so good to see you!"

"Yes, it is good to be here," cried Joel, feasting his eyes on her. "Well, where's Polly?"

"Gone to town," said Phronsie; "and she said we were not to wait luncheon for her."

"That's too bad," said Joel, "for I must be off this afternoon;" and he pulled out his watch. "And now I'll tell you, Phronsie, what I've come for. I want you and Grandpapa to go back with me for a few weeks. I can't tell you why now, only that I want you both. I'm dead tired of being alone. Now, do persuade him to come, Phronsie." Joel took her hand and held it close, his other arm being around her.

"O Joel!" cried Phronsie in great dismay, "I can't go just now. Could you wait a few days, perhaps a week; could you, Joey dear?"

A sound very much like a groan came from the

room behind them.   Phronsie tore herself away
from Joel, stepped back, and shut the door.   "Oh,
how could I be so careless!" she said remorsefully.   Now she's heard every word we said,
poor thing."

CHAPTER VIII.

ALEXIA COLLECTS THE NEWS.

JOEL ran off for a little visit to Grandma Bascom, at which time he unloaded himself of
various packages, to find places for them on her
cupboard shelves alongside the cracked sugar-bowl
that had been supposed to contain Mirandy's
"wedding cake receet." Then he shut up his
disappointment to himself as best he might, and
took the last train for New York alone.

"It can't be helped, Joe," old Mr. King had
said; "Phronsie has her hands full with that girl.
So you must wait for us."

"Bother that girl!" Joel looked. Then he
thought better of it. "All right; come when you
can," he had replied, as his brow cleared. On the
way to the station he ran across Alexia, who had
just arrived, as usual in a terrible hurry to see
Polly.

"Goodness me, Joel, you here!" she exclaimed

with no show of ceremony. " Don't I wish I had
a parish, and could run about the country as you
do ; and here I am tied to a husband and a baby."

"Poor husband and baby!" said Joel with a
grin, who liked Alexia immensely, but always
kept her on short commons of flattery.

"The most dreadful thing, Joel, you can imagine," gasped Alexia. "Oh, dear me! I've hurried so — to tell Polly — there's a girl who wormed
herself into her reception, and " —

"Whose reception — the girl's, or Polly's ? "
asked Joel.

"You know — Polly's of course. She pretended
to be" —

"Who — Polly, or the girl ?"

"Joe Pepper, if you don't stop and listen, I'll
never, never speak to you again!" cried Alexia in
a pet.

"That would be terrible," said Joel with a
laugh. "Good-by, Alexia," putting out his hand,
"I shall lose my train if I stay to get to the end
of that recital."

"Joe, Joe!" cried Alexia, running after him.
But he strode off, calling back, "I'll trust Polly."
And his train approaching the depot, Alexia, be-

moaning her fate in not getting out to Badgertown
earlier, skipped off to "The Oaks" in no very
pleasant frame of mind.

"Where's Polly?" she cried to Phronsie in the
conservatory as she ran through the library.

"Polly's gone to town," said Phronsie, cutting
off some blossoms to add to the bunch in her
hand.

"To town! Oh, dear me!" screamed Alexia.
"And I've only just come out! What *did* she
want to go to town to-day for, Phronsie?"

"She had to go, Alexia," said Phronsie, pausing
as she saw Alexia was really distressed; "what is
the matter?"

"Oh! then I must tell you," said Alexia. "Oh,
my! I'm so hot, as if I'd run every speck of
the way."

"I'll get you a fan," said Phronsie, coming into
the library. "There are some, Alexia, on the
table."

"Whew!" Alexia possessed herself of one,
and fanned vigorously, so that she set all the
feathers on her much-betrimmed hat into a violent
flutter. "Oh! it's all over town, Phronsie," she
said.

"Polly 's gone to town," said Phronsie, cutting off some blossoms
to add to the bundle in her hand.

"What is all over town?" asked Phronsie quietly.

"Oh, about that dreadful Strange, or Tupper girl — how she wormed herself in here at Polly's reception. I heard of it this afternoon, and I just stopped to run home and tell Baby I was coming out here to let Polly know. Oh, dear me!"

"I'm sorry for Grace," breathed Phronsie pityingly. "Oh! I hope she won't know anything about it."

"Sorry for Grace," repeated Alexia, throwing down the fan, "well, I should say! I believe it was all a plan between Mrs. Atherton and that Mrs. Drysdale, to get her here."

"Oh, no, Alexia! it wasn't," said Phronsie decidedly, shaking her head; "because Grace has told us all about it. It was nobody's fault but her own."

"Well, I can't abide that Mrs. Drysdale," declared Alexia, who had reasons of her own for not being in love with that lady; "and as for Mrs. Atherton, why, she's well enough, I suppose, only a trifle weak in the upper story. Well, and oh, dear me! Miss Fitzwilliam said" —

"Did Miss Fitzwilliam tell you," asked Phronsie quietly, "the story of Grace's coming here?"

"Yes," said Alexia; "she told us all. And she said she saw through her disguise, and that it was Mrs. Atherton's niece."

"Who are all?" asked Phronsie.

"Why, all of us in the Campbell's drawing-room, child. What makes you question a body up so close. It doesn't make any difference, does it, where or how I heard it, if everybody's talking of it?"

"Everybody isn't a few people in Mrs. Campbell's drawing-room, Alexia," said Phronsie; yet she sighed, and the bunch of flowers in her hand trembled a little.

This made Alexia more vexed than ever. "Well, there was Captain Sledges; he's home on a furlough, you know; and, oh! the Romeynes from New York, and two or three others, besides some of our Berton set," said Alexia. "Oh! there was quite a nice little lot, Phronsie, to hear the news. And I just tore out, I was so vexed, and only stopped to tell Baby, and" —

Phronsie turned her brown eyes full on Alexia. "I hope you stood up for poor Grace

She's only sixteen, and she didn't stop to think, she says."

"I stand up for her — how could I ?" cried Alexia. "I never saw the girl. Oh, dear me! now you're going to take her part, and comfort and pet her. It's just like you, Phronsie; I wouldn't go near that Atherton house, nor even send a word to her."

"It isn't necessary," said Phronsie, in the quietest of tones; "for Grace hasn't been home, and she's going to stay here, I hope, a good while."

"She's in this house ?" screamed Alexia, tumbling off the sofa to gain her feet, "oh, my good gracious me, Phronsie Pepper !"

"Yes," said Phronsie; "she's in this house, Alexia. She fell yesterday, and hurt her foot very badly; and Dr. Phillips said this morning when he saw it, that she ought not to be moved for a week or two. And Polly's had her clothes sent out, and I hope she's going to stay a good while; for I like her, Alexia, very much indeed."

It was a long speech for Phronsie to make; and she sat quite still after it was over, and looked at Mrs. Dodge.

"Oh, dear me! and now you'll give up all your

time to taking care of her, and coddling her up. How do you know but what she will go and do something just as bad when she gets well again?" cried Alexia.

"Ah, but I know she won't, Alexia," said Phronsie, shaking her head decidedly. "She's awfully sorry and ashamed, and she's been made almost sick by it."

"So she ought to be," cried Alexia wrathfully. "Now I know what Polly's doing in town to-day, running about in the heat — she's fixing up the trouble this girl made."

"Alexia," said Phronsie in a tone indicative of the deepest distress, and leaning forward to whisper the words, "I almost know that Grace's mother never told her about what was right and wrong — I really believe she didn't."

"Well, supposing she didn't; are you going to take other people's children, and bring them up?" exclaimed Alexia. "Phronsie Pepper, I should think you'd enough on your hands with that Orphan Home down at Bedford, without any more young ones to look after!"

"And Grace has been away at boarding-school ever since she was six years old," mourned Phronsie, without paying the slightest heed to Alexia; "dear, dear, just think of it, Alexia."

"Well, I suppose I might as well talk to the wind," exclaimed Alexia, "as to try to reason you and Polly against such a Quixotic scheme. Dear, dear, I can't do anything with either of you."

"No," said Phronsie, "you can't, Alexia. And now I want you to come up and see Grace — how nice she is. And you must tell her something lively to amuse her. Do, dear Alexia."

She got off from the sofa, and put her arm around the tall, slim figure.

"Ugh! — no, I can't." Alexia edged off. "It's bad enough for you to pet and coddle her; I'm going home."

"Come, Alexia," said Phronsie, holding out her hand; and Mrs. Dodge, grumbling all the way, went up the stairs after her.

"And just to think," she said, when they reached the top, — "wait a minute, Phronsie, — how it's all over town about her getting in here so; and you're giving up your time, and Polly's too, to take care of her, I " —

"Hush!" warned Phronsie, picking Alexia's sleeve, and pointing to the door of the little room.

"Ugh!—oh, goodness me! I thought she was in the west wing," gasped Alexia, in a stage whisper. "Well, I don't believe she heard anything."

"Please remember Alexia, to tell her amusing things, for Grace has been so sad," said Phronsie, softly drawing Alexia into the room. There was no one in the little white bed.

Out in the dressing-room they found her, crying bitterly, and trying to pull her clothes out of her trunk. "I'm going home," she exclaimed passionately between her sobs.

"O Grace!" cried Phronsie, hurrying forward to lay a restraining hand upon her.

"Oh, me — oh, my!" exclaimed Alexia, backing up for support against the door.

"Please call Mrs. Higby, Alexia," said Phronsie. And Alexia, glad to do something, fled with long steps, and presently brought Mrs. Higby, who, without any more ado, just picked up Grace, with a "Poor lamb, there, there, don't cry!" and deposited her on the little white bed again, where she shook with the passionate declarations that she was going home, and no one should stop her.

Mrs. Higby examined critically the bandaged

foot. "Lucky if she hain't hurt it," and she drew
a long breath, "I don't b'lieve she did, Miss
Phronsie."

"No, I didn't," sobbed Grace; "I hopped on
the other foot. Oh, dear, dear!"

"Please go out," begged Phronsie. When the
door was closed she put her hand on the hot
brow. "Grace," she said, "I am disappointed
in you."

"I heard what she said," cried Grace in a
gust, and throwing both arms suddenly around
Phronsie. "O Miss Pepper, just get me to
Aunt's — do! I'll make her let me go home.
And I never'll trouble any one any more."

"You can't be moved yet," said Phronsie;
"and it remains with you to say whether or no
you will be a good girl, Grace, and be a comfort
to us." Grace could take but one look at her
face, it was such a disapproving one, and she
disappeared as far as she could beneath the bedclothes. "I heard what she said," she reiterated
faintly.

"Ah, Grace," said Phronsie sadly, "when we
have done wrongly, we must just make up our
minds to bear what people say."

Alexia knocked timidly at the door. "Come in," called Phronsie.

"I'm awfully sorry you heard what I said," she mumbled, going up to the foot of the bed, "everybody don't know it — only a few people, I guess. And anyway, I suppose Polly, Mrs. King, will fix it up, and I'm real sorry for you, and I'll help you — oh, dear me!"

Phronsie looked at her gratefully. "Alexia, will you tell her about your baby," she asked suddenly.

"Oh, that blessed child!" began Alexia in delight; "yes, indeed, that is, if you'll take your head out of those bedclothes. I never could talk to any one unless I could see at least their nose. Well, now, that's something like. You know, Miss — Miss" —

"My name is Grace Tupper," said Grace, who had pulled up a very red face to lay it against the pillow.

"Oh, yes; well, you must know, Miss Tupper," ran on Alexia, "that I really have the best baby in the whole world. He's a perfect beauty to begin with, and he's ever so many teeth, and he talks, and what do you suppose he was doing when I got home? — I only ran out to pay a few visits, you know."

"I don't know," said Grace faintly, as Alexia waited for her to speak.

"Why, he was trying to brush his own hair," said Mrs. Dodge. "Now, that blessed child must have known his hair didn't look good. Bonny, that's his nurse, lets him muss it up dreadfully, and so the poor dear was just doing it for himself."

"I suppose she gave him the brush to play with," said Grace, interested at once.

"Never mind how he got it," cried Alexia, "he was brushing his hair. Now, I call that very smart indeed; I'm almost afraid to think what he will become, Miss Tupper, when he grows up. There isn't anything that'll be quite the thing for him."

"I suppose he can be President of the United States," said Grace.

"Oh, dear me, no!" cried Alexia hastily. "There have been twenty-four of them already. I want my boy to be something new, and ahead of other people. And just think, it won't be but a little while before he'll be in college, and then he'll be through, and then I'm sure he'll want to be something quite unusual; I'm sure he will."

"What's his name?" asked Grace, wishing she could see this wonderful baby.

"Algernon Rhys Dodge," said Alexia; "isn't it just a beautiful name? I wanted to call him after his father, 'Pickering;' but I knew it would be 'Pick' all the time to distinguish him, so I gave it up. Well, you'll see him often, because we're going to move out to Badgertown next week."

"Are you?" cried Grace, "how nice!"

"Yes," said Alexia, pleased at the effect of her efforts to entertain, "we are; into the dearest little yellow cottage, with barberry-bushes in front. I've named it, 'The Pumpkin' and"—

"O Alexia! you are only in fun now," said Phronsie with a little laugh.

"Indeed, and I'm not," said Alexia; "I'm having my cards engraved so. Why shouldn't I have that name, when it's just the color of a pumpkin, and not much bigger? and lots and lots of places have the most ridiculous names, and no rhyme nor reason for them either. You must come and visit me at 'The Pumpkin,' Miss

Tupper, when we get in nicely. Then you'll see for yourself, if you ever knew such a baby as that blessed child of mine. Oh, here's Polly!"

Polly came in swiftly. She had a little white look around her mouth, as if she were very tired, but she smiled brightly. "It's all right," she said to Grace. "Oh, how nice and cheery you are here! Alexia," and she beamed on her, "you're as good as gold, to come out and be a comfort."

"Ugh!" exclaimed Alexia, "don't praise me, Polly."

"Go and take your things off, do, Polly," begged Phronsie.

Alexia sprang after Polly as she went out.

"Oh! I've been a horrid mean thing, Polly," she cried, when safe in Polly's room, "and I messed things up generally. But I'll help you now, and she's a dear, that Grace Tupper is, and you must go for that dreadful Fitzwilliam to-morrow;" and then she told Polly the story of her afternoon.

CHAPTER IX.

PHRONSIE SETTLES THE MATTER.

BUT Polly didn't take Miss Fitzwilliam in charge; for Phronsie came to early breakfast the next morning with her little brown bonnet on, that, with the walking-suit, meant a day in town. "I am going to Berton," she said, "with Jasper."

The small red breakfast-room at "The Oaks" was always cosey for the early meal that Jasper took every morning before he grasped the "little publishing bag" and hurried off for his train. Polly sat behind the coffee-urn, pouring a cup for him.

"Why, Phronsie!" she exclaimed in surprise; then she asked, "does Grandpapa know?"

"Yes," said Phronsie; "I told him last night. I was going to tell you, Polly, but you were busy in the den with Jasper."

"Then I'll pour you a cup of coffee," said Polly.

"No," said Phronsie; "I'll have just a glass of milk, the same as every day, Polly."

"O Phronsie!" remonstrated Polly, "take the coffee, do, dear; it will be a hard day in town."

But Phronsie shook her head. "Polly," she said, as she got into her chair, and the butler had gone out and closed the door, as he always did that Polly and Jasper might talk through the meal, "I am going to town to see Miss Fitzwilliam."

"Phronsie!" exclaimed Polly in great dismay, letting fall her spoon; Jasper set down his cup to look at Phronsie.

"Yes, I am," said Phronsie, beginning to drink her milk. Then she took a piece of toast and buttered it.

"If you are going to town, Phronsie," began Polly quickly, "do have a hot chop, dear."

"No," said Phronsie; "I do not want it, Polly. I am going to take an orange in my bag. Please, Polly, let me tell you about it."

Polly looked over at Jasper in despair. His eyes said, "Don't worry, dear. Perhaps she won't do it."

"You see," said Phronsie deliberately, "Miss

Fitzwilliam must not be left to spread the story about Grace. And she won't want to when I tell her all about it. She'll feel sorry that she told in the first place."

"You don't know Miss Fitzwilliam, Phronsie, if you say so," burst out Polly. "She's the veriest gossip there is in all Berton — or the universe either. It won't do a bit of good for you to go to see her. She can't change, child; she's too old."

"Ah, but she must," said Phronsie, shaking her head; "and if nobody tells her how wrong it is to set people against Grace — why, she will go on doing so all the time."

"Phronsie," said Polly desperately, and leaning past the coffee-urn, "I can't bear to have you put yourself in that old gossip's house. Oh, dear me! why is it that nobody puts her down? Everybody hates her; and then they listen to her stories just the same."

"That's just it," said Jasper, pushing back his chair; "they listen to her stories, Polly, as you say. They're as bad as she is, every whit."

"But I can't see them all, I'm afraid," said Phronsie, setting down her empty glass. " Miss

Fitzwilliam started it, so I ought to talk with her."

"Phronsie, does Grandpapa know you're going to see Miss Fitzwilliam?" asked Polly, seeing here a ray of hope that the visit to town would be given up.

"Oh, yes! did you think I would go to see her without telling Grandpapa, Polly?" asked Phronsie with a grieved look in her brown eyes.

"No, dear," said Polly hastily.

Then she got out of her chair, and ran around to drop a kiss on Phronsie's yellow hair; but Phronsie moving just then, the kiss fell on the little bunch of brown flowers on the top of her bonnet. "Dear me!" said Polly with a laugh, "well, I'm sure I'm willing to kiss your bonnet, Phronsie, as it isn't all decked up with birds' wings. I knew, of course, you'd tell Grandpapa everything, Phronsie."

"Oh, I couldn't wear a bird's wings on my bonnet; you know I couldn't, Polly!" exclaimed Phronsie in horror.

"No more could I," declared Polly. "I should feel as if I'd murdered the sweetest thing on earth, to perk a bird up on my bonnet. Oh, dear me!" aghast at the thought. "Jasper, what shall we do," as Phronsie got up and went over to the sideboard to get an orange for her bag, "to keep Phronsie from going to town?"

"I don't believe we better try any more, Polly," said Jasper, going over to take his wife's hand. "I really believe it's best to let Phronsie alone, for she thinks that she ought to go."

"But that old thing!" began Polly impulsively, "and our Phronsie."

"It won't hurt Phronsie," said Jasper wisely, putting his arm around Polly's waist, to look into her eyes. "No, Polly, I don't believe we ought to say any more. Come, Phronsie, are you ready?"

"Yes, I am," said Phronsie, patting her little bag; "all ready, Jasper. Polly, I'll get your red wool; you said you didn't have time yesterday."

"Oh, you dear!" cried Polly, comforted by Jasper's words. "But don't tire yourself, Phronsie; it's no matter; I can wait."

"If anybody is going to town with me, she must hurry up; that's all I say," called Jasper, giving Polly a kiss and, running off.

Polly ached to say, "Don't go to Miss Fitz-william's," as Phronsie set a kiss on her cheek; but remembering Jasper's words, she smothered the longing with a sigh. "Well, good-by, child," as Phronsie ran down the path to the dog-cart that was to carry them to the train.

When Phronsie left Jasper as he turned off into the business section, and she waited for the electric car bound for the old residential part of the town, he gave her a bright smile. "Success to you, Phronsie dear! What train are you coming out on?"

"I don't know," said Phronsie; "don't wait for me. I wish you wouldn't, Jasper."

"All right. It shall be as you wish, Phronsie. Good-by, dear." He flashed her another smile, and was off, to plunge into the work of the day.

"I do think Jasper is the dearest brother that ever lived," said Phronsie to herself as she hurried on her car. A little old woman, whose back was bent, and the ends of whose white hair had escaped from her rusty black bonnet, stood in her way, clutching one of the leather straps that hung from the bar that ran across the top of the car.

"Move up in front," shouted the conductor, giving a push to the little old woman's back; "this lady can't get in."

Phronsie led the little old white-haired woman to the vacated seat.

"Never mind," said Phronsie; "I can stand here just as well."

"Move up, I say," repeated the conductor, with another shove.

Thereupon three or four collegians, bound for the university a few miles off, precipitated themselves out of their seats, the fortunate one who was first, hustling against the little old woman in black. "Will you take my seat?" taking off his cap to Phronsie.

"Thank you," said Phronsie gravely. Then she touched the bent shoulder gently, and took hold of the pinched hand clinging to the strap; the other one she could now see was filled with bundles. "Here is a seat for you;" and before any one could say anything, she had led the little old white-haired woman to the vacated seat, arranged her bundles more comfortably in in her lap, and gone down to the end of the car again.

The collegians' faces got dreadfully red. No one of them dared to try it again, for an old gentleman who had seen it all had gotten out of his seat, and with a courtly bow was proffering it to her.

"Thank you," Phronsie was saying, refusing it, with a smile. "I really do not mind standing." And the three collegians melted out suddenly to the front platform, and away the car flew, and

Phronsie was soon at the corner down which she was to turn to the three story brick house that had the honor to be owned by Miss Honora Fitzwilliam.

She was in, the trim maid said; and Phronsie gave a sigh of relief, as she stumbled on down the darkened hall, to find a seat in the still more darkened drawing-room, whose door the maid opened deferentially.

"What name?" she asked in the same manner.

Phronsie took out a card from her plain brown leather case. The maid departed, bearing this evidence that Miss Sophronia Pepper, The Oaks, Badgertown, was awaiting Miss Fitzwilliam's pleasure.

It was fully half an hour before that lady made her appearance, with everything as fresh as possible about her, her side-curls beautifully gotten up. Even the lorgnette was ready.

"Oh! I am *so glad* to see you, my dear Miss Pepper," she began effusively, extending both hands, "Phronsie, I may call you, may I not?" Phronsie did not answer, only to say, "Good-morning;" so Miss Fitzwilliam exclaimed hastily, "That stupid Eliza! this room is as black as midnight." She stepped to the other side of the apartment, and gave a nervous twitch to the bell. " Let some light into this room," as the maid came in; " how careless of you not to open the shutters by this time."

Eliza opened her mouth to say something, but evidently was too frightened to carry out her intention, and throwing the shutters wide, hurried out of the room as if glad to get away.

The morning sunlight flooded the long drawing-room, whose faded coverings looked tired out; several thin places very near to becoming holes could plainly be seen on the furniture, while even the mantel ornaments looked depressed.

Miss Fitzwilliam sprang to her feet, and energetically thrust the shutters half way to. " That stupid Eliza!" she ejaculated again. " I hope, Miss Pepper, that you are not troubled as I am with servants. They are really the plague of my life, although I change every fortnight or so." Then she came back and sat down on the faded red sofa by Phronsie's side. " What a most beautiful reception your sister's was, to be sure!" she cried rapturously. "I always make it a point to exert myself to go to Badgertown whenever she

gives one. And I'm so sorry for you, that you
were all so annoyed Tuesday by that" —

"Miss Fitzwilliam," said Phronsie, breaking in
to the stream of talk. "I have come to see you
about that very thing." Then she looked steadily
into the little steel-gray eyes before her.

"And have you, my dear?" cried Miss Fitzwilliam delightedly. "I suppose you want my advice what to do." She tried to lay her pinched and
restless fingers on the quiet gloved ones in Phronsie's lap, to show her sympathy; but the young
girl not stirring, Miss Fitzwilliam pulled hers
back, and went on rapidly, "As it was such an
outrageous thing, I would " —

"Miss Fitzwilliam," Phronsie did not pause
now, but went swiftly on to the end, not remov-
ing her gaze from the other's face, "I've come to
see you about this matter, because I know that
after you've heard all about it, you'll be sorry for
the young girl who did such a wrong thing. Just
think, she's only sixteen, and she hasn't been with
her mother only vacations when she was home
from school, since she was six years old. And as
soon as she did it, and got there to the reception,
she'd have undone it all if she could, — oh, a thou-

sand times! And she made Bella Drysdale take
her. Mrs. Drysdale didn't know anything about
it, but thought she was a parlor-boarder at Miss
Willoughby's; and Mrs. Atherton didn't know
either. Grace has told it all to us, and that she
alone was to blame. It was the first time that
she has ever done such a thing, and she didn't
stop to think before she did it. And now she
can't forgive herself; she must always be sorry
to the end of her life: so all of us must help her
to bear it."

"Miss Phronsie Pepper!" screamed Miss Fitzwilliam, throwing away her self-control as Phronsie paused, "you don't mean to say that you think
people should take up this Tupper girl; why, I've
told everybody I could about it! I went around
yesterday, and I'm going again this afternoon."
Her thin face glowed, and her pinched-up nose
was set high in the air with positive delight.

"I know you did tell them yesterday," said
Phronsie quietly; "but I think you'll be sorry for
that when you come to think it over."

"Sorry? Indeed, no!" sniffed Miss Fitzwilliam.
"I shall get as many as I can to know it before
nightfall. It's my duty. Sorry, indeed!"

Phronsie surveyed her gravely. "You will be very sorry, I think, Miss Fitzwilliam," she said again quietly; "it will spoil that young girl's whole life, to repeat that story."

"And you'll be very glad," cried Miss Fitzwilliam shrilly, "that I did take the pains to tell it, and to warn people against such a little impostor. How do you know that she won't repeat this experiment again at your house?"

"She will not, because"—

"And that stuff about hurting her foot was half of it made up," said Miss Fitzwilliam; "that's the reason I wanted to stay and help you. I found her out long before." She gave a little triumphant cackle; "and I wanted to see her foot, if that wasn't all a pretence, so"—

"Oh, no, it wasn't!" said Phronsie, who couldn't help interrupting; "because she"—

"But you wouldn't let me stay. However, I have started the story about her, I am glad to say; I suppose she went home soon after, didn't she?" she asked quickly, greedy for the last bit of news.

"No," said Phronsie; "she did not."

"That shows what kind of a girl she is!"

exclaimed Miss Fitzwilliam with venom, "after worming herself in there, to hang on until you had to send her home."

"Miss Fitzwilliam," said Phronsie so decidedly that Miss Fitzwilliam pulled herself up at the beginning of another harangue, "don't you understand — can't you understand, that Grace Tupper is not that kind of a girl at all? She began this as a childish freak; she is most dreadfully sorry for it, and she would give everything — yes, the whole world," said Phronsie, clasping her hands while her face drooped sorrowfully, "if she hadn't done it."

"Pshaw!" exclaimed Miss Fitzwilliam in disdain. Then she put back her head on her spare shoulders, and laughed loud and long. "Anyway, Miss Pepper, I shall do as I think best about it. And I do think best to tell this story wherever I have a good opportunity." She set her thin lips together unpleasantly.

"In that case," said Phronsie, rising, "I will trouble you no further. And will you be so very good, Miss Fitzwilliam, as to discontinue calling at 'The Oaks'? Grace Tupper is our guest, our *dear* guest; and my sister, Mrs. King and I hope that she will stay there a long time, for we are both already very fond of her. I will bid you good-morning."

It was impossible for Miss Fitzwilliam to get her breath to speak. Twice she essayed it, but no words came; and vexed that she had made such a terrible blunder, and with her own hand cut off visiting relations with Mrs. Jasper King and her sister, Miss Pepper, she made another effort, this time even managing a ghastly smile.

"Of course if you are going to take her up, why I will let the matter drop," she gasped. But Miss Pepper did not appear to notice, nor to observe the outstretched hand, but went swiftly out. On the old-fashioned table in the hall was the morning paper, still unread. Wild with chagrin, Miss Fitzwilliam seized it to divert her mind, as the door closed after Phronsie; and whirling the sheet to the social news, read: "Miss Grace Strange Tupper, niece of Mrs. Carroll Atherton, is the guest of Mrs. Jasper King at 'The Oaks' Badgertown."

When Phronsie completed her round of calls, beginning with Mrs. Coyle Campbell, everybody knew that it was to be the fashion to take up

Grace Tupper. And each one vied with the others, to be ahead in the matter of sympathy and help.

Then Phronsie hurried down town to buy Polly's red worsted.

CHAPTER X.

SUCCESS FOR POLLY.

THE grand extra concert, the best of the year, given by the Symphony Orchestra, with Mrs. Jasper King as pianist, was over, and only a delightful memory. Every member of the orchestra declared no such performer on the piano had it ever been their good fortune to accompany, and musical critics went a little wild in their efforts to find adequate expressions to describe her treatment of the theme she had chosen.

It was a great society event; all the fashionable world of Berton being in evidence, with good sprinklings from New York and other towns to overcrowd the house. But Polly, although her heart responded, most especially for Jasper's sake, to these tokens of cordial interest and admiration, felt her whole soul drawn to the old friends who, here and there, were in conspicuous seats among the audience. They were all there, as far as was possible. Miss Salisbury, who had left her school and the duties that never before allowed her to wander, recklessly dropped all this time into the sub-principal's hands, and went off to hear her dear old pupil, Polly Pepper.

Cathie Harrison, living in the South with her grandmother, made that old lady pick up her belongings, and take a two weeks' jaunt, that included Berton on its return. Amy Loughead in New York, under the care of her aunt, Mrs. Montgomery, of course was there; the two happening to take the same train on with the Rev. Joel Pepper, who had collected his friend Robert Bingley for that very purpose.

The Cabots and Van Meters, besides Ben Pepper, who represented that house now, the Alstynes, Mr. and Mrs. Hamilton Dyce, and a score or more of other old friends, all turned up at the last minute, and electrified Polly with swift glances of recognition across the crowded hall, that cheered her on over the difficult passages better than any applause could possibly have done. Charlotte Chatterton seemed to be the only one left out. She was in Europe, turning out something wonderful, if accounts were true, with her voice —

"unlocked by Phronsie's golden key," Charlotte always said, in telling how Phronsie's generous gift of a portion of old Lady Chatterton's money had made it possible for her to cultivate her one talent. Charlotte's love for Phronsie was so passionate it seemed to outrun her love for music, making it a dreary exile for her to stay and study abroad. Only the hope of seeing Dr. Fisher and Mother Fisher kept her from running off with a homesick heart to the dear old friends.

Mr. and Mrs. Mason Whitney of course were there, and Van, mightily proud of being in his father's business, and engaged to one of the sweetest girls born and brought up in his set, "the little blue-and-white creature," whom Joel so desperately entertained at the Welcome-Home-party years ago. Van had regularly offered himself to Phronsie at any and every opportunity that had presented itself in the past three years, to be as regularly but more gently refused. And now he had wisely concluded to pass that pleasing attention down to Dick, or rather Dick had taken it upon himself, with small care whether or no Mr. Van passed it along. And Van had looked around for the best way to settle in life, to

get ready for that partnership with his father
which he fondly hoped was just ahead of him;
so he proposed and was accepted promptly by
Gladys Ray, who had, it seems, been waiting for
him all the time; and everybody was delighted;
and Van was so important with it all, his mother
having brought along little Miss Ray in the party,
that Percy, a newly fledged lawyer with his shin-
gle just out, who was in the party also, found it
hard to bear with equanimity his unimportance,
and the trouble of his monocle, just assumed.

Dick brought along a whole lot of his jolly
brother collegians, among them the three who
figured in Phronsie's car episode, and who trusted
not to be recognized; but Dick, not knowing
anything of it, hauled along this identical trio,
after the concert, and presented them, " Mr. Fox,
Mr. Beresford, and Mr. Sargent," when they immediately had the appearance of desiring to melt
away again.

Dick was here, there, and everywhere on this
occasion, bubbling over with jubilation. Was he
not to go into the house of Marlowe & King " the
very day after graduation — yes, sir ! " to begin
his dream of being a publisher.

But the best of all, in Polly's eyes, was the
presence of Jasper's and her dear friend David
Marlowe, who sat in one of the front rows. Mr.
Marlowe never took his eyes from Polly; but
sat quietly through it all, when it became impossible for the other friends to control their intense
interest. But how his keen gray eyes glistened!
And when it was all over, he put his good right
hand on Jasper's, "My boy!" said he in that
strong, clear voice of his; and Jasper knew all
his friend's heart better than if many words had
been uttered.

The only disappointment in certain quarters
was that Polly had issued her command that no
flowers should be given, thus throwing Dick, as
well as some other friends, into incipient rebellion.

"No, indeed," said Polly, who dearly loved to
be elegant in just the right way, when some ink-
ling of Dick's extravagant plans had come to
her, "not so much as a solitary sprig — now
remember, Dicky," one glance of her brown eyes,
and Dicky and everybody else knew that offence
in this respect meant a terrible thing.

But afterward, when they got Polly away from
"the mob," as the collegians called it, of those

swarming up to congratulate, then Jasper took matters into his own hands, and disclosed the surprise he had planned for Polly; and with Mr. Marlowe's aid, he piloted all the old friends, and a goodly number of new ones, to the special cars waiting for them, and away they all went for dinner, and to top off the evening at "The Oaks."

Phronsie had sent a very special invitation to Mr. and Mrs. Carroll Atherton, to Mrs. Drysdale and to Bella, and also to "Cousin Charley Swan;" so they all came. And Miss Willougby was there, and she found an old schoolfellow in Miss Salisbury before the evening was half out; and everything went merrily as possible in every section of the big company.

And Alexia, whose little "Pumpkin" was bursting with guests, up for the occasion, — she having stipulated that Cathie Harrison and Cathie Harrison's grandmother should be part of her especial share, — was there in full force, helping, with Mrs. Fargo and Pickering, to receive and do the honors, having "told the baby all about it before," and consigned him to Bonny's tender mercies.

And when the dinner had proceeded to the toasts, Jasper looked across the table into his wife's eyes, "Yes, Polly," he said to her questioning look, "I cabled Mamsie the very minute you finished playing."

"Indeed he did!" cried Mr. Marlowe, smiling into her rosy face.

"O Jasper, how lovely of you!" cried Polly with dewy eyes. "And is that what you signalled the usher for?"

"Yes, dear," he said, smiling at her; "I had it all written before. You didn't think I could leave the dear Mamsie a minute longer than was necessary without the news?"

"No, Jasper," she said; "but oh, how lovely in you to do it!"

Phronsie, opposite Grandpapa, who was stately and resplendent at the head of one of the other tables, looked over happily, "O Jasper!" she exclaimed, clasping her hands, "does Mamsie really know it now?"

"Yes, Phronsie," said Jasper, beaming at her; "she really does."

Phronsie sat quite still, her hands remaining clasped. It was as if the dear Mamsie's face was really there before her, with the light and cheer that always made everything bright; and a tender

look came into Phronsie's eyes and around the
curves of her mouth. And then her face drooped;
and the dreadful longing that she had had every
minute since Mother Fisher had sailed, just to see
her again, settled down upon her. "Mamsie!"
she breathed slowly, but in a way to make everybody turn and look at her.

Just then the heavy brass knocker on the front
door clanged sharply. One of the maids brought
in a yellow envelope, which she handed to Jasper. He tore it open quickly. "O Polly!" and
across the table it sped to her. "Give it to
Phronsie; let her read it first, dear. It's from
Mamsie!"

When they all came out of the babel of confused delight, Phronsie still sitting with clasped
hands but radiant face, Jasper stood up and
read: —

"To my dear Polly, I send my proud and loving word.
I knew she would do it. And give my love to Phronsie.

MAMSIE."

"We'll drink her health," cried Jasper. "Sim-
mons, pass the loving-cup."

So the butler took down the massive silver

loving-cup, that had been for generation after generation in the King family, from the oaken sideboard, and filled it with pure cold water to the brim, "The only thing worthy of it," said Polly; and all the company stood up, and Jasper lifted

The loving cup was filled with pure cold water to the brim, "The only thing worthy of it," said Polly.

it high, with "Our Mamsie, now as always our guide, our comfort, and our delight; we pledge ourselves anew to her in loyal love." And then the cup went around silently to every one.

And Ben proposed Father Fisher, and everybody drank his health and happiness; and then Polly turned a happy face over toward old Mr. King. " Our dear Grandpapa was *everything*," she said; " I don't know what we should ever have done without him."

And around went the loving-cup again. And this neat little speech so touched the old gentleman that he got out of his chair, and responded right gallantly to his daughter, and to the rest of the " Five Little Peppers." And Jasper's eyes shone with proud delight, and everybody applauded to the echo. And then Davie, the new instructor in literature at a Western university, and already booked in the minds of all present for the professor's chair, was called out for a speech; and a right good one it was too, the Rev. Joel pounding vigorously his approval above all the others on the festal board.

And Hamilton Dyce tried his hand at talking a bit, and brought down the house with many funny reminiscences; and Mr. Marlowe said, as he always did, exactly the right word in the right place; and Joel was called for loudly, but he had slipped away just then, so several of the others talked; and then Jasper brought down his improvised gavel, the handle of Grandpapa's cane, "Speeches declared over! We will now adjourn to the little brown house;" and Polly led off proudly with Grandpapa, as was quite right, Phronsie and Mr. Marlowe following, the rest of the company falling in as they chose, with Jasper at the rear corralling all the stragglers into line.

"Let's march all around it, father dear," whispered Polly, gleefully as a child. So they led off in the moonlight the long procession around and around the little brown house, till some one proposed unwinding and going the other way. But they didn't do it, but just broke ranks, and rushed unceremoniously into the old kitchen.

And there were Polly's two hundred candles she longed for in the old days, all alight most merrily, which explained the Rev. Joel's absence from the last part of the speech-making; and after that there was no more quiet. The old kitchen resounded to the babel of happy voices, until at last everybody drew up in a circle of chairs, getting the Peppers in the centre, whom they besieged for stories of those old times.

"I'm a Pepper!" cried Jasper, scrambling

into the charmed circle. "I was in those happy days."

"Yes, Jappy belongs to us," said Phronsie.

"Jap always felt so smart," declared Van enviously, "because he knew the Peppers first." Percy looked as if he wanted to say as much, but concluded to keep still, and only readjusted his monocle to his satisfaction.

"We shouldn't any of us have had or done anything if it hadn't been for Jappy; hey, old fellow," declared Ben, clapping him on the shoulder.

"And dear Grandpapa," cried Phronsie, with a world of affection in her eyes, looking over at him.

"Well, Phronsie did it with her gingerbread boy," said Jasper quickly. "It was Phronsie, after all, who brought us all together."

And then everybody clamored for the story of the gingerbread boy again; so off they rushed on that, old Mr. King edging his chair a little nearer to the Pepper circle. And then Polly's old stove had to come in for a share of attention, and how she had to stuff all the cracks with paper, and Ben stuffed it with putty, and — "Davie gave boot-tops," broke in Joel, grimly even now

at the remembrance of how he felt because he
hadn't any to give.

And then that brought up Mamsie's birthday
cake, and the momentous work of getting ready
for its baking; and how Phronsie's toe was
pounded; and how good Grandma Bascom was,
and how she wasn't able now to get out of her
bed because of the rheumatism, but that those
guests who stayed over were to go down the
lane to see her to-morrow.

And how the cake, compounded after "Mirandy's weddin' receet" was at last made, and
hidden in the old cupboard.

"Joe was such a precious nuisance in those
days," said Jasper, "always poking and peering
around; I suppose they were afraid he'd find it
out."

"We truly had a dreadful time," said Polly,
shaking her head, "to keep him away from that
cupboard."

"That old cupboard!" declared Joel, bounding
out of the circle to swing wide the upper door.
"Oh, what a lot of conniving, and how many
dark conspiracies it might tell!"

And how the dreadful measles fell upon the

whole Pepper flock, and the dear mother was almost in despair, and how good, dear Doctor Fisher was, and how he saved Polly's eyes, and then got her her stove. And then how the wonderful Christmas had come from Jappy and Grandpapa, and Polly had her bird and her flowers, and Ben had made a Santa Claus wig out of the hair in Mamsie's old cushion, sprinkling it snowy white with flour. And how Mamsie had hidden all the splendid presents over at Parson Henderson's.

"Such a time as we had," breathed both the parson and his wife, who had run up from the Orphan Home at Dunraven for the occasion.

Well — and how Phronsie had her doll, such a gorgeous affair she was afraid for days to show her to Seraphina, for fear of hurting the feelings of the latter. And then Phronsie had to get out of her chair, and make her way out of the circle surrounding the Pepper group, and go into the bedroom, where, kneeling down before the old bureau, she drew with a loving hand from the lowest drawer the two dolls.

"Bring the little red-topped shoes, too, Phronsie," called Polly; "do, dear."

So Phronsie reached back into the farthest corner, and carefully drew out a tissue paper bundle

With her arms full, Phronsie entered the kitchen.

that held the precious shoes, just as she had worn them last; and with her arms full, she **was** just entering the kitchen, all eyes upon her,

when Polly said in answer to some question,
"Yes, Mamsie wrote they would be in Rome
next month."

Grace Tupper sprang suddenly from her chair.
"O Mrs. King! will they, will they? Then perhaps they will see my cousin Roslyn May."

CHAPTER XI.

ON THE WAY TO THE BEEBES.

"I'M going down to see dear Mr. Beebe and dear Mrs. Beebe," cried Elyot suddenly the next morning; and he threw down the small trowel with which he had been spatting his mud-pie into shape, and jumped up, "Come along, Barby, you may go too," he said. "We won't trouble anybody to take us, 'cause they're all busy. I know the way."

"I know the way too," declared Barby sturdily; and deserting the spatting of her mud-pie which she had been engaged in without the aid of a trowel, she stood straight, and thoughtfully rubbed her fingers on her brown linen pinafore.

"Huh — you're too little to know the way," laughed Elyot; "but then I'm here, I can take you down," he added patronizingly.

"I don't want to be tooken; I'm going myself," said Barby decidedly; "this very one minute

I'm going;" and she trudged off in the direction of the high road, not once looking back.

Elyot ran after her in alarm, and twitched her pinafore, "That isn't the way; we've got to go down through the lane."

"I'm going to see my own Mr. Beebe, and my very own Mrs. Beebe, all alone by myself," declared Barby, keeping on. And presently, coming to a descent in the ground, she dropped flat, and rolled over and over, her usual method of going down hill; at the bottom picking herself up to resume her journey.

"I'll scream right out, and then they'll come after us, and we won't either of us get there," said Elyot, taking long steps down the bank after her.

Barby stopped at this, and waited for him to come up. "You may come too," she said ; and she put out her fat little hand to him.

Elyot took it contentedly. "You see, Barby," he said, "you couldn't get along without me. We must keep out of the road at first, because it would worry folks to see us going alone. But I know the way perfectly ; and then how glad dear Mr. Beebe and dear Mrs. Beebe will be when they see us coming in."

"Oh, so glad!" hummed Barby; "I guess they'll be very glad, Elyot. And I shall just kiss dear Mr. Beebe, and say, 'How do you do, dear Mr. Beebe, pretty well I thank you mostly.'"

"No, Barby, you don't say the things together like that," corrected Elyot; "that isn't right."

"Yes, it is," contradicted Barby sturdily. "And I shall say, 'How do you do, my dear very own Mrs. Beebe, and pretty well I thank you mostly. I've heard Mrs. Higby say it."

"You mustn't say such things, Barby," ordered Elyot, shaking her small sleeve with determination. "You don't know how to make calls yet. Mamma wouldn't like you to talk that way."

"My mummy would," declared Barby, shaking herself free, and panting **from** her exertions. "My mummy loves dear Mr. Beebe and dear Mrs. Beeby, and Barby loves them too. And I shall see all the shoes, all the little wee baby ones, and the great big ones, and I'm going to stay all day, and have pink sticks **for** dinner." She turned her hot little face up at him, and stiuck off bravely again, but her feet dragged.

"You're getting awfully tired," said **Elyot;** "let's go back."

"No, no, no!" protested Barby, making all possible speed. So Elyot had nothing to do but to follow, which he did smartly, keeping close at her side.

"And they'll be so s'prised to see us," went on Barby, growing confidential. "Oh, dear me! why don't their home ever come, I wonder."

"Oh! we're not half way there yet," said Elyot cheerfully; "it's off that way, so," waving his arm down the winding road, "then it's down this way," sweeping off in the opposite direction.

"Oh, dear me!" said Barby, with a small sigh she could not suppress, "why is it so long, I wonder? Won't it come sooner?"

"You better give me your hand," said Elyot, looking down into the tired little face.

So Barby gave him her hand; and not caring much where she planted her feet, she pattered unsteadily on over the dusty road, letting Elyot do all the talking.

Presently she said, "I'm tired, Elyot, truly I am," and tumbled down, a sleepy little heap, in a thicket of blackberry-bushes.

"Oh, you mustn't!" cried Elyot, pulling her arm; "wake up, Barby. Mamsie wouldn't like

you to go to sleep here by the road." But
Barby only hummed once, "I'm so tired, truly
I am;" and tucking her hand under her chin,
she fell fast asleep.

Elyot looked up and down the road. There
was nobody in sight. It was too far to carry
her, that he knew from his recollection of the
distance as he had been taken there in the carriage. Nevertheless, he got her somehow up in
his arms, and staggered off a few steps; but she
slipped out, and rolled up more of a heap than
ever on the ground.

At last he ran out into the middle of the road,
and watched for some one to come by; and as
no one appeared, he gathered up his small soul
with the best courage he could muster, and sat
down on a big stone by the side of the road.

"Some one has got to come by pretty soon,"
he said.

How long he waited no one knew. It seemed
to him hours, when, "Gee-lang — there, sho,
now," struck upon his ears, and an old farmer
came around a bend in the road with a wagon-
load of grain.

Elyot got off his stone, and dashed over to

him on unsteady little legs. "Oh, say, Mr. Man!
please would you take us, my sister and me,
please?"

"Sho," cried the farmer, pulling up his old
gray horse, "sho there — why, who be ye?"
staring at him.

Elyot gatherd up his small soul with the best courage he could muster,
and sat down on a big stone by the side of the road.

"Oh, please, Mr. Man, take us in your wagon!"
begged Elyot quickly, and not thinking it best
to answer any questions, "I'll bring her;" and he
ran over to Barby. "Sit up now, you must;
there's a good, kind man going to carry us in

his wagon," while the farmer rested his hands, with the ends of the old leather reins, in his lap, and scratched his shock of light hair in perplexity.

"We're coming," cried Elyot at last, tugging Barby along. Her eyes were half closed, and she protested every inch of the way, but he got ner up to the side of the wagon.

"Land o' Goshen!" exclaimed the farmer, jumping out, "I'll help ye; there ye be." He picked Barby up, and lifted her over among the grain-bags. "Curl up, now — she can sleep easy as a kitten," he said. Elyot had already clambered up to the driver's seat in great satisfaction; so presently they were off, rattling down the turnpike.

"Wher' ye goin' to in Hingham?" at last asked the farmer; "mebbe now ye want to be dropped this side o' th' town?"

"We don't want to be dropped at all," cried Elyot, hanging to the wagon-seat with both hands. "Oh, please don't drop us, Mr. Man!" He glanced over his shoulder at Barby, peacefully asleep, her head on a grain-bag.

"I mean, where d'ye want to be let out?

Mebbe this side o' th' town," explained the farmer; "or shall I carry ye to Hingham?"

"Oh, we don't want to go to Hingham at all," said Elyot, hanging on for dear life.

The old farmer pulled up so suddenly that despite his care, Elyot nearly fell out. "Don't want to go to Hingham!" he roared; "what did ye ask me to take ye there for, then?"

"Oh, I didn't!" said Elyot stoutly; "I asked you to take us in your wagon. And you're so good, thank you, Mr. Man."

"Well, an' that's the same thing; for my wagon's goin' to Hingham; that's where I live. Where in thunder do you want to go, you an' th' girl?" he pointed with his thumb over his shoulder to Barby.

"Oh! we want to go to see dear Mr. Beebe and dear Mrs. Beebe, you know. We've been wanting to go for a good many days; and Johnny couldn't come over to our house this morning, and everybody was busy, so it was a good time;" Elyot kept on talking, under the impression that the farmer wouldn't look so if conversation went on.

"Well, where's Mr. Beebe live?" demanded the farmer after an interval of despair.

"Why, don't you know? I know the place just as easy," exclaimed Elyot with a little laugh.

"Where is't?"

"It's down about there;" Elyot gave a wide sweep to his arm, thereby almost knocking off the farmer's broad-brimmed straw hat; "and he has such lots and lots of shoes"—as an after. thought.

"Shoes? be ye talkin' of a shoe-shop?" asked the farmer.

"Why, of course. I thought you knew that," remarked Elyot in disdain. "And dear Mr. Beebe will say"—

"Never mind what he'll say till he gets ye," said the farmer grimly. "Now, can't ye remember where that Mr. Beebe lives? I'll be switched, if I don't b'lieve it's Badgertown."

"Yes, yes, that's it; of course he lives there," said Elyot, nodding furiously. "And please, aren't we most there? I like your wagon; but we ought to hurry, 'cause Mr. and Mrs. Beebe will ask us to dinner, and"—

"Land o' Goshen, I am in a scrape!" exclaimed the old farmer, slapping his knee with a dingy hand. "Here I be with two young ones on my

hands, an' don't know no more'n one o' them
what to do. An' I can't go clear back to them
shoe-shop Beebes, an' I don't durst go forrards.
Well, mebbe some one'll heave along, who's goin'
to Badgertown, an'll take 'em."

But no one "heaving along" for a good half
hour, the old farmer was just about to turn his
old gray horse in despair, when an ancient gig
appeared, whose swaying top gave him a delicious
hope long before it came within talking distance;
and he cried joyfully, "Well, if this here ain't
luck! Now, there's Miss Sally an' Belindy Scrannage a-goin' over to Badgertown of course."

Long before the old gig got alongside the
wagon, the farmer had begun to shout out the
story; and by the time it was all over, Miss
Belinda, who wasn't driving, had made a place
on the old leather seat between her sister and
herself; and sleepy little Barby being set thereon,
the small head was cuddled up against that lady's
spencer waist, with one mitted hand put carefully
around the little figure to hold her close.

"You get up an' set on that basket," said Miss
Sally, who held the reins, and who was always
under the impression that the ancient horse was

just going to run away. "It's good we took the flat-covered one to-day; 'twon't hurt it; there's some garden-sass we're a-carryin' to our folks in Badgertown. There, get up."

"Can't I sit on behind?" begged Elyot, who didn't view the basket with great affection. It would be fine to swing his legs in freedom, instead of being cooped up with the old ladies.

"No, you can't," said Miss Sally with authority; "we might drop you off and never know it. I'm a-goin' to have you where I can see you. Get in, an' set still."

"They're to go to Mr. Beebe's shoe-store, ye know, on High Street," roared the old farmer after them from his high wagon.

"Yes, yes, we're goin' right past there," called back Miss Sally in a thin, high voice, firmly grasping the reins, and keeping an eye for danger ahead. "Go easy there, Billy."

Elyot, from his perch on the flat basket, with his back to Billy, surveyed her carefully. He could tell by the big mole on her chin that it was no one whom he had ever seen before. He was quite sure he should have remembered that mole; and then he looked Miss Belinda over. Mean-

time he had to cling to the basket tightly; for
the cover, even though flat, was quite slippery,
and Billy had a way of putting his heels down
unexpectedly with a thud, and not always so
evenly as one ought to expect.

"Now, ain't that a nice seat?" asked Miss
Sally briskly, when they had plodded along in
this fashion for a mile or so.

"No; I do not think it is," said Elyot, hanging
on, and wishing he could turn around, or jump
out and rest his legs just once.

"Tush-tush! little boys shouldn't be so free
with their tongues," said Miss Sally, slapping
the reins smartly up and down Billy's back.
"Land! when I was a little girl I always set in
front on a basket like that when pa and ma
took me ridin'."

"Was it slippery?" asked Elyot, feeling a
little less miserable since some one would talk,
"just like this one?" patting it.

"Yes, just as like it as two peas. Sho, now,
Billy! An' I remember when pa took me to
Cornwall Centre, and I never moved once on my
basket, but sat just as pretty. An' I didn't muss
my pelisse a mite. Don't you remember their

telling on't when we got home, Belindy?" turning to her sister in pride.

"Yes, I remember," said Miss Belinda, with a glance of veneration at the big square figure; "an' I know ma alwus said you were a proper child to take away, Sally."

"Didn't you ask to get down once, and just stretch your legs just once?" asked Elyot, who felt that the time had now arrived when he must beg that favor.

"Oh, dear me, no!" said Miss Sally in horror. "Why, that wouldn't have been proper, child. No, indeed, I just set pretty all the way."

CHAPTER XII.

AT THE BEEBES.

WHEN they turned the corner of High Street, which was the former post-road of the old town, and began to descend its somewhat crooked slope, Elyot flew off from his basket, and began to shout excitedly, " Oh, there it is — there it is, oh, *please* stop ! "

" Set down, child ! " commanded Miss Sally sharply; and gathering the leather reins in one hand, she picked him energetically by the blouse. Miss Belinda exclaimed faintly, " Oh, he'll fall out ! " and put out her mitted fingers to help.

" You keep quiet, Belindy," said Miss Sally brusquely; " you got one child to look after; I'll see to this one. Now, set still," to Elyot, " till we get there. Then, goodness knows I'll be glad enough to let you out."

Elyot tried to still his throbbing heart and hang to the basket, craning his neck to watch the Beebe shop, while Billy leisurely picked his way over the cobble-stones.

"There, here you be!" exclaimed Miss Sally, as at last they drew up in front of the little shop, "to home; and, my land, I'm thankful enough!"

Elyot was out over the wheel long before she finished, and holding up his arms for Barby.

"That boy can't carry her," cried Miss Belinda nervously from the depths of the gig; "let me get out, Sally, and take her in."

"Nonsense!" exclaimed Miss Sally, who knew very well what settling Miss Belinda in again would be; "she'll wake up soon's she's on the ground. And her folks'll come out and get her. Give her to me."

With that she bundled Barby out, a sleepy little heap, into Elyot's outstretched arms. "Now, run right along in to home," she commanded; and slapping the reins over Billy's back, the gig passed slowly down the street, Miss Belinda working her spare figure around to apply her eye to the square of dingy glass at the back.

"I hope they'll get in safe," she breathed anxiously.

"Nonsense!" said Miss Sally again. "Well, now, Belindy," and she took up the interrupted thread of their morning's business, "I b'lieve we better not take up this jell to Mrs. Jasper King's till afternoon. Seein' we're here, we better do a mite o' tradin'."

"Very well," said Miss Belindy meekly, who would have said, "Very well" if the other way had been proposed.

Meanwhile Elyot, not taking one blissful moment to stretch his legs, staggered over the uneven pavement, and set Barby on the broad, flat doorstone. Then he doubled up his little fist, being too short to reach the old knocker, and too polite to enter the shop without any summons at all, and rapped with all his force on the green door. Nobody coming, he propped Barby safely up against the upper step so that she would not fall over on her nose, and ran and peered into the little window strung with shoes and boots and rubbers of every description.

"Mr. Beebe!" he cried in a shrill little voice, and plastering his face against the small panes of glass, "oh. my dear Mr. Beebe, please let me in!"

"Open the door, and go in, child," said a good-natured woman coming along; "folks don't knock when they're going to th' shop. Th' knocker's for Sundays, when you're goin' to call." With that she reached over Barby, and threw wide the door. "Mr. Beebe," she called, "here's somebody wants to see you."

"Oh, let me tell 'em first!" screamed Elyot, running past her, and precipitating himself into a fat old lady in a white cap with a good deal of pink ribbon. "We've come all this way to see you!"

"Oh, my good gracious me!" exclaimed Mrs. Beebe, raising both hands in astonishment, then clasping him close. "Pa! pa!" she screamed, "here's the little King boy come to see us! Is your ma out there in the carriage?" all in the same breath.

"Oh, no!" cried Elyot, in the greatest pride; "we came all alone by ourselfs — and Barby's out on the step;" and he dragged Mrs. Beebe along by the apron.

Old Mr. Beebe, a good deal slower than he used to be, came leaning on his cane, out from the little room at the back, and over to the green front door.

He propped Barby up against the upper step, and ran and peered into
the little window strung with shoes.

"Well, now, my little dear," he kept saying all the way with a pleased smile, and beaming kindly over his big silver spectacles, "that's nice to see you to-day."

"You poor lamb, you," Mrs. Beebe was saying to Barby, and trying to lean over to lift her up, "there, there, oh, you pretty creeter, you! Pa, I don't s'pose you can carry her. Oh, dear, I'm such a stout old woman, an' good for nothin'!"

"Oh! I'll get her in," said Elyot, really afraid that Mrs. Beebe would tumble over; and before Mr. Beebe could remonstrate, he had lifted Barby, and rolled her in over the sill, both of the Beebes "ohing" and "ahing" all the time.

"Now, dear, there ain't no manner o' use in askin' you how you come," said Mrs. Beebe, restraining her curiosity, "the first thing to do is to see after that poor lamb there. Do you s'pose, Elyot, you could manage to get her onto the sofy, an' I'll off with her shoes an' bathe them poor tired little feet. Oh, you poor lamb, you!"

"Yes, I can," said Elyot manfully; and between the help that old Mr. Beebe gave and old Mrs. Beebe contributed, Barby was soon on the old chintz sofa.

"Now, says I," declared old Mr. Beebe, rubbing his hands, "that's something like it. I'll take off her shoes, wife, that's in my line; an' you get the hot water an' bathe her feet." So he drew up a chair to the side of the sofa, and putting Barby's little dusty boots on his knee, he drew them off, and the stockings; and Mrs. Beebe, coming out with a big bowl, and a towel over her arm, sat down in the chair that Elyot drew up for her. "Oh, me! oh, my!" she exclaimed compassionately, "the poor precious little toes!" caressing them.

Elyot threw himself on the floor, and rolled and stretched in perfect abandon.

"And he's so tired too," said old Mrs. Beebe, stopping in her work to peer at him over her spectacles.

"Yes, I am," declared Elyot; "so awfully tired sitting on a basket."

"Sitting on a basket!" ejaculated both of the Beebes together.

Elyot nodded, and took another roll.

Just then Barby pulled away the white toes that Mrs. Beebe had submerged with the warm cloth. "Oh!" she exclaimed, opening her eyes dewy with sleep, and regarding them fixedly, "I want some pink sticks for dinner; I'm hungry, truly I am."

"I'd rather have one of the sugar doughnuts, please," said Elyot, now that his legs began to feel better, finding that he was very hungry too.

Old Mr. Beebe laughed till his sides shook and his spectacles tumbled off, and Mrs. Beebe laughed too, and Elyot began to laugh, for he was so comforted with it all, and he knew the doughnuts were coming; and Barby laughed too, and it was so very jolly, that no one heard a customer come in, until he said rather gruffly, "Is my boot half-soled, Mr. Beebe?"

"Oh, bless you, yes!" said Mr. Beebe, getting up and hobbling over to the other side of the room, and he lifted a curtain that concealed a shelf where the repaired articles were kept; "yes, I had that done yist'day, Mr. Coombs," he said, bringing it out.

"You come along with me," whispered old Mrs. Beebe to Elyot, "an' we'll git the doughnuts. Lucky I made a big lot yist'day; I must 'a' known you were comin';" and she laughed again.

"And bring the pink sticks," cried Barby after

them. Then she leaned back on the old chintz pillow, and gazed entranced at the beautiful rows and rows of shoes dangling from strings across the room, and strung across the little window. And great green things, that afterward old Mr. Beebe showed her were boxes that contained shoes and rubbers; each had one of the articles hanging to it. And there, on the top shelf of all, was a long row of big rubber boots — oh, and it smelt so very lovely! Barby lay quite still, and sniffed and sniffed in delight. And even when a long pink cinnamon stick was brought and put into her chubby little hand, she held it loosely and still gazed on.

"It's a pink stick," shouted Elyot at her, his mouth full, and taking his face out from behind a big doughnut.

"Isn't it beautiful!" hummed Barby in delight. "An' oh! how do you do, my dear very own Mrs. Beebe, and pretty well I thank you mostly," remembering her manners.

"She will say such dreadful things," broke in Elyot, quite mortified, notwithstanding his satisfaction; "but you must excuse her, dear Mrs. Beebe, 'cause she's very little, you know."

"You blessed dear!" cried old Mrs. Beebe, quite overcome with admiration, and covering the little round face with kisses till her cap-border trembled.

"And I shall say just the very same thing to dear Mr. Beebe," declared Barby decidedly. Then she began on her pink stick.

"There ain't no mortal use askin' them blessed dears how they come here nor anythin', till they gits rested, Jotham," said Mrs. Beebe, taking her good man by the arm as the customer departed, and whispering violently. "And my! they're as hungry — " she glanced around at them as she spoke.

"They better 'a' had somethin' more solid 'n candy," said old Mr. Beebe, critically eying them too.

"Goodness me!" cried old Mrs. Beebe, "I wouldn't 'a' kept that blessed child from her pink stick a minute more'n I could help. Look at her suck it now!"

Barby's face was wreathed in smiles, as she lay on her back, in the fullest enjoyment of her pink stick, that was rapidly melting, and adding considerable of itself to the dust that the mud-

pie baking and the travel had given her small
countenance.

"Time enough to give 'em somethin' solid when
they've got what they wanted," said the old lady
wisely. "Now, Jotham, we must let Mrs. King
know as soon as we can that them childern are
here. Think how she's a-worritin'."

"To be sure — to *be* sure!" exclaimed old Mr.
Beebe thoughtfully; "well, how'll we do it, Sarah.
I can't get down there, an' now we don't keep
no horse — well, I d'no what to do."

"We must get some one to go for us," said Mrs.
Beebe determinedly; and going to the door, she
peered anxiously up and down the street. "Now,
there's them two old ladies who come over from
Hingham every week or so, — the Scrannages, —
I see their gig in front o' Simons's shop. I wonder if they'd go for us. I mean to ask 'em."

She untied her apron, and threw it over her
shoulders, it being more elegant than to go out
with nothing over her waist, and waddled down
the street.

The Misses Scrannage were selecting a new
calico dress apiece at Mr. Simons's shop; and he
had taken them down to the extreme end, to see

the beautiful new stock he had just gotten in. They were now in a complete state of bewilderment, not knowing whether or no to get a bright pink with purple spots on it for Sally, as they were afraid it wouldn't wash, Mr. Simons solemnly assuring them every minute in which there was a lull in their consultations, that he knew for an absolute certainty that it *couldn't* fade. And when this was decided and cut off, there was the choosing of Miss Belinda's gown. She had set her heart on two shades of green worked in together, with little white dots all over the whole.

"I know that won't wash," declared Miss Sally scornfully; "an' then how 'twill look when it streaks," she was saying as old Mrs. Beebe stepped into the shop.

"It never'll do to interrupt 'em when they're choosin' caliker gownds," said the old lady to herself; "s'posin' they shouldn't get the right ones, they'd blame me every blessed time they put 'em on. Oh, dear me! I must wait; p'r'aps they're most through."

But it was a good three-quarters of an hour before Mr. Simons clicked his scissors through the two pieces of calico, and they were torn off be-

yond recall. Every minute old Mrs. Beebe had
been on the point of rushing home, or rather
waddling, and had restrained herself, thinking
she heard the supreme moment of decision approaching. "Pa knows where the cold meat, an'
the pies, an' the bread is," she comforted herself,
when she got nervous sitting on the wooden stool
they brought her to wait on. Now she hurried
as fast as she could down to the end of the
shop.

"How d'ye do, Miss Sally and Miss Belindy
Scrannage?" she said in her most polite way, "I
want to ask a gret favor;" trying to pull Miss
Sally, as the woman of business in the family,
aside, that no one might overhear.

"The little King children, Mrs. Jasper King's,
are at my house. Poor things! they must 'a'
walked clear down here, when no one knew it,
and " —

"I brung 'em in our gig," proclaimed Miss
Sally in a loud voice. ' Oh, my land. an' good
gracious me!"

CHAPTER XIII.

FOUND.

"OH, now," cried King joyfully, "I can go and play with Elyot and Barby!" He sprang up, and began to skip to the door.

"Oh, no, dear!" said Phronsie gently; "you had three words spelled badly, you know. That column must be right, and then you can go."

"O sister Phronsie!" King began to whine. And then he grumbled, "I wish there weren't any lessons in the world. I just hate 'em, I do."

Joel thrust his head in the doorway. "May I come in?" he asked Phronsie.

"Yes, indeed," she said with a smile.

"Well, well, King," he said, going over to the little desk, and laying his hand on it, "do you know I said just those words you've used, once to Mamsie; and I wish I could forget it."

"You said you hated books!" repeated King

in amazement, and forgetting to cry, a thing he had just made up his mind to do. "Why, you know just everything."

"Not quite that," said Joel, bursting into a laugh; "but I know considerably more because of what Mamsie said to me then."

"And what did Mamsie say?" asked King, intensely interested, and leaning across his little desk.

"She said study didn't amount to much unless one was glad of the chance, and that she would stick to it if she had to work herself to skin and bone. I tell you, King, that just about killed me for Mamsie to have to tell me that."

King drew a long breath. "Do you s'pose she'd have to say so to me, if she was here now?" he asked presently.

"I verily do," said Joel, with a keen glance out of his black eyes that looked so very like his mother's, that King quailed immediately. "I'll — I'll study, brother Joel," he said, reaching for the neglected spelling-book."

Joel gave him a pat on his stubby head. "Good for you," he said.

Outside, Alexia was saying to Amy Loughead

in the hall, "Oh! no use to try to get a squint at Phronsie in the morning till ten o'clock."

"What is she doing?" asked Amy.

"Oh! she hears King's lessons for an hour, and studies with him; he's her care, you know, while Mrs. Fisher is away. But she might slip off a few minutes once in a while, and he'd study by himself. But horses can't drag her away till the hour is up."

"No," said Amy slowly, "I shouldn't think they could."

"Umph!" said Alexia, remembering Polly's frightful trials with her little music-scholar. Then she added kindly, "Oh! of course not; but we do want her just awfully this morning. We're going to have a driving-party down to the Glen; and of course no one can do anything without Phronsie."

"Oh! of course not," said Amy.

"Well, it won't make that tiresome clock go ahead any faster," observed Alexia, "to watch it," tearing off her gaze from the tall clock in an angle of the hall, "so I'm going off to find Cathie."

Amy sat down in a niche by the window, and

busied herself with a little book she drew out of her pocket. How long she read she did not know, but King rushed past in a whirlwind of delight. "Phronsie said I could go! Hooray!" and Phronsie came out into the hall, followed by Joel.

"Now," said Phronsie, "we must hurry and get up the Glen driving-party. Joel, please see that Johnson understands that the horses are brought around for those who are to ride. And, O Joel! please see that the drag is ready, and my cart."

"Oh, yes! and the trap, and the whole list of them. You ride Firefly, Phronsie, of course; and I'm going to take one of the black horses, Polly said I could, and ride with you."

"No," said Phronsie; "Grace Tupper is to ride Firefly."

"Oh, no, Phron!" protested Joel.

"I asked her to," said Phronsie. "She used to ride a good deal, and she hasn't had a chance for a long while. I want her to, Joel."

"Any other time would do just as well," began Joel. But Phronsie looked at him, and he hastened to add, "But of course it's just as you please. Well, then, I shall drive you."

"Yes, so you may," cried Phronsie, well pleased, "and Amy too. Take us both, Joel, do." She put her arm around the young girl affectionately.

Joel suppressed what he felt, and said, " All right," and was just rushing out, when in ran King.

"Phronsie, where are Elyot and Barby?"

"Just over the east terrace," said Phronsie. "I saw them a little while ago when you were at your lesson."

"Well, they aren't there now," declared King in an injured tone. Now, I know they meant to run away from me."

"Oh, no, King dear!" said Phronsie, putting a gentle hand on his hot face.

"Well, where are they, then? " demanded King wrathfully.

"I'll go and hunt for them," said Phronsie merrily. "Come, Amy, let us find those babies."

So Amy Loughead and Phronsie picked up their skirts and sped over the terraces, King racing on ahead, all three calling, "Bar-*by!* Ely-*ot!*" at the top of their voices.

"There, they aren't here, you can see for your-

self," said King, turning a hot and flushed face
upon them after a while.

"No," said Phronsie, the pink color deserting
her cheek, "I see they are not, King." Then, as
he began to look frightened, she brightened up,
and said cheerily, "Do you run up to the house,
Amy dear, and get the horn from Mrs. Higby;
then, King, you shall blow it, and that'll surely
bring them back."

"I'm going to get brother Joel first," cried
King, scampering off in the direction of the
stables.

"And tell him to set Patsy to hunting on the
grounds," called Phronsie after him.

But despite the vigorous horn-blowing presently set up, King puffing out his cheeks with
all his might, and Patsy and two or three of the
other stable-men scouring the grounds, headed by
Joel; and notwithstanding that Phronsie and Amy
ran hither and thither spreading the alarm, till
Polly and nearly all the guests in the house were
just so many searching-parties, exploring the little
brown house and every other place that would be
likely to attract the children, no trace of the two
children could be found. And King threw him-

self disconsolately into Phronsie's arms, crying as if his heart would break.

Miss Salisbury was up on the front veranda; she so far forgot herself as to wring her hands, when she thought no one observed her.

"O Miss Salisbury!" cried Amy Loughead, running up, "will you be so very good as to tell Aunt Montgomery that I'm going down the road to hunt for the children. I may not be back, you know, for some time."

"Hey, what's that?" cried Robert Bingley, sauntering along the side veranda. He was waiting for the assembling of the driving-party, and hadn't heard a word of the bad news.

"The two children are lost," said Amy briefly, before she ran off.

"Great Cæsar's ghost!" cried Robert Bingley. "Excuse me, Miss Salisbury," as he now saw her; and clearing the veranda railing with one bound, he struck off for the group on the lawn. Just below lay the deserted mud-pies and the two little trowels.

Meantime Amy, gathering up her skirts with one shaking hand, skipped down the road, only one feeling uppermost in her heart, — to find

Polly's children. "I must, or I shall die," sobbed Amy to herself, the tears splashing over her pretty blue lawn gown.

An old scissors-grinder came down the road, ringing his bell violently. "Oh, sir!" cried Amy, rushing up at him, "have you seen two little children, a boy and a girl? they're lost, and we don't know where to find them." She wrung her hands now, and cried all over her dress.

"Hey?" cried the scissors-grinder.

"Oh! please, sir, do tell me if you have seen them," begged Amy.

"I'm deaf," said the scissors-grinder, "and I don't know what you're saying, Miss;" and he put his hand behind his ear, and opened his mouth, as if in that way his hearing might be improved. So Amy got up on tiptoe, and shouted it all into his ear; and he shook his head, and declared he hadn't seen a child on the road that morning, and he had just come from Badgertown Centre.

"I'll tell you what I'll do," he said. "I'll ring my bell, and then I'll cry, 'Child lost' — no, 'two children lo-ost,' and then everybody'll know it, and look out for 'em." So he went on, ringing and jingling, and calling it out, while she flew down along the road.

"There isn't any use in your doing this," said a voice back of her as she sped along; and Robert Bingley dashed up in a dog-cart. "Here, Miss Loughead, jump in, and we'll search for those two kids together."

"They're Polly's children," announced Amy, as if stating a wholly new fact, and turning her sorrowful face, down which the tears were chasing, to him; "and it will just kill her, Mr. Bingley, if they're not found."

"Jump in," said Mr. Bingley, extending his hand to help her; "excuse my not getting out, but this horse is bound to go. There, now," as she was seated, "which way, of all the ways in the universe, would those children be likely to take — that's the question. Then I should take the other."

"The scissors-man said he hadn't seen a child on this road; and he has just come from Badgertown," said Amy.

"I saw you interviewing him," said Robert Bingley. "Well, as that remarkably stupid individual did give utterance to that fact, I should state my private opinion to be that those children took this very road. He's too stupid to know a child when he sees it."

"Mr. Bingley," cried Amy, all the color deserting her cheek, and in her sudden terror she seized his arm, "oh, I've just thought — there's the pond, you know."

"No, I don't know," said Bingley, distressed at her fright, but outwardly as cool as ice.

"Why, Spot Pond, they call it," said Amy with a little gasp. "Phronsie was telling me about it — what a pretty place it was, and how they would take me fishing there, and "—

"Were the children about so that they heard you?" he asked abruptly.

"Yes — no, I believe not," she said, racking her brain to remember; "but they may have gone there just the same."

"Where is it, do you know?" asked Bingley, slackening speed a little.

"It's on this road. After you get by the schoolhouse, then turn to the right — that is, it's just a little off the road," said Amy; "she told me all about it at the breakfast-table. O Mr. Bingley, do let us go there!"

"There's the schoolhouse," said Bingley, spying it a little distance away; "so as the pond is a short bit away, we better try it, instead of going home for assistance." He gave the whip to the pony, and off they spun.

But Spot Pond was still and lovely and serene. Not a ripple disturbed its clear surface, and only a cat-bird screamed at them overhead.

"They couldn't have walked clear down here by this time," said Robert Bingley; "besides, there are no little boot-tracks anywhere." Amy clasped her hands tightly together.

"Now I shall interview the schoolmarm," said Robert Bingley, driving back; and rapping on the schoolhouse door, he brought out the teacher, book in hand, and a fringe of scholars, older and younger, around her.

"No," she said to his question; "we haven't any of us seen any little children. Have you," turning to some big boys who sat by the window, " seen any go by ? "

"No'm," they said; and Bingley, feeling sure that nothing could have escaped a boy at such a vantage-ground, set his teeth together hard, and turned irresolutely.

Amy Loughead now sat up quite straight. "Oh! I can't go home, Mr. Bingley," she said, "and see Polly, and not take the children to her. Please take me into the town, and I'll ask everybody there, in all the shops, and along the streets and houses. Somebody must know."

"Not a bad idea," said Robert Bingley, whipping up, "and at least your plan has action in it; and I confess myself that I don't want to go home either without something to show for it."

It was well past midday when Amy, who had asked at every farmhouse and each smarter residence within the village itself, now began to traverse the High Street, where all the shops were crowded together as a trading centre. Bingley had begged to get out and do this for her; but she had refused so decidedly, and plodded on so persistently, that he was forced to obey her, and he watched her little figure and pale, set face, compassionately. She had just asked at the milliner's, gay with its spring and summer ribbons and flowers, and smart in the perky hats adorning the big window, and had turned away despairingly, going into the neighboring shops, and asking the same question, to leave

everybody sad and anxious to help, when they
knew Mr. Jasper King's children were lost. Me-
chanically she turned up the next step of a little

There was Barby in a little wooden chair, eating bread and butter with a
very sticky face.

shop, wedged in between two taller ones, and
having on the sign above the green door, —

J. BEEBE.

BOOTS AND SHOES.

"Have you seen," she began, with no hope
of success, "two little" — and there was Barby

in a little wooden chair, eating bread and butter with a very sticky face, while Elyot was
capering around the small shop on a cane, an
old man with big silver spectacles laughing to
see him go.

CHAPTER XIV

HOME AGAIN.

THE "Scrannage girls," as their neighbors called them, were seated in high-back chairs in the big hall at "The Oaks;" their gig, in which they had followed as best they could the swift pony-cart bearing home the children, was tied at the end of the carriage-drive. They had cups of tea in their hands, from which they drew long draughts of inspiration and refreshment to help along their part of the tale.

Polly sat down in front of them on a low cushioned seat, clasping her baby in her arms, and Elyot crouched on the floor, his arms in his mother's lap; the rest of the household and guests crowding up for the recital, old Mr. King at the visitors' right hand, and Amy Loughead modestly selecting the background.

"Ye see," said Miss Sally, who as usual was spokeswoman, "it was jest this way. We made up our minds to go to town this mornin'; one thing on account o' bringin' you the jell you'd ordered, marm," bobbing her large bonnet at Mrs. King.

"Yes," said Polly. "Well, and where did you meet the children, Miss Scrannage?" clasping Barby very closely.

"I was a-goin' to tell you. Land! but this tea is proper good, Mis' King," taking a long draught of it, and smacking her lips. "Well, we made up our minds to come to town as I was a-sayin'."

"My good woman," said Mr. King, "we do not care for all those particulars. What we do want to know is where you met those children?" pointing to Elyot and Barby.

Miss Sally Scrannage turned her large face and looked at him. Wasn't she a Scrannage of Hingham, Jabez Scrannage's daughter? and was she going to be put down that way, even if this was the great Mr. King, and he worth his millions? She set down her teacup, and gathered up the crumbs of cake carefully in a little heap in her napkin before she was ready to open her mouth. Phronsie stepped softly out of the group, and going up to the two old ladies, she laid her hand gently on the big, square shoulder, "Don't you understand, dear Miss Scrannage," she said, " that we are all so anxious to know at once, just as soon as we possibly can, when you first saw the children. Their poor mother cannot bear to wait."

Miss Sally followed the hand that pointed to Polly. When she saw the tears on the cheek usually so bright, her own face softened, and her battle feathers, so to speak, drooped. " And I'll tell you quick's I can, my dear," she said, " seein' you ask so pretty. But I ain't accustomed to be spoke to like a dog, an' ordered 'round, you know. Let's see; 'twas after we'd got by the Hammatt place, Belindy, warn't it, when we saw Abiel Babbidge driv up by the side o' the road, an' he a-settin' still, an' his horse not movin' a hoof, an' sez I — you remember what I sez, Belindy, says I " —

" Did Mr. Babbidge have the children in his wagon ? " asked Phronsie, still standing by her side.

"Yes, he did; we was quite a piece by the Hammatt place."

" A *good* piece," said Miss Belinda.

" Yes, just as I say, a good piece."

"How far is the Hammatt place from here? Ask her, Phronsie," said old Mr. King.

"How many miles do you think the Hammatt place is from here, Miss Scrannage?" asked Phronsie.

"Well, I d'no. It might be six mile, and then again it might be five. I hain't heard folks say."

"Never mind," said Mr. King.

"Well, Jabez he was a-sittin' stock still as a stun, an' it scart me. I didn't know but what he was dead. If it had 'a' been cold weather, I should suppose he'd fruz. And I says to him, says "—

"Where did he say he found the children?" asked Phronsie.

"I was a-comin' to that," said Miss Sally shortly; and picking up her tea again, she took a good swallow. "Well, Jabez he says to me, he says, 'Get these childern home, will ye, Miss Scrannage?' I'm very sure he said home, ain't you, B'lindy."

"I don't remember," said Miss Belinda.

Miss Sally tossed her a look of scorn. "Well, I do," she sniffed. "He says, 'Get these chil-dern home, will ye, Miss Scrannage, down to Mr.

Beebe's shoeshop?' An' sister an' me said of course we would; an' he an' I got the childern in, an'" —

"The 'Scrannage Girls,' as their neighbors called them."

"And she put me on a slippery basket, and I couldn't see the horse," said Elyot; "and I didn't like it!"

"O Elyot!" said his mother gently, patting his

head; "just think how kind dear Miss Sally was. You couldn't have gotten home without her, dear."

Elyot grunted feebly something that was inaudible, especially as Miss Sally, much mollified by Mrs. King's words, proceeded, —

"So B'lindy took care of the little girl," — Polly glanced over with a smile at "sister's" meek face, — "an' I had the wust, 'cause I had to drive, an' I had that boy. Well, an' we went fust of all to the shoe-shop. I was a-comin' here with the jell fust, but then I thought, bein' you said you warn't " —

"Oh! I didn't need the jelly," said Polly hastily; "thank you for going to Mr. Beebe's first."

"An' I jest let the childern out, of course, as I s'posed 'twas their home, an' that's all I know, 'cept that old Mis' Beebe run in to Simons's with an apun over her head, — we was tradin,' gettin' some new calikers, you know," said Miss Sally in an important way, "an' " —

"She asked you to let us know, did she?" asked Phronsie.

"Yes, she did; an' then I told her I was the one that brung them childern to her shop, an'

then we heard a squeal, an' that boy there,"
pointing her long finger at Elyot, "come runnin'
in the shop, an' said he'd come to bid old Mis'
Beebe good-by, and the little girl come along too,
an' he said they'd sent for 'em to come home
right away, an' he was a-comin' again some time
— but I know one thing, an' that is, that I won't
bring him."

"Sally, Sally," ventured Miss Belinda in a
shocked tone.

"Dear Miss Scrannage," cried Polly, rushing
out of her seat, and clinging to Barby, while
Elyot dragged after, clutching her gown, "and
dear Miss Belinda, you don't know how grateful
I am to you for all your lovely care of my little
ones. I wish — oh, how I wish my husband was
home to thank you too! Oh! we never can repay
you." She took their withered and hard hands
in her soft, warm ones.

"And I'd like to kiss you," said Barby, putting
up her rosy lips, "anyway her — I would like to
kiss her," pointing to Miss Belinda, who was
blushing like a winter apple, and beaming at her.

"No, we never can repay you," repeated Polly
out of a full heart.

Miss Sally received all this with the greatest satisfaction, but her cup of happiness was quite full when Grandpapa got deliberately out of his chair and advanced to her.

"And you mustn't mind what an old fellow says, Miss Scrannage," he said, holding out his hand with a courtly bow. "Goodness me, my dear woman, can you guess what we've suffered when those blessed babies couldn't be found? And so shake hands, and forgive whatever you didn't like in my words."

"Oh, I'll forgive!" said Miss Scrannage, putting out her toil-worn hand with just as much pride; "an' mebbe I hadn't orter been so quick myself; but I can't help it, for I've got it from the Scrannage side o' th' house, an' it's hard to pull up. Well, now, B'lindy, seein' all's comfortable, we better be a-goin'. We're goin' to stay all night, ye know," she said, addressing the company, "down to our cousin's in town; but we got to go to one or two more o' th' shops, an' then we want to visit some before supper."

Mr. King did not dare to interrupt; but he kept fingering his pocket-book nervously, well concealed as it was. His eyes sought Phronsie's

face and Polly's, and finding no encouragement
in either, he cleared his throat, "Hem! well, now,
Miss Scrannage, I don't want to hinder you; but
what sort of a man is this Mr. Babbidge, I believe
you said his name was, that gave the children
to you?"

"Oh! he's a good sort o' man, 'Biel Babbidge
is," replied Miss Sally, "dretful poor he is,
an'"—

"Poor, is he?" cried old Mr. King with interest.

"Land, yes! never was forehanded; couldn't be,
with that sick wife of his."

"Is she sick?" asked Phronsie pityingly.

"Yes; hain't done a hand's turn for a year,
with rheumatiz, an' before that 'twas newmony,
an' before that"—

"Poor man!" said Polly; "of course he could-
n't get along, with a sick wife."

"That's so," assented Miss Sally; "an' he
hain't got along; has to hire whatever help he
gets in the house. He's dretful good to his wife;
sets a store by her, an' treats her jest like a baby.
She was a Potter, lived down to th'"—

"Now, Miss Scrannage," said old Mr. King

desperately, and bringing the pocket-book out to the surface, "I want to reward somebody for all their goodness to me and to my family in bringing our children home. Do help me to do it."

"You better give it to 'Biel Babbidge, then," said Miss Sally with a stiffening in her back, as she looked in his eyes. Then she glanced at her sister, who straightened herself involuntarily. "Land, yes! he's dretful poor, an' needs it." She stepped out of her chair with the air of being able to buy up all Badgertown. "Come, B'lindy, we reelly must be a-goin'. I thank you for that cup o' tea, Mis' King; 'twas reel pa'ticler good, and you, Miss Phronsie, thank you. Goodday," with an old-time courtesy to the company.

Elyot rushed after her. "I'm sorry I said that about the basket," he cried.

"Now," said Phronsie, as they all turned back and went slowly over the lawn, the whole company having escorted the old ladies to their carriage, the gentlemen vying in their attentions, and David securing the honor of unhitching Billy, "why cannot we take our driving-party over to Hingham to-morrow, instead of to the Glen, and see Mr. and Mrs. Babbidge?"

"And do up the business with them," finished old Mr. King. "The very thing, Phronsie," with a grateful smile at her. "I only wish I could wind up my debt to that Miss Scrannage as easily," he groaned.

"O Phronsie!" cried Polly ecstatically; "that's a lovely plan. Oh, you dear, for thinking of it!"

And every one of the company thereupon expressed their great delight. Suddenly Elyot glanced down the road. "Oh, I see papa!" he howled; "he's on top of the stage."

"Well, well, what is the whole family drawn up here in parade for?" cried Jasper, swinging himself down from Mr. Tisbett's side. And "O Jasper! what has brought you so early?" from Polly. And then all the story had to be gone over and over, with many things interspersed by Elyot and Barby, who felt that half enough attention had not been paid to the Beebes, and who clamored for every one to hear what a splendid time they'd had in the little shop.

"And I sat in the little chair that Aunt Phronsie sat in," cried Barby. "Truly I did, papa," pulling his sleeve.

"Yes, she did," said Elyot; "the same little

wooden chair that Aunt Phronsie sat in when she got her red-topped shoes; Mr. Beebe said so. And I had doughnuts — all I wanted."

Polly viewed him in alarm, while Joel smacked his lips. "We remember those doughnuts, don't we, Dave," poking the college instructor in the ribs.

And then they all hurried in, Jasper's arm around Polly, while his children hung to his hand; for he had brought out a new piece of music he wanted to try with Polly before dinner.

On the way to the music-room, Joel picked up a little book from one of the window-niches in the big hall. "Whose is this?" he asked, carelessly whirling the leaves of a Greek poem.

"That's Miss Loughead's, I believe," said Robert Bingley, who stood next, and looking over his shoulder.

"Impossible!" exclaimed Joel impulsively. "What, belong to that little thing! Why, man alive, she never knew enough to understand that there was such a book." And then he turned and met Amy Loughead's blue eyes.

CHAPTER XV.

SOME HINGHAM CALLS

"PHRONSIE," said Joel desperately, "I can't take Miss Loughead with us."

"O Joey! you promised," said Phronsie in a grieved way.

"But I can't do it — do beg off for me some way. Why, it's impossible for me to look the girl in the face after what I've said. How I could ever have spoken so, I don't see," went on Joel remorsefully.

Phronsie was about to say something; but thinking better of it, she only smiled comfortingly.

"Do, will you, Phronsie?" begged Joel in a wheedling way.

"I think you ought to take Amy all the more because you did speak so, Joel," said Phronsie quietly, "so I cannot speak for you, dear."

Joel turned off, and ground his boot into the

gravel. "All right, Phronsie," he said, turning around.

But just here Grandpapa came around the curve in the path. "Phronsie, you will drive me in your cart," he said.

"Shall I, Grandpapa?"

"Yes, dear; and tell Johnson to put my bay in."

"Yes, Grandpapa." Phronsie looked at Joel. His black eyes said, just as when a boy he had been delighted at anything, "Oh, goody! now I sha'n't have to drive that girl to Hingham."

Phronsie answered the look by, "O Joel! now it will help to make up for what you said; as you can take Amy Loughead over alone, and that'll show her you are sorry."

Joel's face lengthened. "Really, Phronsie?"

"I would," said Phronsie; then she ran off to get ready.

"Miss Loughead," said Joel awkwardly, going into the music-room where she stood alone, turning over some of Polly's music, "I don't know as you'll go with me — I'm sure I shouldn't, if the cases were reversed; but I was to take my sister Phronsie and you on the driving-party to the Glen yesterday, you know." He paused, having come to the length of his chain, and stared helplessly at her.

"Yes," said Amy.

"Well, now it's Hingham, instead; and Grandpapa wants Phronsie to go with him, so it leaves you and me out in the cold," he said with an attempt at a laugh.

Amy said nothing, so he had to plunge on. "And if you'll be willing under the circumstances to let me drive you, why, I'll do it," finished Joel desperately.

"Do you wish to, Mr. Pepper?" asked Amy, raising a pair of clear blue eyes to his, "because do not really try to do it — to — make up — for anything. I'd rather you didn't," she said earnestly.

"I do wish it," said Joel heartily, "if you are willing — that's the question. Miss Loughead, I never was so sorry in all my life for anything," he declared; and he hung his head, wishing he were small enough to be whipped, and be done with it.

"Don't feel distressed about it," said Amy. "I was a little goose, Mr. Pepper, in the old days; and I just wasted my time, and I wouldn't study; and I worried Polly dreadfully." It was now her turn to look distressed, and Joel cried out, "Don't look so, I beg of you."

"And you were quite right in believing I couldn't, or I wouldn't, study now," said Amy. "I don't blame you, Mr. Pepper." She put out her hand, which Joel seized remorsefully.

"Will you go?" he cried eagerly, and hanging to it, — "will you?"

"Yes, I will go," said Amy Loughead, pulling away her hand, and smiling brightly.

"Oh, beg pardon!" ejaculated Joel, backing off," "I was thinking it was Phronsie." Then in hurried Robert Bingley.

"Miss Loughead, I've been looking everywhere for you. May I have the pleasure of driving you to Hingham this morning?"

"I am going with Mr. Joel Pepper," said Amy. And Joel heard his friend Bingley say, "Whew!" and he meant to have it out with him some time for that.

At last they were off, — Mrs. Higby, shading her eyes with her hand, watched them from the upper door, — all but Jasper, who went as usual with the "little publishing bag" to town in the early train. The children were distributed evenly throughout the party on the drag; Polly and Grace Tupper, Ben and David were on horse-back; and Grandpapa and Phronsie led off in the dog-cart merrily; while Joel and Amy Loug-head brought up the rear, the interval being filled by a big beach-wagon. When Robert Bing-ley found how it was, he clambered into this last, without a sign on his face that he didn't choose that place to begin with.

"Well, really," observed Percy, adjusting his monocle with importance, "this road looks ex-actly like all country roads — don't you know."

Van, on the back seat with Gladys Ray, grinned. "Astonishing fact," he whispered to her. "It's his monocle that does that."

"Polly wouldn't like it to have you make fun of your brother," she said.

Van colored up to the roots of his light hair. "I'm glad you're going to be like Polly, Gladys," he said, "and keep me straight."

"Indeed, I'm not going to keep you straight," she cried with spirit; "you've got to keep your-self straight. But I shall say things that I've heard the Peppers say, for it's good for you to hear them."

"Isn't this fine," cried David, riding up to the side of the trap — "eh, Joe? Doesn't it take you back to the days when we used to race barefoot along this Hingham road?"

"That it does," cried Joel, in huge delight, and raised back to his self-esteem by the quiet poise of the girl beside him, who evidently meant to take everything as it had been before his cruel and unlucky speech. "She's one girl in a thousand for sense and a good heart," said Joel to himself many times on the drive. "Nobody else but Polly and Phronsie could have done it."

When they reached Hingham, as they did in good time, it was an easy matter to find Abiel Babbidge's house. Everybody knew him, and could tell the old yellow house, run down at the heel, as it were, set back from the side road. All around it lay one of the New England farms, whose principal crop seemed to be stones, which, if removed, would leave not much else. "Good gracious me!" ejaculated old Mr. King, as Phronsie turned the bay up the scraggly wagon-path to the door.

The whole procession came to a halt. "Phronsie," said Grandpapa, "you'd better ask to see
Mrs. Babbidge. I'll tackle him if he is home."

"Shall I, Grandpapa?" asked Phronsie, getting out.

"Oh, let me!" howled Elyot, trying to spring
off from the drag. "I want to see my nice Mr.
Babbidge."

"And me too," cried Barby; "let me too!"

King was consumed with envy, and so was
Johnny Fargo, because they had no former acquaintance to plead. "I wouldn't," he said, laying a restraining hand on Elyot's jacket.

"You let me alone," cried Elyot crossly, and
twitching himself free. "You don't know my
Mr. Babbidge. Oh, *do* let me get down!"

"So you shall, dear," said Polly, riding up to
the side of the drag, "and Barby. Run along
now, chickens," as somebody lifted Barby down
and set her on the ground, "and call your Mr.
Babbidge out. We all want to see him."

Thereupon King and Johnny screamed for permission to get down, which being accorded, they
whooped off also, and disappeared around the
house in the direction of the dilapidated barn.

Presently Abiel Babbidge appeared, shambling and shamefaced, with one of the King children hanging to either hand, — the other boys trying to catch on somewhere, and not succeeding very well.

Polly reined her horse up to his side. "How do you do, Mr. Babbidge?" she said, putting out her dainty riding-glove. "I am the children's mother, and I want to thank you for all the kind care you gave them yesterday."

"O Moses and Methuselah!" exclaimed Abiel Babbidge, startled out of any sort of manners; "ye be! Why, I can't tech ye're hand with this." He extricated one of his horny palms from Barby's grasp, and held it up to her.

Polly shook it warmly. "I cannot thank you, Mr. Babbidge, as I want to. May I see your wife?" and she rode up to the old horse-block and dismounted.

Abiel Babbidge's face fell. "My wife is sick," he said slowly, and something like a tear fell from his eye. Elyot pulled away his hand, and looked up in astonishment at him.

"I know she is not well," said Polly gently; "but I thought perhaps you would think she could

see me and my sister," taking Phronsie's hand.
" But not if you do not think best, Mr. Babbidge."

" Ye may," said Mr. Babbidge abruptly. " I
declar to gracious I sh'd be glad to have her see
ye both. 'Twould bring her right up, mebbe."

Old Mr. King got slowly out of the dog-cart
while Mr. Babbidge was escorting Polly and
Phronsie in. On the top step, Polly turned and
said softly, " Now run away, children, and don't
make a noise under the window."

" Oh, we're going in ! " cried Elyot, pushing
with all his might to get in first.

" Mamma says not," said Polly; and they
tumbled back quickly, and swarmed into the dog-
cart to wait with Grandmpa.

In a few minutes out came Mr. Babbidge's
head and shoulders in the doorway. " They want
ye," he nodded to old Mr. King; who, mightily
pleased to be summoned, wended his way to the
steps.

" Somebody come and sit with those youngsters," he cried, shaking his walking-stick at the
bunch of them in the cart. So Ben got out of
the drag, and ran up just in time to save the

bay from getting a smart thwack from the whip that Johnny Fargo had captured.

"The next boy that gets hold of that whip will tumble out of this cart," said Ben decidedly.

Polly sat by the side of the bed in the old bed-room that opened out of the kitchen, Phronsie stood by the foot, as Abiel Babbidge said to Mr. King, "There's my wife, sir," and pointed to the bed. Under the old patched bedquilt she lay, propped up by pillows; everything marvellously neat, but oh, so coarse and poor! She had a smile on her thin face; and her hand, all drawn up with rheumatism, was extended in simple courtesy of an old-time pattern.

"Oh! how do you do, madam?" said old Mr. King much shocked, and for the life of him not knowing what to say.

But Mrs. Babbidge knew no embarrassment. She asked her husband to get some more chairs from the kitchen and bring in; and when he, big and awkward, knocked down more things in the carrying out of this request than he could pause to pick up, she passed it serenely over, and smiled at him just the same.

Polly felt the tears in her eyes, in spite of all

her efforts to keep them out. "Dear Mrs. Babbidge," she said gently, "you know a mother
who has had her little children restored to her as
I have, and largely through your good husband's
kindness," — here Mrs. Babbidge sent a proud
glance over at him, at which he blushed like a
girl under his big farmer's hat he forgot to take
off, — "finds it hard to express her thanks; and
so I brought you, from my husband and from me,
a little gift." Here Polly laid down a small parcel on the patched bedquilt, and tucked it under
one of the drawn and twisted hands.

"How about the Scrannage ladies?" asked old
Mr. King, drawing Abiel off to a corner; "they're
pretty well off, I expect."

"They hain't got much but pride," said Abiel,
shifting from one foot to another, "but enough
o' that to carry this hull town."

"Poor, are they?" asked the old gentleman.

"Poor — well I should say so; why, I guess
it comes hard on 'em to keep a cat. But then
they'd rather starve themselves than to scrimp
her. But they're monstrous ginteel."

"Dear, dear!" said the old gentleman, with
great concern.

"Ye see, they're a-workin' to pay off that there mortgage the old squire left; been a-workin' on't for twenty year now, an' mos' likely they'll die a-workin' on't; but then 'we *will* die a-workin' on't,' as Miss Sally said to me only t'other day; and bless my buttons, so she will," declared Mr. Babbidge, slapping his knee.

"How much is it?" asked old Mr. King.

"Five hundred dollars," said Abiel.

"Five hundred dollars!" repeated the old gentleman.

"Yes, 'tis, every bit; awful, ain't it; 'cause they're wimmen, an' there ain't no way for 'em to arn money, only to make jell."

"They wouldn't accept a little gift, you think?" asked the old gentleman suddenly, "not if she was to give it," pointing to Polly, "or her sister?"

"Massy sakes — no," cried Abiel in alarm; "they'd set the dorg on you; that is, Miss Sally would, if she had a dorg. They wouldn't take it from the angel Gabrel."

Nevertheless, when they went out of the Babbidge household, the old gentleman had made up his mind to something; and, by the time they were on the way homeward, he announced to the

"There now, it's done, Grandpapa, dear," said Phronsie, tucking the bit of paper under the old door.

rest of the procession, "We are going down to the Scrannage house."

And down to the "Scrannage house" they went. There it stood, by the lilac-bushes, with its flag walk between the rows of ancient box; its blue-green blinds, and its big-knockered door — just as it had stood in the old squire's time, with a mortgage on it.

The whole procession drew up silently. "You all sit still," commanded the old gentleman. "Phronsie, you come with me." So, Ben hopping into the dog-cart again to hold the bay, the two passed up between the rows of box, and halted at the blue-green door.

"Now, Phronsie, I want you to help me," said Grandpapa, "because that Miss Sally Scrannage is truly awful to deal with. But whether she likes it or not, child, I'm going to lift that mortgage."

"O Grandpapa, I'm so glad!" exclaimed Phronsie, the sunlight all in her eyes.

"So," said the old gentleman, "get behind the lilac-bush here, child;" and he took out a paper from his pocketbook that proved to be a check, filled it out, and handed it to Phronsie. "Now stick it under the door, Phronsie; the crack's big enough. And when they get home, and find it, and that Miss Sally comes for me, I can tell her you did it."

"I will do it, Grandpapa," said Phronsie, running off happily, to tuck the bit of paper under the old door. "There, now, it's done, Grandpapa dear. And I am so glad."

"And now let us get in, and drive off like hot shot," exclaimed the old gentleman, hurrying down the path. "I really feel as if I heard Miss Sally after us now."

CHAPTER XVI.

MR. MARLOWE HELPS MATTERS ALONG.

PHRONSIE passed slowly up the path to the little brown house door. The last of the party of guests at "The Oaks" had just departed. She turned the key in the lock and went in, picking up, on her way, the playthings the children had left the afternoon before, strewn on the old kitchen floor.

Phronsie sat down on a low seat, and leaned her head in Mamsie's old rocking-chair. Outside, a little gray squirrel ran up and down the big apple-tree, and peered in the window chattering loudly; the china basket of sweetbrier noiselessly dropped a petal now and then on the old kitchen table, and the clock ticked away busily; and still Phronsie did not move.

"Mamsie," she was saying softly to herself, "is it very wicked for me to *want* to see Roslyn? I will stay with Grandpapa; but oh, I want so to just see Roslyn."

And after a long pause she said, " I could not ask Grace all she knows about him — oh, to think that he is her cousin ! because that would not be right to Grandpapa, who did not want me to see him. But oh! I cannot help thinking of him; and is it very wicked, Mamsie, just to think of him?"

Still Phronsie did not move. When she did lift her head, there were no traces of tears upon her cheek, only her hands were clasped upon her knee, and a white line settled around the droop-ing mouth.

" Dear Grandpapa," she said softly, " he has done everything for us, and all his comfort is in us. He needs me; and I'll try again not to think of Roslyn. But oh, Mamsie! " She laid her head once more upon the old cushion in the rocking-chair, and kept it there for a long time.

Old Mr. King had gone to town in the early morning train with Jasper. Having not only a great delight in Mr. Marlowe, so that he seized every possible opportunity to be with him, Mr. King had absorbed such a violent pride in the whole publishing business as conducted by Mar-lowe and King, that he had become a silent partner, and contributed such a generous amount of funds as to make possible the great breadth and extension that had been longed for by its founder.

Phronsie leaned her head upon Mamsie's old rocking-chair.

"And I don't want anything to say about the working of the capital," the old gentleman had cried. "Gracious, man alive," to Mr. Marlowe, "I don't know anything about business; and I can trust you, who have brought it up to this."

So Mr. King resolutely kept **away from all** business conferences to which he was always asked; and he pinched his lips under his white mustache very tightly together whenever the fit seized him to give advice. Whenever this was particularly strong upon him, he invariably kept away from town, working it off by scolding at the editorials in the morning paper. At other times he would sometimes take an early morning train with Jasper, and spend hours in wandering over the big establishment, in which he was a great favorite, and in reading and examining the books and periodicals turned out; swelling with pride more and more at the splendid character of the work he saw before him.

Sometimes Phronsie was with him, and often Polly came; and now and then Elyot or King hung to his hand, and listened to his delighted praise of the whole thing.

But this day he announced that he was going alone with Jasper. And when they arrived at the publishing house, he said, in a very different tone from that he had used on his first visit, — "And what a first-class fool I was then, to be sure," he reflected, — "Jasper, my boy, see if Mr.

Marlowe would like to talk with me now. If not, I'll go up into the bindery and see that new machine."

Mr. Marlowe wasn't ready to see him, being, as on the former occasion, occupied with a gentleman who had made the appointment for that hour; so Mr. King did go up into the bindery, whereat all the working-people looked up with a smile, as the old gentleman made them his courtliest bow.

"Father," cried Jasper, springing up the stairs two at a time, "Mr. Marlowe is ready now. He is dreadfully sorry to keep you waiting so long, but it couldn't be helped. Mr. Strong did not get through, but lapped over on the agent of the new paper company, who had an appointment."

"Say no more, my boy," cried his father. "I don't mind waiting a half-hour. I've nothing special to do, and it's pleasant up here."

"A half-hour?" repeated Jasper, taking out his watch. "You've been up here just three hours, father!"

"To be sure," cried the old gentleman, glancing at it, and then whipping out his own, when he burst out laughing, and took Jasper's arm, and went down stairs.

"I move that we all three go out to luncheon," said Mr. Marlowe, as they came into his small private office. "What do you say, Mr. King?"

"Yes, yes, to be sure; a good plan," assented the old gentleman, who always said "yes" nowadays to everything Mr. Marlowe proposed.

"And we can begin our talk there, and finish it here," said the publisher, putting down his desk-cover.

"Now, Jasper, my boy," said old Mr. King, when the three were together in a quiet corner at the restaurant, "I'm going to say something that will perhaps make you feel badly a bit."

Jasper put up his hand involuntarily.

"It won't make a thing come a minute the sooner for talking of it," said the old gentleman cheerily; "but I'm not going to live forever, and that's a fact. I never should have lasted half so long if it hadn't been for you, my boy," laying his hand across the little table on Jasper's, who grasped it eagerly, "and for those blessed Peppers. And, dear me, I mean to go right straight on living a long while yet," he added, with a glance at Jasper's pale face. "But I want a good talk with both of you to-day. I don't mind saying that a certain thing troubles me, and I want to get it off my mind."

Mr. Marlowe said nothing, his clear-cut face quietly turned to the old gentleman, waiting for him to proceed.

"There's no man living, Marlowe, that I'd ask advice from sooner than you," said Mr. King; "and that you know."

A bright smile shot over the publisher's face, lighting up the keen gray eyes with a world of affection. "I know," he said simply.

"It's about Phronsie," said old Mr. King brokenly, and his handsome white head drooped.

"Don't, father," began Jasper, dreadfully distressed; "Phronsie wouldn't want you to feel badly."

"I would let your father speak what is on his mind, Jasper," said Mr. Marlowe quietly.

"She — she — oh, you know it already," said the old gentleman with difficulty, "formed an attachment with a young sculptor when we were last abroad. I introduced them myself. He's General May's nephew, working in Rome; got a high degree of talent, and all that. But, oh, Phronsie!"

Mr. Marlowe's imperturbable countenance gave no hint to any onlooker that anything but the most ordinary conversation was in progress; the other two sitting with their faces to the wall.

"And now that precious child is really and absolutely in love with that man," said Mr. King in a subdued but dreadful voice. "I didn't believe it until I saw her face the other night when little Grace said he was her cousin. Marlowe, what *can* I do?" He grasped the strong right hand lying on the table.

"Mr. King," said the publisher, with a lightning-like gleam in the gray eyes, "I can only tell you certain ways of looking at the matter that seem right to me. You may not like what I say."

"You will say it all the same," said the old gentleman grimly.

"I shall say it all the same," said Mr. Marlowe.

"That's what I like you for," broke in Mr. King. "Why, if I hadn't wanted the truth, I wouldn't have come to you, man." He leaned forward, and gazed into the clear gray eyes.

"You approve of Roslyn May as a man?" asked Mr. Marlowe.

"Dear me, yes. Why, if I hadn't, do you suppose I would have introduced him to Phronsie," cried the old gentleman, somewhat irately.

"Certainly not. Now, what is there that you disapprove of in him?" asked the publisher.

"Nothing; that is, the young fellow is all right, I suppose, only — why Phronsie is a mere child yet. She's my little one!"

"Miss Phronsie is twenty years old," said Mr. Marlowe.

"Bless me, why so she is!" exclaimed Mr. King. And then, as if a wholly new idea had struck him, he kept repeating to himself at intervals as the waiter brought the luncheon, "Phronsie is twenty years old. Phronsie is twenty years old!"

"It doesn't seem a day since that child sent me her gingerbread boy," he said aloud, when the meal was half over.

"I suppose so. That's a way time has of treating us all," said Mr. Marlowe. "Well, I am glad you broached this subject, Mr. King; and now, with your permission, we will finish it when we get back to my office."

Jasper shot him a grateful glance; and quite easy in his mind about his father, now that the

ice was really broken, and the dreaded subject
open for future discussion, he gave a sigh of relief as he saw the countenance of the old gentleman lighten.

"I take it, Mr. King," observed Mr. Marlowe,
when they were once more in the little private
office with orders for no callers to be admitted,
"that Phronsie's welfare is what you are most
concerned about?"

"Yes, yes," cried the old gentleman; "it is,
Marlowe."

"Then, that is really the only thing for us to
consider in this conversation.   You admit that
you believe Phronsie to be deeply in love with
this young sculptor?"

Old Mr. King whirled abruptly around on Jasper. "What say you, Jasper?" he cried. "Perhaps she isn't," with a sudden hope that Jasper
might confirm this.   But Jasper looked him steadily in the eyes. "You are right, father. Phronsie
has loved him ever since you brought her home, I
believe."

The old gentleman groaned aloud, and caught at
the table for support.

"And it is only her love for you," said Jasper,

seeing in Mr. Marlowe's eyes the counsel that the whole of the truth had better be spoken, "that has made her able not to show it."

Old Mr. King got out of his chair, and took as many turns around the small room as its space would allow, fuming like a caged animal.

"And what do you want me to do about it, Marlowe ? " he demanded presently, stopping short in front of that gentleman's office-chair.

"I do not want, nor advise anything," said Mr. Marlow calmly.

"Well, what do you think I ought to do," he fumed — "that's the same thing. Come, speak out and be done with it, man."

For answer, Mr. Marlowe turned to his desk full of papers. "I've talked enough," he said with his bright smile. "Think it out for yourself, King; you'll do the right thing." And he put out his strong hand kindly. The old gentleman grasped it without a word, and hung to it a moment, then clapped on his hat. "I won't wait for you, Jasper," he said. "I'm going home."

"Don't you want me to go with you, father ? " cried Jasper with a glance at Mr. Marlowe.

"You can go just as well as not," said that

gentleman; "there is nothing pressing this afternoon."

"No, no," said the old gentleman imperiously;
"I'll go by myself. Good-day, Marlowe."

"Jasper," said his friend, as the tall, stately
figure passed rapidly out down the long salesroom,
"don't be troubled," glancing into Jasper's overcast face; "it is better as it is. Let him think it
out by himself. And believe me, my boy, the
greatest kindness one can do your father, is to pre-
vent him from being untrue to himself."

"I know it," said Jasper; "but, O Mr. Marlowe! you do know, because you've seen it, how he
just worships Phronsie. We all do for that matter; but father — well, that's different. She's just
everything to him."

"And that's just the very reason he wants to
show her that he is worthy of it," said the publisher gravely; "and no one must point it out to
him. He must travel that way alone, till he can
think only of her good. And he'll do it."

CHAPTER XVII.

ALEXIA HAS GRACE TO HERSELF.

"WELL, if I'm not glad to get you here!" cried Alexia that same morning, dragging Grace into the front doorway of "The Pumpkin." "Now you shall make me such a visit! Dear me, won't we have good times together," making all sorts of wild plans in her mind on the spot, to atone for any former coldness.

"I can't stay but two days," cried Grace in alarm. "I'm to go back to 'The Oaks' then."

"Nonsense! Why, it would take you two days to see that blessed child alone. You've no idea how he's grown this last week," said Alexia.

"Hadn't I better see him now?" asked Grace, feeling it unsafe to put off such a wonderful sight any longer.

"That you had!" exclaimed Alexia, delighted at such enthusiasm. "Come right up into the nursery this very minute, Grace."

So the two ran up the winding stairs into the tiny box of a room called the nursery. There on the floor, sprawling after a red rubber ball, was Algernon. His mother seized him, and covered his round red face with kisses. " The blessed, precious baby!" she cried.

" Ar-goo-goo-goo!" screamed Algernon in a passion, and kicking fearfully.

" See how he tries to talk — how he *does* talk!" cried Alexia, whirling around with him till his arms and legs appeared to Grace like so many spokes to a wheel in rapid motion. "Oh, my dear! So he should tell his old mother all about it. Grace, isn't he perfectly wonderful?"

"He *is* a baby," said Grace, saying the first thing that came into her mind.

" I knew you'd say so when you came to see him," declared Alexia, with a triumphant flush on her sallow face. "That isn't half he can do, either."

She set Algernon on the floor, and dropped there herself, regardless of her elaborate morningdress. "Crawl over mummy, now," she commanded.

But Algernon preferred to crawl just the other way, after his ball.

"That's just it!" cried Alexia delightedly. "Now, you see he's not to be led. He's going to think for himself. Oh, I expect great things from that boy, Grace!"

A placid-looking woman in a big stiff white cap sat by the window sewing.

"Now, there's Bonny," said Alexia, still sitting on the floor, and looking over at her, "she's thoroughly commonplace, and can't rise to the superiority of that blessed child. And strange to say, Grace, his father can't either. But I can; oh, you dear!" with that she caught Algernon by one of his fat little legs, and drew him to her. And then ensued a wild screaming on Algernon's part, and a petting on Alexia's, Grace backing off to the door, feeling that the room was too small for so much action.

"Now I'm going to have a talk with you, Grace," said Alexia presently, and hanging tightly to her baby, "come," in one of the lulls when Algernon paused to take breath, "let's go into your room."

"Can we talk with the baby?" asked Grace with wide eyes.

"Nonsense; yes, indeed! Algernon loves to hear

conversation, and he really understands a good deal," said Alexia, tucking her "blessed child" under one arm, and going off. "This is your room, right next, so you can hear his dear little voice the first thing in the morning. Oh, you darling!" stopping to kiss Algernon. Then she ran with him into Grace's small apartment room, and dumped him into the middle of the bed. "Now, then, Grace, he's all right. Come in, dear, this is your room."

"Will he stay there?" asked Grace fearfully.

"Dear me, yes," said Alexia; "he's so very sensible. And I'm going to sit this side to make it absolutely sure. Well, now, Grace, take off your bonnet, and come here. I want to ask you something."

Grace took off her bonnet, and came round by the side of the bed.

"Sit on the foot there, will you," said Alexia. "That's a dear. Well, now, Grace, do tell me about Rosyln May. I've been dying to know, and couldn't get a chance with all this swarm of company around our ears, ever since you said he was your cousin the other night. How did that ever happen?"

"Why, he was born so," said Grace.

"Of course, you stupid child," cried Alexia; "why, even Algernon would know that! But I mean — oh, isn't it just the most wonderful thing in all the world that it turns out that Roslyn May is your cousin?"

"Why, no; I don't see how it is very wonderful," said Grace in a perplexed way.

"Oh, dear me! well, you are stupid — I mean! well, I wish I could tell you, but I suppose I mustn't."

"And what made everybody look so queer when I spoke his name, when Mrs. King said that the Fishers were going to Rome?" asked Grace, recognizing here a mystery, and meaning to get at the bottom of it. "Why did they, Mrs. Dodge?"

"Oh, dear me! Algernon, would you tell her?" asked his mother.

"Ar-goo!" said Algernon, having recovered himself, and finding it very pleasant to pull at the pillow-shams.

"There, since that blessed child says so, I believe I ought to tell you, Grace!" said Alexia; "and besides, all our set, the old friends I mean,

know it.   Why, Phronsie Pepper and Roslyn May
are lovers."

Grace gave a squeal that entirely threw Algernon's into the shade, as she hopped off from the
bed, and ran around into Alexia's arms.   "Oh,

"Ar-goo!" said Algernon, finding it very pleasant to pull at the pillow-
shams.

say that again — do say it again, dear Mrs.
Dodge!" she cried with blazing cheeks.

"Oh, my goodness me!" cried Alexia, feeling
of her throat; "how you scared me, Grace! And
you've frightened this blessed child;" as Algernon

put up his little lip, and scuttled over like a rabbit to the side of the bed next to his mother.

"I can't help it — I can't help it," cried Grace wildly, and spinning around the room on her toes; "to think that my dear Miss Phronsie Pepper loves my cousin Roslyn May — oh, oh!"

"Do stop!" cried Alexia, picking off her boy from the bed to go after her and pluck her by the sleeve. "Hush, hush — Bonny will hear. And besides, it can't ever be — no, never in all this world, I tell you; so what's the use of hopping so."

"Can't ever be?" asked Grace, coming to such a dead stop that she nearly overturned Alexia, baby and all. "Didn't you say, Mrs. Dodge, that they loved each other?"

"Yes; oh, dreadfully!" said Alexia, backing up against the wall; "but it won't ever be that they will be married, because Grandpapa King don't want Phronsie to be married."

"He don't want Miss Phronsie to be married when she loves somebody?" gasped Grace.

"Oh, well! he doesn't exactly believe that she does love him," said Alexia testily, who had privately berated him so many times when talking

it all over with Pickering that she was now sore
on the subject, "and he wants her to himself."

Grace Tupper sat down on the first thing that
she could see, which proved to be the scrap-basket. "Doesn't old Mr. King love Miss Phronsie?" she gasped.

"Yes, yes," gasped Alexia, running to pull
at her; "but get out of that scrap-basket. Polly
Pepper made that for me years ago, and you are
mussing all the ribbons." And calling to Bonny,
who came without a ripple on her placid countenance, she bundled the baby into her arms, and
began to pull out the big pink bows from which
Grace gave a bound.

"I'll tell you all about it, and then you must
tell *me* all about it," she said, when the pink
bows were found not to be much crushed after all.
"There, come over here to the sofa. It's a mercy
that you didn't ruin that basket. If you had, I'd
never have forgiven you, Grace Tupper, in all
this world. Well, you see, it all happened three
years ago when they were abroad, — Phronsie and
Grandpapa King and David, and the Fishers and
Charlotte Chatterton, — there was a perfect mob
of them; Charlotte was just going over to be-

gin to study in Germany. And although Polly and Jasper heard something of it in Mother Fisher's letters, it wasn't till they all got home that we knew how it was. And then Roslyn May came over twice to see her. And then the most awful thing, Grace Tupper, in all this world, you can't think," she leaned her elbows on her knees and regarded Grace fixedly, " happened, and I've been worried to death about it ever since."

" What ? " Grace scarcely breathed it, while her large blue eyes dilated fearfully.

" Why, Roslyn May came across just a few weeks ago," said Alexia in a stage whisper, "actually came to this side of the Atlantic, and didn't come to see Phronsie ! And I think — I really and truly do, Grace Tupper — that Grand-papa King had something to do about it; for Roslyn May didn't stay but one day. What do you think of that ? "

It was so very dreadful, that Grace couldn't think of anything for the space of a minute; then she said, in a puzzled way, " But how could old Mr. King have done anything when he didn't see Roslyn — I don't see."

"I don't see either," said Alexia irritably, "but it's my private opinion publicly confessed that Grandpapa King is mixed up in it some way. It worries me to skin and bone. And Pickering won't do anything when I beg him to, and everything is just as horrid as it can be. Well, now, tell me all about your cousin Roslyn May," she added, brightening up, and eager for the news.

"Why, you see he is my very own cousin," cried Grace in the greatest pride.

"How?" interrupted Alexia; "is General May your uncle?"

"Yes," said Grace; "he is my mother's brother. And Cousin Roslyn is awfully smart. Why, when he was a little boy he got hold of some clay, and he made dogs and pigs and horses just as natural. And Uncle May took him abroad—you know his mother died when he was a baby."

"Oh, dear!" said Alexia.

"Yes, she did," said Grace. "Well, and Uncle May took him abroad to see if it was really in him to be a sculptor, he said, and everybody was perfectly astonished. But Roslyn was determined to come home to be educated."

"Good for him!" cried Alexia.

"Yes; and so he waited till after he'd got through college before he really did much sculpturing. Then he went abroad to stay; and I tell you he's just worked! Why, haven't you heard of the things he has done?"

She opened her blue eyes widely at Alexia now.

"Yes — yes, child, of course," said Alexia; "I don't want you to tell me that newspaper talk, I want to hear about *him*. Is he nice?"

"Oh, he's splendid!" cried Grace, beating her hands together. "If he were to come into the room now, you'd say you never saw such a handsome man."

"I don't know about that," said Alexia, who had ideas of her own as to manly beauty. "Well, go on."

"And all the girls are in love with him," said Grace; "but he's just devoted to his art, and he don't care anything for any of them."

"Except Phronsie," said Alexia.

"Except Miss Phronsie," cried Grace, hugging herself at the thought. "Well, and the first bit of money he ever earned, — it was for a fountain or something, and it took the prize, — the design,

I mean, — he gave it to a poor boy he knew at
home, who hadn't any money to study with.
And mamma is going over next fall to see him;
and I've been teasing her to take me, but she
said I must stay with Aunt Atherton another
year and go to school.   And now — O Mrs.
Dodge! 1 didn't tell you, for this other news
scared it all out of my head — Mrs. King has
asked me to stay at 'The Oaks.' "

"You don't mean it, Grace ? " cried Alexia,
catching her by the arm; "why, I meant to
have you myself."

"Well, I'm to be with dear Mrs. King, and go
in every day to Miss Willoughby," said Grace
in great satisfaction; "for mamma answered Mrs.
King's letter and said so, and Miss Willoughby
says she wants me back again.   She really did,
Mrs. Dodge."

"I don't doubt it, child," said Alexia.   "I
rather like you myself.   Well, now, Grace, this
troubles me."   She nursed her knee with her
long arms, and gazed into Grace's face.   "Roslyn
May is your cousin, and I am just determined
to do something to help Phronsie.   I can't keep
still any longer; I shall fly out of my head if I

do. Now, can't you write to him, and ask him why he didn't come to see Phronsie when he was over last time. That will bring some sort of an answer, and at least tell us the reason."

"Oh, so I will!" cried Grace, springing up; "1 will write it now, this very minute." Then she stopped suddenly, and her face turned scarlet. "Mrs. Dodge," she said, "I'd rather not. I've just been silly, you know, and — and — I don't mean to do anything I don't ask Miss Phronsie or Mrs. King about first."

"And you blessed child," cried Alexia, kissing her, "I knew the minute I'd asked you I'd said the wrong thing. To tell you the truth, Grace, I never do a single thing without asking Pickering first. Oh, dear me! but what *shall* we do? Things can't be left to themselves so. Something must be done."

CHAPTER XVIII.

GRANDPAPA DOES THE RIGHT THING.

THE little brown house door opened slowly, and some one came in. Phronsie raised her head. "Why, Grandpapa!" she exclaimed, "have you come home?"

"Yes; I thought I would, Phronsie; there wasn't much to detain me, and I finished early."

Phronsie had risen and hurried over to him, putting her hand affectionately through his arm. "You are not sick, Grandpapa dear?" she asked, anxiously looking up into his face.

"No, no, child; that is, only sick of myself," he answered with a short laugh. Phronsie stood quite still in a puzzled way, regarding him closely. "There's nothing to worry about, Phronsie, nothing at all. Only I thought I'd have a little talk with you. Come here, child." He took a seat in a big easy-chair, and drew her to his knee. "There, now we can be comfortable."

Phronsie fixed her brown eyes upon him wonderingly.

"Phronsie, I've always been a curious old chap.
I wouldn't say so to any one else, only to you,
dear; but I have."

"O Grandpapa!" cried Phronsie convulsively,
and throwing her arms around his neck, "don't,
don't, dear Grandpapa! You've always and ever
been beautiful," she sobbed in great distress.

"Well, there, there, child," said the old gentleman, patting her back as if she were three years
old, and mightily pleased with her tribute, "you
love the old man, and that's enough. But what
I should have done without you, child, no living
mortal knows. I'm sure I cannot tell. Well;
and now, Phronsie, I want to say something, and
you must hear me. Sit up, dear, and let me see
your eyes."

So Phronsie sat up quite straight on his knee,
and he held her hands, and she never took her
eyes from his face, but listened attentively to
every word.

"You see, Phronsie, it's just this way. I've been
thinking over many things lately, and I've come
to the conclusion that I made a mistake in send-

ing Roslyn May off. So I've just been writing to him that it strikes me he would better run across again."

All the pink color had gone from Phronsie's cheek long ago, and she now sat pale and still, her brown eyes fastened on his face.

"Does that please you, child?" asked old Mr. King after a pause, and smoothing her yellow hair.

"Grandpapa, has some one been speaking to you about it, and wanting you to write to Roslyn?" she asked suddenly; the brown eyes flashed, and she looked at him steadily.

"No indeed; I thought it all out by myself," he answered with conscious pride, "and it seems to me the best thing to be done. Really it does, Phronsie."

"Do *you* wish it, Grandpapa?" she asked slowly.

"Yes, I do, child. Listen, now, Phronsie. You are not to cry, child, nor to feel badly; but you know Grandpapa is an old man, and cannot last forever, and "—

For answer, Phronsie dropped her head upon his breast, and cried bitterly. It was some time

before he could soothe her, though he tried every
means in his power. At last he said, " This is
making me ill, child."

Phronsie took up her head quickly, and put her
hand caressingly over his white hair. " Does it,
Grandpapa ? " she asked, her face working convulsively.

" Yes; that is, I shall be," said the old gentleman artfully, "if you cry. And if you want to
please me, Phronsie, you will be very glad that
I wrote to Roslyn. I want to see you happily
settled myself, child, and to enjoy it all. Why, I
expect to live years and years, Phronsie; " and
he sat erect, and looked so handsome and strong,
that Phronsie smiled through her tears. " Don't
you love him, child ? " he asked abruptly.

" Yes, Grandpapa," said Phronsie, " I do."

" Very much ? " asked old Mr. King, with a
dreadful pang at his heart.

" Very much indeed," said Phronsie.

" Child, child, why didn't you tell me ? " he
cried, holding her to him remorsefully. "Oh,
why didn't you tell your old Grandpapa ? " he
groaned.

It was now Phronsie's turn to comfort him; for

he felt so very badly, that it was some time before she could get him out of the dreadful state into which he was plunged. But at last they emerged from the little brown house hand in hand, Phronsie looking up into his smiling face.

"I've been hunting just everywhere for you, father dear," cried Polly, running down the terrace to meet them, and waving a yellow envelope. "It's from Mamsie, of course. Do open it, Grandpapa," lapsing, as she often did, into the old familiar title, "and see what she says."

With a merry laugh, and holding it so that Phronsie could see, the old gentleman tore it open, and stared blankly at the words: —

HOTEL CONSTANZI, ROME, *June* 22, 18 —.

"Roslyn May very ill with low fever. Come and bring Phronsie.   ADONIRAM FISHER."

They were off the next morning, Grandpapa and Phronsie, hurrying down to New York to sail on the following day. Joel, informed of it by telegram, got a brother minister to take his place for a fortnight or so, and determined to go too. And hardly before Polly and the rest of the home people at "The Oaks" had accustomed them selves to think of it as a settled thing surely to be, the little party were off on the waste of waters, that lengthened every day into a terribl. distance between them and their dear home. But they were going to Mamsie and to Roslyn! And although Mr. King was dreadfully overcome at the thought of what might meet them at the end of the journey, as a result (he now felt quite sure) of his meddling with Phronsie's happiness, he kept up pluckily on her account, and never let a sign of his inward trepidation be seen.

"Oh, how do you do" — Joel was saying very carelessly, as Phronsie came up to him on deck, to a very elegant-looking person, who extended two fingers to her — "Mr. Bayley, Mr. Livingston Bayley, you remember, Phronsie."

"And Mrs. Livingston Bayley," said that gentleman, as the young girl bowed, presenting a handsome, showily dressed person, who eyed Phronsie all over. "Well, 'pon me honor, this is not half bad, don't you know, to meet in this way."

Phronsie, not knowing exactly what to reply, left it to Joel, who didn't care to, but stood gazing blankly out to sea.

"We have only been in America a week," said

the lady in a sweet little drawl, "and I made Mr. Bayley bring me directly to London again. I absolutely could not exist unless he did."

"A beastly boat, ain't it now?" said Mr. Bayley with a yawn.

"Haven't tried it yet enough to say," replied Joel with a short laugh.

"How are all your family?" asked Mr. Bayley a trifle awkwardly, which so disconcerted him that he paused mid-air for another idea.

"All very well, thank you," said Joel.

"Your sister, Mrs. King, is she well now?" pursued Mr. Bayley, trying to be very nonchalant, and fumbling at his cigarette case.

"Very well indeed, thank you," said Joel.

"Mr. Bayley, I think I must have my constitutional now," said his wife with another drawl, and putting her hand on his arm.

"Oh, yes, certainly — certainly," said Mr. Bayley. "Well, I'm awfully glad, don't you know, that we've met again," making elaborate adieux.

"And I hope we shall see much of each other on the voyage," said Mrs. Bayley sweetly, with no eyes for any one but Phronsie.

"Thanks," said Joel as they swept off.

"If you please, miss," said the deck-steward, coming up and touching his cap respectfully to Phronsie, "there's an old woman who says she wishes you would come to see her. She's in her stateroom."

"An old woman?" asked Phronsie wonderingly.

"Yes, miss. She didn't give her name, but said she saw you come on board yesterday. And she's very urgent, miss."

"I'll go with you to the door, and you can find out who she is," said Joel.

Phronsie moved off after the steward, and held out her hand to Joel. "You can wait for me outside."

The stateroom, small and uncomfortable, into which she was ushered, while Joel paced up and down outside, was so dark, that at first Phronsie could not see distinctly its occupant.

"O miss!" cried an old lady, trying to rise in her berth, and brushing away the straying white hair from her cheek, "you don't remember me. But I'll never forget you nor your face." It was Phronsie's little old woman of the Berton electric car.

"What can I do for you?" asked Phronsie

gently, and standing by the berth she smoothed the straying hair.

"O miss, I'm afraid I'm going to die, and I can't when I'm just going home."

"I don't think you will die," said Phronsie, "and I am sorry you feel ill."

"It is just this way, miss. I'm all worn out with gladness to get home and put my feet on English ground," said the little old woman hungrily. "But I must tell you about it; because if I should die, I want you to know all about it. You see, my husband and I came over because he didn't want to live on his sons, and he fancied America, and being independent there in a new country. And so we came a good many years ago; and our sons felt dreadfully, for they wanted us to stay with them. But John, he's my husband, said 'no,' and you couldn't move him. Well, we were very happy living in a little home of our own, and my husband worked the ground to suit himself as best he could; and though I worried some, and I know he did, only he was always still like, to see the grandchildren, they were so cunning when we came away, we did pretty well. Only English ways of farming are different from yours, and John was too old to learn new ways, and so we began to get behind. And we didn't care to make new friends, and we didn't know how, and so when John was taken away there wasn't any one to advise me, and the property was sold off for almost nothing. And after I'd got a letter, I had it in my pocket the day you were kind to me in the car, I was all so in a tremble I hadn't read it, I just sat down and answered it when I got home. It was from one of my sons; and I told him the whole truth, and he sent me the money, and told me to come on this boat. But I'm trembling so, miss," she held up her thin arm that shook like a leaf, "that I'm afraid I won't last till I get there. And I want you to see my boy, who'll be there to meet me, and tell him for me that his father said he was sorry we came away, before he died, and he sent his love to both of 'em, and he blessed all the grandchildren, and so do I;" and her voice sank to a whisper.

Phronsie knelt down by the berth, and put her face very near to the troubled one. "Don't be worried," she said, as if to a child. "You are lonely, I think, but not very ill."

"Ain't I ill, miss?" cried the little old woman pleadingly. "Oh, I'm so glad! I thought I was going to be most dreadfully sick, and I was afraid to call the doctor to hear him say so;" and she gave a sigh of relief.

"No," said Phronsie; "I do not really think you are very ill, but I do believe you want something to eat. Now, I am going to tell you what I think you had better do, if you want to have me."

"I wish you would, miss," said the little old woman gratefully, and clinging to her.

"A cup of beef tea is the first thing," said Phronsie cheerfully; and getting to her feet she touched the electric button, and on the appearance of the deck steward, ordered it; "and then I will brush your hair, and you shall sit up in bed, and I will talk to you."

"O miss, how good you are!" exclaimed the little old woman, leaning back against her pillows, while two tears coursed down her cheeks.

"Joey, dear," said Phronsie, going to the door of the stateroom, "I am going to stay here now a little while. It is all right, dear," as Joel took a look within. The next moment he marched in, and up to the side of the berth, and put out his hand.

"Well, my good Mrs. Benson, how did you get here?"

The little old woman gave a scream of delight. "O Mr. Pepper!" she exclaimed, seizing his hand.

"It's one of my good parishioners, Phronsie," said Joel, taking both of the thin little hands in his big strong one; "but I lost sight of her, and nobody could tell me where she went."

"I didn't want to let you know," said Mrs. Benson shamefacedly; "so I was going to write you as soon as I got to England, and my son was going to write too, and thank you for all your kindness to me."

"Ah, but you don't know how I looked for you," said Joel, shaking his crop of short black curls, that was a dreadful cross for him to carry, as he admired straight hair intensely, especially "in the ministry," as he said.

"Well, I went up to Berton," said little Mrs. Benson, "because folks said that there I could get a place as matron in an orphan asylum. But I didn't — and then came my son's letter."

CHAPTER XIX.

TRYING TO BE CHEERY.

"OH, dear, dear!" King struggled manfully with his sobs, and then wailed outright; and running into Polly's room he crouched behind the door.

Grace Tupper came after him. "King, you mustn't," she whispered, leaning over to pull him out.

"Let me be!" cried King, wriggling away from her; and he roared on.

"Your sister Polly will hear you," cried Grace desperately.

"She can't; she's got comp'ny," sobbed King in a fresh burst. "I wa — want Phronsie, I do!"

"So we all want her," said Grace with set teeth; "but, O King! don't cry, dear. There, there, I'm sorry for you." She smoothed his stubby head with a kind hand, wishing she could say something to comfort.

"Who'll he — hear my lessons?" olubbered King, who never had been known to worry over them before; "and if I don't say 'em, Mamsie won't tell me I've been a good boy. Oh, dear!"

"Now, there is something I can do," cried Grace joyfully, "I can hear those lessons, King; and just as soon as Mrs. King's company has gone, I mean to ask her if I mayn't."

"I don't want you," said King, with one eye on her, the other obscured by his arm, and feeling dreadfully sorry that he had mentioned lessons anyway.

"But I can help Mrs. King," cried Grace in a transport, flying around the room; "for of course she will have to hear them now. And, O King! I'll make you pictures of the countries you study about, and the natives, and " —

"What's natifs?" asked King, bringing the other eye out.

"Why, the people who live there, and " —

"And make bears, will you, Miss Grace?" cried King, dreadfully excited, and springing out in front of her. "Oh, say, *please* do — and have 'em catch some of the natifs, and chew 'em, and 'most eat 'em up. Will you, Miss Grace?"

"Yes, I'll make bears," said Grace, glad now of her power to sketch, "and ever so many other things, King; that is, if you are good," she said hastily.

"Oh! I'll be just as good as everything," said King, clasping his hands. "Begin now, do, Miss Grace;" and he began to pull her along to the little room where the lessons were always said.

"No, King," said Grace, "I can't begin those lessons until I ask your sister Polly first. But I'll draw you a picture of anything you choose."

"Oh, goody!" exclaimed King, jumping up and down, and making so much noise that Elyot came running in, and after him Barby, trailing her doll by one leg.

"Stop, you mustn't come in here!" shouted King, with a very red face, and trying to slam the door against them; "Miss Grace and I are going to do something."

"What you going to do?" demanded Elyot, crowding in.

"What going to do?" asked Barby, wriggling and pushing.

"Go right straight out!" demanded King, pushing the door with all his might.

"O King, King!" cried Grace, pulling at his sailor collar.

"This is my mamma's room," said Elyot stoutly; "and I am not going out — so there!"

"My mummy's room," declared Barby, shaking her curls at him; "an' I'm coming in, I am."

"You sha'n't. We're going to draw the most beautiful pictures of bears — and eating men up, and everything," howled King quite beside himself, and beginning to use his teeth and finger-nails.

"Oh, dear me!" cried Grace Tupper, unable to do a thing to stop them. And she sat right down in the middle of the floor, and began to cry.

Polly's company just departing, Polly ran lightly over the stairs. "Why — children!" she exclaimed, pausing at the landing.

"He's going to draw be-yewtiful bears, mummy," cried Barby, dreadfully excited; and being the nearest to the hall, she ran out, and threw herself into her mother's arms.

"O boys — boys!" cried Polly sorrowfully, coming in, Barby hanging to her gown.

Both boys, now engaged in a lively tussle,

stopped pulling each other's hair, and sat up. Grace Tupper sat still and cried on.

"He wouldn't let me come in and see it all," cried Elyot with flashing eyes.

"No, he wouldn't, mummy," said Barby, shaking her head.

"And Miss Grace was going to draw 'em for me," screamed King; "and they pushed and scrouged dreadfully."

"What?" said Polly. "Where did you learn that word, King?"

"Oh, dear, dear!" wailed Grace. "I'm afraid I'm to blame, dear Mrs. King; but I said I'd draw him some bears — I wanted to help; and now I've only made you trouble."

"Oh, no, Grace dear!" said Polly gently, "you haven't made any trouble. It was very nice and kind of you to offer to do that."

She had such a sorrowful look in her face as she sat down, that the boys crept near, and hung their heads.

"I — I — didn't mean to," said King, trying not to whimper, "sister Polly, I really didn't." And he was quite near now; but Polly didn't look at him nor stir.

"Please don't look like that, mamma," begged Elyot, feeling cold creeps down his back, "I never'll do so again."

"Never'll do so again," hummed Barby, playing with her mother's rings.

"To think that when Mamsie is away, and she trusts us all," said Polly, when she could find her voice, "that we should do such dreadful things."

The boys wriggled and twisted, and hid their faces.

"And then, when Phronsie has had to go off with Grandpapa — oh, it quite breaks me down," said Polly, and there was a tremble in her voice.

At this, both boys precipitated themselves into her lap, where they burrowed in speechless misery, Barby yielding herself to it all with a happy little crow as if part of the play.

"No, no, Barby," said Polly gently, and shaking her head a' her; "mamma is not playing now. We have been very naughty. Go and get your little chairs, boys, and sit down quietly."

So the two boys went out and dragged in their two little cane-seat chairs, and planted themselves down in them, Barby being put on a corner of the lounge. And Polly took Grace out into another room and heard all about it.

"Sister Polly!" called King presently, "oh, do come here!" There was such a cry in his voice that Polly hurried in, and found him sobbing as if his heart would break. "I can't sit here any longer — don't make me," and he hid his face on her neck. "I think of everything bad I ever did. O sister Polly! I'm so sorry."

"Then that is as long as I want you to sit here," said Polly, helping him out.

"I've got to sit longer," said Elyot gloomily, "because I'm not sorry," as King rushed to kiss him. "I wanted to hear about the bears too."

"And I want bears too," declared Barby from her sofa; "bad, naughty King."

"You shall have the bears," cried King radiantly, running up to her; "yes, you shall, Barby; the very first picture Miss Grace draws you shall have it — and Elyot shall have the next," he said, after a minute's hard thinking.

Polly sent him a happy little smile that warmed every corner of his small heart.

"Mayn't Elyot get out now, sister Polly?" he asked pleadingly.

"I'm not sorry," said Elyot stoutly.   'No; I've got to stay."

"You may go out, King, and you too, Barby," said Polly slowly, "and shut the door."

"No; I'm going to stay," said Barby perversely.

"Barbara."

Barby slipped to the ground and edged out, and King closed the door, feeling that it wasn't so easy to undo being naughty after all.

In a minute the door was opened slowly, and King's head appeared. "Sister Polly," he said, "it truly wasn't Elyot's fault, because if I'd let them in, he would have been good."

"Go out, dear," said Polly gently, "and close the door."

When the door was opened again, Elyot walked into the little room where they were all waiting for him. No one had done anything, and Grace's hands were idle in her lap. Elyot walked up to her. "I'm sorry I made you feel badly, Miss Grace," he said; and then he ran and threw his arms around King. "I don't want the bears; I'd rather you had them," he cried.

Barby hurried over to Grace. "I'm sorry too," she said; "and I'll take the bears if nobody wants

'em." So a space being cleared in the middle of
the room, Polly had her little sewing-table brought
in; and presently there was a delightful hum, and
everybody talking and laughing at once. And it

" Barby hurried over to Grace. ' I'm sorry too,' she said; ' and I'll take
the bears.' "

was found that Grace Tupper could draw everything in the most delightful fashion. And bears
pursuing men and women and children in the
most impossible places, were executed, and all

sorts of hair-breadth escapes were indulged. And then the children wanted to color the pictures with their crayons, and then to cut them out; until the first thing they knew, the "little publishing bag" was swung over their heads.

"O papa!" screamed the two, and "O brother Jasper!" howled King, "is it so late?" And then they all swarmed around him to show their work; and Grace Tupper's face flushed rosier yet at the praise, for Polly had come in, and was hanging on her husband's arm.

And in the midst of the noise and bustle the children made, — for they seized their papa, and made him play "bear-garden" in earnest, — Grace made bold to proffer her request to Polly that she might try to hear King's lessons.

"I'm afraid I don't know enough," she said humbly; "but oh! won't you let me try, dear Mrs. King?"

And Polly, looking into the blue eyes, said, "Yes;" and Grace ran off on happy feet, resolved to do her very best, and to put in practice all that she had ever learned at school. How she wished now that there were no idle hours to think of! "But Mrs. King would say that it was of no use to spend time to think of that now," she said to herself, "but to take hold of the books at once."

"What a comfort Grace is!" said Polly to Jasper, as they were beginning to try a new duet, and just as he was setting it in place on the music-rest, "isn't she, Jasper?"

"Yes indeed," he said heartily.

But in spite of all their efforts to be cheerful and gay, time dragged heavily enough. And the first few days after Grandpapa and Phronsie went, Jasper had hard work to leave Polly when he ran off to business in the early train.

"I'll stay home with you, dear," he said on the third morning, as he saw the pale face, and the sorrowful look in the usually laughing eyes, "and we will go and drive, Polly;" cut to the heart to see her so.

"Oh, no, Jasper!" she said quickly, the color flooding her face, "oh, how could I be so selfish! I didn't think it would worry you so, and I'll make myself look cheerful. Oh! it would just kill me to have you leave your work. Indeed, Jasper, it would."

"Then I won't, Polly," said Jasper reluctantly; "and don't worry about Roslyn May. I do believe they'll find things better than they fear, when they get there."

"But supposing they shouldn't," breathed Polly fearfully.

"They will, I verily believe," said Jasper in ringing tones. "And just think, Polly, if all goes well, and the boat makes her usual time, they'll be there on Monday."

Polly counted the days and hours, and "even minutes" Alexia said, and was surprised herself to see how swiftly they flew by.

"It's such a comfort to think that Joey could go with them," she said one day, when Alexia ran over and up into her pretty room to bewail her woes over a new gown the dressmaker had sent home. Alexia had worn it over to show it to Polly; and she now turned this way and that, declaring each side was just so much worse than the other.

"Did you ever see such a fright, Polly Pepper?" she cried, quite overcome, and sinking into the first chair she could find — "and to think it was to be my very best gown."

"Take care," warned Polly, "you will spoil all that ruching."

"I don't care," said Alexia recklessly, with a vicious pull at a refractory bow. "Now, look at that; everything sticks up that should lie down, and flops where it ought to stand out. Oh, dear me! I just had to wear it over to show you before Pickering sees it, and to let off steam, because I don't want to worry him, poor boy. It's quite bad enough to pay the bills. Oh, that horrible old Miss Flint! Polly Pepper, what *shall* I do?"

Polly dropped the brush with which she was brushing out her bright brown hair, and ran over. "I'll tell you what, Alexia," she said cheerily, "I think it's these dreadful bows that are not put on rightly, that make half the trouble," picking out one of them; "and then she has the shoulder-puffs too big."

"They're enormous!" exclaimed Alexia, rolling her eyes to compass them both. "I look just like a toad, Polly."

"Now, if those were down in the right place," said Polly, taking little puckers in them, and then standing back to view the effect, "it would make ever so much difference in that gown; you can't think, Alexia."

"Well, I begin to see hope for it," said Alexia, sitting up straight with her usual air; "but when I came in, actually, Polly, I was all gone to pieces, I was so blue. Oh! what were you saying as I came in? I remember now; it was about Joel."

"I was saying it was such a comfort to think that Joey could go with Grandpapa and Phronsie," said Polly, flying over to the toilet-table to her hair again.

"I should think so," cried Alexia, between whom and Joel there had always been a great friendship, though nothing could be farther from their thoughts than to show it to each other. "My goodness me! Joel Pepper is just the most splendid man that ever lived, except Pickering and Jasper."

CHAPTER XX.

FIRE!

"MISS PEPPER," Mrs. Livingston Bayley called sweetly but insistently as Phronsie hurried by.

"I cannot stop now," said Phronsie.

Mrs. Bayley reserved her anger, and picked up her novel, until her husband sauntered up. Then she turned on him furiously from her steamer-chair.

"Livingston," she said, forgetting to drawl, "it is perfectly preposterous in Phronsie Pepper to go on so. I don't see what Mr. King is thinking of to allow it."

"Oh, I don't have anything to do with Phronsie Pepper," declared Mr. Bayley, in a very bad temper, and sitting down, after carefully adjusting the creases along his trousers legs, "don't you know; so what is the use of pitching into a fellow, Celestine."

"In all our conversation, I have observed you are always very cross if I allude to the Peppers in any way. It is extremely uncomfortable for

'Now, Celestine," said Mr. Bayley, rolling a fresh cigarette, "the Peppers are perfectly well able to take care of themselves."

me, Livingston, to have you assume such an attitude toward me."

Mr. Bayley said something way down in his

throat, and got out of his steamer-chair for a turn or two on deck.

"Now, Celestine," he said, coming back and rolling a fresh cigarette as he stood over her, "I want you to understand, once for all, that I'm not going to be drawn into collision with the Peppers, don't you know. They are perfectly well able to take care of themselves; and I wouldn't advise you to try it on, either."

"She has no mother with her, or"—

"And you'll be a mother to her. Celestine, that's too good, don't you know. Ha, ha, ha!"

"Your mirth is always as ill-timed as your other attempts at ideas," remarked his wife angrily. "I repeat, Phronsie Pepper has no mother with her to advise her."

"But she has old Mr. King; and he's just the very—well, if you want to tackle him, go ahead."

"I certainly shall speak to her," said Mrs. Bayley with dignity.

"And when the old man gets through with you, perhaps you'd like to try your hand on her brother, Joel Pepper. But I don't believe you will, Celestine, I give you my word for it."

He tossed that cigarette overboard, it not having been rolled to suit him, and began on another.

"To think of that girl, with her beauty and advantages, taking up with a miserable old dowdy of a woman whom nobody knows a thing about, and spending all her time on her."

"When she might be with you," cut in Mr. Bayley, getting into his steamer-chair again, and leaning his elbows on his knees to assist him through his arduous labor.

"When she might be with me," repeated Celestine calmly; "think what I could be to that girl," she added complacently, and playing with her rings.

"She isn't awake to those immense advantages," observed her husband; "that is, don't appear to be."

"Well, I'll make her, then," declared Mrs. Bayley, setting her teeth hard together.

Mr. Bayley laughed softly to himself.

"Hush! here she comes," said Mrs. Bayley under her breath. "O Miss Phronsie!" she smiled sweetly on her.

"Did you want to see me?" asked Phronsie. "I beg your pardon for not stopping."

Mr. Bayley got out of his steamer-chair, and pressed it upon her elaborately. "Do sit down, Miss Phronsie," begged his wife cordially.

"Thank you," said Phronsie, "but I cannot, Mrs. Bayley."

"You never give me any of your time," said that lady, calling to her aid a reproachful look, an expression that had always brought down other victims, "and you know I have some claim upon you, as my husband is an old friend of your family." She hadn't meant to say this when she began, but for some unaccountable reason her supply of words seemed to give out.

As this required no answer, Phronsie did not give any, but remained silent, standing by the steamer-chair.

"You have sufficient time for *new* friends," said the lady with emphasis; "I have seen you with an old woman on the deck several times the last two days."

"She needs me," said Phronsie quietly; "she is all alone."

"Well, that is just it," exclaimed Mrs. Bayley eagerly, welcoming her chance; and throwing back her head, she said rapidly, "do you know

I don't think it is wise to take up with that old thing. Nobody knows who she is, and it's an awful bore for you — wastes your time and all that. Now, let me give you a piece of advice, Miss Phronsie."

"Thank you," said Phronsie; "but my Grandpapa is here, you know, and my brother," she did not finish, "to whom I can apply for advice."

Mrs. Bayley colored angrily. "But they are men, and they don't think. Now, there are some very desirable people on board here, and Mr. Bayley and I could put you in the way of making some of the best of friends — the very best."

Mr. Bayley made a sudden movement, and said something to his wife of which "don't you know" was all that came to the surface.

"And at any rate," hurried on Mrs. Bayley, as she saw Phronsie's face, "you might amuse me. I am awfully *desolée*, Miss Pepper, and don't know what to do with myself."

Phronsie instinctively glanced at Mr. Bayley.

"Oh, he is no good!" exclaimed his wife petulantly; "all he thinks of is his cigarettes, and how soon he will be ashore to get to the horse-races."

"Thank you," said Livingston Bayley with a

bow, "much obliged, I'm sure. Miss Pepper, don't look shocked; it's all right, don't you know, I'm quite used to it, only I didn't think she'd ring up the curtain for your benefit." And as Phronsie made her excuses and went back, he said, "Well, that's number one, Celestine. Wonder if you'll try it again, don't you know;" and strolled off.

Phronsie was back, tucking up the steamer-rug over the thin little figure in the chair marked "Miss Pepper." "Now," she said gayly, "you are all comfortable, you are sure, Mrs. Benson?"

"Indeed, deary, I couldn't be more so," said the little old lady gratefully. "And now, don't you stay with me any more, but just go and enjoy yourself. I saw you talking with some of your fine friends just now, and you've left them to come to me. And it worries me, Miss Pepper."

"I do not want to go back," said Phronsie; "and they are no special friends of ours."

Joel came up just then, and brought a steamer-chair for Phronsie, and put her in it. He smiled at her and at old Mrs. Benson, but Phronsie looked up in his face quickly. "Joel," she exclaimed as he bent over her, "what is it? Is Grandpapa all right?"

"Yes indeed; right and sound as a nut," he said quickly. "He's deep in his book, and won't stir for an hour you may depend."

Phronsie leaned back in her chair only half-satisfied, as Joel gave her another smile and hurried off.

He didn't appear at dinner; and Grandpapa, who always ate his three meals a day on ship-board, and knew that Joel did the same, thought it odd. "Ah, Joel's knocked over," he said with a laugh, "now we'll take him down, Phronsie, for being a poor sailor."

Phronsie glanced across at his vacant place with a sigh; but she smiled cheerily to the old gentle-man, and the meal went on, old Mr. King being in the best of spirits, and the life of the captain's table.

At nightfall, as little Mrs. Benson slipped off to her stateroom, Phronsie parted with her at the door. "Now I know, deary, the Lord means me to see my old home once more. Seems as if I could smell the green grass;" she grasped the young girl's hands eagerly, and there was a world of longing in her quiet eyes. "O Miss Pepper ! there's no grass like the green grass of old England, and there's no sun like the sun that shines over old England. I've been hungry for it, dear," her voice sank to a happy whisper; "but now I'm almost there."

"Yes," said Phronsie, happy in the other's happiness, and feeling a little of her own dreadful load of suspense lifted; "we shall be in port day after to-morrow if all goes well."

"Only one more day after to-morrow," said the little old lady with a sudden cry of joy, "and I shall see my two boys. Praise the Lord! Well, will you kiss me good-night, deary, and forgive an old woman for keeping you standing so long?"

Phronsie bent over, and laid her fresh young lips on the withered cheek.

"Good-night, deary; and the Lord give you all you want."

Phronsie went back to stay with Grandpapa on deck. It was a beautiful night, and he wanted nothing so much as to pace up and down proudly with her on his arm. "It passes my mind where Joel is," he said after a little pause. "He's not in his stateroom; I went there after dinner. Sly dog! I suppose he's working off his seasickness somewhere, and hopes to keep it from us. But

we'll take the wind out of Master Joel's sails — eh,
Phronsie ; " and he chuckled at the delight in prospect over laughing at Joel's boast that he'd never
been seasick in his life, "and nothing can make
me seasick, sir ! "

" Bless the Lord, Phronsie," he lifted his sea-cap reverently, "we're
almost there."

" And now, child, I can't say how thankful I am
we're nearly across. It's been the longest voyage ;
can't help but be, when one is anxious to have it
over. But bless the Lord, Phronsie," he lifted
his sea-cap reverently and looked out into the

beautiful night, "we're almost there. And, my child," here he pressed Phronsie's arm tenderly, "I can't tell you how I feel, to see you bearing with the old man all these days, after what I've caused you. Oh, I can't, Phronsie!" His voice broke, and Phronsie could feel the thrill that went all over him.

"Grandpapa," she begged, and made him look into her face. "Why, how can you," she cried brightly, "when we're almost there? And you've borne up so well, Grandpapa dear."

"To be sure — to be sure!" exclaimed the old gentleman, pulling up his stately figure to its greatest height; "well, where do you suppose that rascal Joel is?"

It was a good two hours after when Grandpapa said, "Good-night, dear," and kissed her. Phronsie threw on her steamer-cloak, and sat down in her stateroom to wait for — she knew not what. But she must see Joel some way.

"I cannot ring for the steward, for Grandpapa will then hear me in the next room. O Joey, Joey! But I know he's not sick," went on Phronsie to herself — "by the way, he looked as if he didn't want me to question him."

Suddenly there came a little knock, and in an instant Joel was in the stateroom. Phronsie started to her feet, and took his hands.

"O Joey!" she cried, trying not to scream; for his face was black with grime, and drawn and haggard. "There, there, don't try to tell me what has happened," as he laid his head on her arm.

"Oh! I've tried my best — we all have," said Joel with a convulsive effort, and raising his head, his face working dreadfully; "but it's gained on us — the ship's on fire, Phronsie! Hush! we can keep it from Grandpapa a little longer, maybe till morning. O Phronsie!" He held her so closely that she could scarcely breathe. "It broke out in the cotton waste this morning —must have been smouldering some time."

"You have been helping?" asked Phronsie, as he paused unable to utter another word.

"Yes; took a hand at the pumps," said Joel, thinking it unnecessary to relate that he had been at them ever since.

"Oh, my poor boy!" cried Phronsie, taking his face in her hands. "Joel, Mamsie would be glad."

"Phronsie, I'm going back. It can be kept under, I think, from the worst, till morning. The people must not know, for all of us would be lost then in the row they'd make." He was whispering hoarsely, and Phronsie laid her hand over his mouth, "Hush, dear, I know," she said.

"There are life-preservers in your rooms," Joel glanced quickly at hers, "and you know how to get them on if anything *suddenly* should happen?"

"Yes, Joey dear."

"But I shall be back to you — never fear about that."

"Yes, Joey."

CHAPTER XXI.

ARE THEY ALL SAFE?

PHRONSIE thought a moment, and then said to herself, "Yes, I think I better bring her here, and then we will all be together." So slipping out of her stateroom, she went hurriedly, making her way with difficulty, as the distance was a good one, and the ship rolled badly, to old Mrs. Benson's door. "Mrs. Benson," she said, gently rapping, "it is I, Phronsie Pepper."

"Yes, deary." The little old lady was not asleep, but lay in a happy doze, in which she was living over again all the beautiful days in her little English cottage with her lads about her. "Yes, deary; I'll be there in a minute."

"Please hurry, Mrs. Benson," begged Phronsie.

"And so I will," said old Mrs. Benson; and presently she opened the door, and appeared before Phronsie in a short gown and petticoat, her white hair tucked under a frilled nightcap.

"Anything happened, deary?" she asked anxiously, looking up into Phronsie's face.

Phronsie drew her in softly to the middle of the stateroom, and closed the door. "Dear Mrs. Benson," she said, taking her hands,— "I want you to go with me to my stateroom, so that we can all be near each other."

"And so I will, deary, if you want me to," said the old woman obediently; "but what is the matter? Has anything happened?"

"Yes," said Phronsie; "but don't make a noise, for the men are working hard to save us all, and the people are not to know yet, for they would be so frightened we should all be lost." She held her mouth close to the cap-frills. "The ship is on fire!"

Old Mrs. Benson broke away from her with a deep groan, and fell on her knees by the berth. "Oh, my pretty lads, my pretty lads!"

"Mrs. Benson," said Phronsie, laying a hand on the thin shoulders, "there isn't a moment to lose, for I cannot be away from Grandpapa. I must go back at once, and you must go with me; come."

"The Lord forgive me for keeping you," said

the old lady, staggering to her feet; "now, deary, I'm ready."

"You better put your dress on," said Phronsie.

"No, deary; I'll not wait for anything, or keep you a minute longer. I'll go as I am." She glanced back around the room, as if bidding everything good-by; then picked up a little picture on the table, and tucked it into her bosom.

"We must take this," said Phronsie, pulling out the life-preserver quickly.

"Yes," said the little old woman with a shiver.

"And you better lock your door," said Phronsie, "and take the key, Mrs. Benson."

"All right, deary," said the old woman with another good-by glance. They were on their way to Phronsie's stateroom, when suddenly the cry arose, "Fire! Fire!" and a heavy body staggered by them, pushing them to right and to left, as he lunged against each stateroom door with a thud, screaming, "Fire! Fire!"

"Oh, hurry, hurry, Mrs. Benson!" exclaimed Phronsie, helping her along. The little old lady sank helplessly to the floor.

"Oh, I can't, deary!" she moaned; "it's struck me here," laying her hand on her heart.

"Then I must carry you," said Phronsie desperately.

By this time the passage was filling with smoke, and a hoarse babel of sounds, like a distant roar, broke upon their ears.

A man, one of the crew, ran by so roughly that he brushed Phronsie's cheek with his arm.

"The sailor roared out, 'The ship's on fire!' and was plunging on."

"Oh, please carry this poor woman to my stateroom!" she cried to him.

"Leave me, leave me, deary," the little old lady was saying. "Good-by, deary; oh, leave the old woman and save yourself!"

The sailor roared out, "The ship's on fire!" and was plunging on.

"I know it," said Phronsie; "oh, carry her for me, please!" The hood of her cloak fell back, and she clasped her hands entreatingly.

"I didn't know 'twas you," exclaimed the sailor, looking at her for the first time; "you're the one that writ me the letter to my folks."

"Yes," said Phronsie.

He seized old Mrs. Benson, and swung her to his shoulder, "Come," he cried to Phronsie, "they're to lower the boats; I'll save ye both."

"I must go to Grandpapa," cried Phronsie, "save her;" and dashed off by herself.

"No use," roared the sailor roughly, "you'll all be lost together. Come this way;" but he followed her with an oath, with the little old lady.

Stateroom doors were being flung open, and heads thrust out. Now and then a woman screamed, and men were shouting and cursing. And above it all that dreadful roar and the blinding smoke!

"Grandpapa! O Grandpapa!" cried Phronsie, reaching the door and kneeling at it, "O Grandpapa, please hurry, and open the door to Phronsie!"

" Leave away," cried the sailor, dropping the little old lady, and pushing Phronsie aside. Then he backed off, and dashed at the door with his fist.

"Oh, what is that?" called old Mr. King, sitting straight in his berth.

" Let me in, Grandpapa dear!" begged Phronsie.

"Er — oh — why, Phronsie, child!" Old Mr. King threw wide the door, and drew her to her feet with a hasty hand.

" Grandpapa," cried Phronsie, "there is not an instant to lose — the ship is on fire, Grandpapa. Quick! get his life-preserver," to the sailor.

Old Mr. King put up a hasty hand, "Not till you have on yours, Phronsie."

"No nonsense!" roared the sailor at him, dragging out the life-preserver to fling it over the handsome white head.

"I'll get mine in a minute," cried Phronsie, fastening old Mrs. Benson's to her trembling figure.

The rushing of feet, the babel of hoarse cries, the awful roar, and the stifling smoke made it well-nigh impossible for them to see and to hear each other. Phronsie knew that the sailor was securing a life-preserver around her; and then, above all the awful confusion, she heard a voice.

" Joel ! " she cried.

" I'll take her," cried Joel, " and the other one. Do you look out, Jim, for the old gentleman. To the boats, my man, to the boats ! "

He gathered Phronsie up, and old Mrs. Benson too, the sailor picking up Mr. King; and never any of them could tell how, but presently they were in the wild confusion of the hurrying throngs, and crowded in together at the side of the ship, where they were lowering the boats.

And here Joel leaped away.

" Stay where you are," he commanded them ; drawing his revolver as he sprang to the captain's side, who single-handed was trying to keep the half-crazed crew from leaping into the boat.

" I'll shoot the first man of you who drops into that boat," yelled Joel at the crew. In their wild fury to get first at the boats as they were lowered, they were knocking the passengers to right and left in their craze. When they saw him, and knew it was the same man who had worked at their side for nine long hours, they sullenly gave up and backed away.

"'I must go to Grandpapa,' cried Phronsie, 'save her;' and dashed off by herself."

"I think I'll go in this boat, don't you know," said a voice close to them.

"O Livingston! don't go and leave me." There was no drawl now in the shrill, thin voice. "O Miss Pepper, save me! save me!" clutching her.

"Take your hands off," roared Joel at her, pulling Phronsie away from her grasp. "No, Bayley, the women and children and old people must go first."

"Oh, mercy !" shrieked Mrs. Bayley, wild with terror; "oh, save me somebody ! I'll give any one a thousand dollars to save me," she screamed. She had her jewels in a small bag, which she huddled up to her bosom. But no one heard her, as all rushed on, trampling down the weaker ones, to get at the boats.

"Is Grandpapa in ? " cried Phronsie, as Joel lifted her high, and handed her over to Jim's long arms ahead.

"Yes, dear."

"And Mrs. Benson ? "

"Yes, Phronsie."

"O Joel — you ! " she cried as she was swung off, and felt herself drop, drop, to be caught by other strong arms. She lifted her eyes, her yellow hair streaming away from her face as she called him ; and he turned his begrimed and haggard one at her an instant as he smiled, and continued to help the women down.

"This boat is full — not another soul comes

on," cried the sailors shoving off, as a woman, more dead than alive, was dropped in.

Phronsie looked up at Joel; he waved his hand at her, and she turned and threw her arms around Grandpapa's neck.

The ship's surgeon bent over the handsome white-haired old gentleman with the young girl clinging to his neck. They had brought them on together in that way when picked up, drifting aimlessly in an open boat, the exhausted sailors drooping over their oars. He listened carefully for their breathing while he applied all the restoratives, but they seemed to have passed on over the tide together.

"Oh, my deary; let me try!" It was the little old woman whom they brought up next, sodden with the salt spray, and laid down beside them. She raised herself by a violent effort, and threw her wet hands over Phronsie's white face. "Oh, my lamb — quick, doctor, now! See, her eyes are moving — oh, my pretty deary!"

"Grandpapa," said Phronsie feebly.

"Yes, my lamb," cried old Mrs. Benson in the energy of hope; "see, she is coming to!"

But Dr. Ransom knew he had a far more diffi-cult case before him to work back the receding life into the old body; and he left her to the woman's care while he applied the restoratives to Mr. King.

" Lend a hand here, will you ? " cried Mrs. Ben-son to a woman who had not ceased to bemoan the loss of her possessions since she had been put, the last passenger, in the boat before they swept off; " do you rub her feet, while I chafe her hands — oh, my lamb ! "

" I cannot do anything," exclaimed the woman petulantly, and turning away her head, as she huddled up against the cabin sofa; " my heart is broken. I've lost all — all — and at the last some villain twitched away my bag of jewels. Oh! what shall I do ? "

" Do you talk of jewels," cried old Mrs. Benson at her, her eyes blazing underneath her white hair, " at such a time as this — oh, my lamb ! " chafing busily the cold hands.

" And I really cannot help you," whined the other, " for I am nearly dead myself."

" Grandpapa ! " Phronsie opened her eyes, and put her hand weakly up.

"Yes, yes, deary," said the old woman comfortingly. "Has he come to?" her lips framing the words over to the surgeon.

"No."

"Oh, my Lord! Yes, yes, deary. There, there, my lamb."

"Where is Grandpapa?" asked Phronsie faintly.

"He's right here, my pretty lamb," said the old woman, her hot tears raining down on Phronsie's cold face.

Phronsie gave a sigh of relief. "Joel," she tried to say, but the sounds died away in her throat.

"Oh, dear me! I wish somebody would take care of me," complained the person on the sofa. "My dear woman, now that Miss Pepper is all right, will you give me a little attention? I am wringing wet, and as cold as ice."

Old Mrs. Benson never turned her head. One of the sailors looked in. "Bring me some hot water," she said.

"Oh, my good sir!" exclaimed the other woman, springing up to a sitting posture, "will you come here? I want you this instant."

"Bring the hot water!" commanded Mrs. Benson — and he disappeared.

"I do not suppose you know who I am, you ignorant, low-down woman," cried the other passionately. "I am Mrs. Livingston Bayley of New York, now of Bayley Manor, England. Now will you cease your insults to me?"

"Any change?"

The surgeon's lips framed the word "no," as he turned his face an instant; in a second he darted back like lightning, and seized a spoonful of restorative which he held to the white lips. A long-drawn sigh, faint but distinct, was heard. Old Mrs. Benson hid her face on Phronsie's arm and cried like a child — this time for joy.

CHAPTER XXII.

THE SHADOW TURNS TO SUNSHINE.

POLLY stood by her window looking out with a happy face.

Barby glanced up from her play on the floor and saw her so, and immediately dropped everything and scrambled off, climbing a chair by Polly's side.

"Mummy," cried Barby, wriggling along till she stood on the broad window-ledge under Polly's arm.

"Oh, you dear!" exclaimed Polly, clasping her closely, and turning a happy face. "Barby, *do* you know that dear Grandpapa and Aunt Phronsie and Uncle Joel are probably safe on the other side now. *Do* you know it, Barbara?"

"You called her Barbara," said Elyot from the floor, and relinquishing the charms of a castle ready to receive its final tower, to look over at them.

"I know it," said Polly happily. "When everything is so beautiful, Elyot, I must call my little girl by her own true name — her papa's dear mamma's name. O Barbara, Barbara!" exclaimed Polly with a final kiss.

"And when she's bad, you call her Barbara," said Elyot thoughtfully.

"And that is to make my little girl grow up good and beautiful like her dear grandmamma," said Polly. "Children, you don't know how beautiful your papa's mamma was; everybody who ever saw her says so."

"She's down-stairs in the drawing-room," said Elyot, as if stating a wholly new fact for the first time; "and when I go in, I run up and kiss her dress, and say, 'How do you do, grandmamma,' and she smiles at me."

"And I say, 'Boo, grandmamma!'" laughed Barby confidentially.

"Well, if the picture is so beautiful," said Polly, "you must remember that dear grandmamma was ever so much more beautiful herself. And she was good and lovely all through, dears."

"Here comes a man to our house," cried

Barby, leaning over Polly's arms to look out of
the window.

"And I say, 'Boo, grandmamma!' laughed Barby confidentially."

"It's Mr. Ferguson," said Polly, glancing over
Barby's shoulder. "I suppose he has come out

on the early train.   Oh! your papa, dear, will
come next train, I verily believe; and then, children, perhaps he will have a cablegram from
Grandpapa and Aunt Phronsie and Uncle Joel.
Just think!"

The maid stood before her saying, "Mr. Ferguson is down-stairs, Mrs. King, and he wants
to see you at once."

So Polly put Barby down, and hurried off.
"Go back, dears," as they rushed along the
upper hall after her.

Mr. Ferguson, their next neighbor a half-mile
or so down the road, stood in the wide hall nervously twirling his hat.

"Won't you come in?" asked Mrs. King.

"N — no, I thank you," said Mr. Ferguson,
edging off to the big front door.   "I just called
going by from the train.   I thought you ought
to know, and there wasn't any time to go to
Mr. King's office and tell him."

"What is it?" asked Polly quietly.

"It's on the bulletin-board," said Mr. Ferguson, twirling his hat worse than ever — "they
were putting it out when I went by for the
train — I thought you ought to know."

Polly felt everything swim before her eyes, but she looked steadily in his face, and clasped her hands tightly together.

"It's on the bulletin-board," repeated Mr. Ferguson, "that the Llewellyn was burned at sea; but the passengers were picked up by one of the Harris line of cattle steamers," he hurried on as he saw her face, "and carried to Liverpool."

"Is that *all?*" gasped Polly hoarsely.

Mr. Ferguson looked into his hat, and then gasped out, "N — no; but perhaps it isn't true, Mrs. King. It said that the Rev. Joel Pepper was among the lost. That's all."

Polly ran through the hall, and out the side door. "*Jasper, Jasper!*" she was saying over and over in her heart, though her white lips did not move. Would she never reach the little brown house! At last she was speeding up the narrow path and over the well-worn flat stone, and through the old doorway and on into the bedroom, where she threw herself on her knees by Mamsie's big four-poster, just as she had thrown herself years ago. "Dear God!" she cried now, her face buried in the gay, patched bed-quilt, just as it had been on that afternoon so long ago, when in that darkened room, her eyes shadowed by a fear of blindness, they had told her of the worse shadow that hung over

Polly threw herself on her knees by Mamsie's big four-poster.

Joel, "make me willing to have anything — yes, *anything* happen; only make me good."

How long she knelt there she never knew. Jasper hurried through the old kitchen, and found her so. "O Polly!" kneeling by her side, he cried, "don't, don't, dear! We have each other."

"O Jasper!" Polly turned, and threw her arms around his neck, burying her face on his breast as he gathered her up closely. "I was going out to watch for you," she cried remorsefully.

"I've only just got home, and they told me you were over here. I'd rather find you here, Polly," he hastened to add, as he saw her face.

And then Polly smiled, "We have each other, and God, Jasper," she said.

"Yes," said Jasper; "and as long as I can say that, Polly, I can bear everything else."

There was a step outside in the old kitchen; Jasper sprang to his feet, Polly by his side.

"It is only I, children," said Mr. Marlowe.

So they ran out to him, getting him into the easiest chair, and trying to comfort him; for although he said nothing, it was easy to see how he was suffering. And sitting one each side, they took a hand and patted it softly between their own.

"I came as soon as I knew," Mr. Marlowe was saying quietly; "can I do anything to help? Have you wired Ben and David ? It's better for them to hear it first from you."

"No," cried Jasper, starting to his feet; "I forgot it."

"He thought only of me," cried Polly.

"I'll attend to it," said Mr. Marlowe, getting up quickly; "on the way to the train I cabled to Liverpool for full particulars."

"Oh, how good you are!" cried Jasper and Polly together.

"But they will cable you from Liverpool probably before this is answered," said Mr. Marlowe; "so keep up heart, children."

"They ?" Polly dared not even think "Father" and "Phronsie," as she clung to Jasper. "Yes, dear Mr. Marlowe," she said with a smile, as he went out.

He came striding in presently, his keen gray eyes alight. "I believe it is good," he said, handing a yellow envelope to Jasper; "this has just come."

Jasper tore it open, one arm around Polly, and together they cried, "Oh, *they're safe*, Mr. Marlowe — all of them — *Joey and all — safe !*"

Mr. Marlowe picked up the yellow sheet as it

dropped from their hands. With a glance like lightning down the page, he gave it back, and rushed off. "I'll telegraph to the boys," they heard him say, as he shot out the doorway.

Polly seized the cablegram hungrily, and dropped a kiss on it. Then over and over they read the blissful words: —

"LIVERPOOL.

We are safe. Joel and the captain and a sailor named Jim were the last to leave the ship. Joel was hurt, but not seriously. Grandpapa was exhausted, but in a day or two we shall leave for Rome. Joel insists on it. He is to stay here a little longer, at the house of a good friend, Mr. Henry Benson, thirty-seven Harley Street.

SOPHRONIA PEPPER."

"Now, you two children are going in the next boat to Liverpool," Mr. Marlowe hurried in with a smile — "if you can catch it;" and he began to rummage in the newspaper-folder behind the door. "Let's see; yes, Thursday the Abyssinia sails; day after to-morrow — plenty of time."

"But, Mr. Marlowe, I cannot be spared," cried Jasper, aghast. "And as long as everything seems to be so well over there, I ought not to leave you."

"I'm going to have my say now, Jasper," de-

clared the publisher deliberately, and drawing up
his chair to their side. "To be sure, all is right,
thank God, over there; but Polly wants to see
Joel for herself, and you need it, too, after all this
anxiety; and then you are to go on to Rome, and
look after them all there."

"O Mr. Marlowe!" Polly and Jasper turned,
and gazed into each other's faces. This was too
good to be true.

"You are sacrificing yourself," said Jasper brokenly. "Stop — don't say a word, sir, I know
just what is to be done; and my work must come
on you. No, no, it isn't right; I cannot go and
leave you; Polly wouldn't wish it under such conditions."

"No," said Polly, throwing her arm around him;
"indeed, I do not wish it, dear Mr. Marlowe. I
wouldn't go for anything."

"Listen, now, Polly," Mr. Marlowe turned his
face with a smile toward her; "you are both
like my children, aren't you?" looking at Jasper now.

"Yes, yes, we are," they both cried.

"Well, then, I'm going to be obeyed," he said,
getting a hand of each, and keeping them close.

"Now, hear me. You are wife and child and everything to me, and it is my happiness to look out for you. Don't go against my plan, children. Remember, I'm all alone in the world, and don't thwart me in this." He set his lips firmly together, while his keen gray eyes held them.

"But, sir " — began Jasper.

"No, no, Jasper, it won't do. I've planned it all coming out on the train. I can get Jacobs; he's out of a job now. He can take some of the detail work you look after, so that I shall not carry that. And I should only worry if you stayed at home. You must go." Mr. Marlowe took away his good right hand a moment from Polly's, to bring it down quickly on his knee.

"Can you get Jacobs ? " asked Jasper joyfully.

"Yes; heard so to-day. I was going to ask you if we better not secure him anyway. So you see the way is open for you to be off."

"But there is plenty more that Jacobs cannot do, Mr. Marlowe," began Jasper anxiously.

"Never mind; I shall plan it so that you're

"'Of course,' cried Polly, with kindling eyes, 'splendid old Joel
would do just that very thing, Davie.'"

not to worry. You must go, Jasper;" and looking in the resolute face with its shining eyes,
they knew it was a settled thing that in two
days, if all went well, they would be off.

And on the next day David came rushing in,
breathless with pride and excitement. "I'm going to Joel," he panted.

"Why, David," Polly cried at him, "oh, you
dear boy! Can you?"

"Can I?" cried David. "Nothing in all this
world is strong enough to keep me from him.
To think that Joel stayed till the very last. O
Polly!"

"I know it," cried Polly with kindling eyes;
"but of course splendid old Joel would do just
that very thing, Davie." She was hugging his
hands now, and laughing and crying together.
"Jasper!" she called, hurrying into the wide hall,
"David has — oh, oh — Ben!" she screamed.

"Well, well," cried Jasper running up, "you
here, Ben?"

"And David," cried Polly, quite overcome,
and laying her head on Ben's shoulder.

"Yes, I'm here, of course," said David, coming
out into the hall.

"Jasper !" cried Ben, his honest eyes shining with pride, and reaching past Polly to give him a handshake such as Ben only could give, "run your hand in my coat pocket here; there's a paper, the *Press-Bulletin* — it's all in there about Joe."

"And I have it in mine," cried David, whirling out a big journal; "here, Jasper, read mine first." He shook it in Jasper's face.

"Softly, there," cried Jasper just as excited. "Polly, hold one of these fellows — take Dave there — while I get this paper out of Ben's pocket."

"Polly read mine — read it," implored Davie. So Polly deserted Ben, and fastened her brown eyes on the sheet Davie held for her, and Jasper read his out too; and no one who hadn't learned it before could hear a word of it all, — how the Rev. Joel Pepper had worked for nine long hours with the sailors to subdue the fire; and when it was found that the ship couldn't be saved, he it was who kept by the captain's side and maintained order, so that everybody got off. And then, at the very last, those three — the captain and the Rev. Joel and a sailor named Jim — had jumped for their lives; and the cattle steamer, after picking up the boat-loads, had come to their rescue, to discover them floating on broken spars. And the clergyman was injured, but was recovering in Liverpool. And Mr. Horatio King and his grand-daughter were passengers. Oh, and it was a marvel that no lives were lost! And then followed glowing praises of Joel.

"Hear, hear!" cried Ben and Davie, pounding for order. "One or the other of you stop." And in ran Alexia and Pickering.

"Oh! what is it?" cried Alexia, rushing up to Polly.

"They are so excited they don't know what they're reading," cried Davie.

"Oh, splendid old Joel!" breathed Polly, turning with shining eyes.

"Good for Joe!" cried Jasper, beginning afresh on his column.

"Give it to me, Polly! give it to me!" exclaimed Alexia, trying to get hold of the sheet. But Polly only whirled away with it, reading happily on.

"Well, that is too splendid for anything," cried Jasper, throwing down the newspaper at last, "Oh, hello, you here, Pick?"

"So you've waked up, have you," cried Pickering, pouncing on the journal, and edging off into a corner with it. "Then I'll have a go at it myself." Alexia seeing this, deserted Polly, and ran over to him.

"Just one little teenty corner of a scrap," she said, laying hold of one edge.

"Get away," said Pickering, holding fast to it. "I can tell you so much quicker, Alexia, than you can read it."

"I'm going to have one corner," she begged. "Oh, what a mean shame!" as Pickering turned a cold shoulder to her.

"He's a shabby little beggar," said Ben, flying around suddenly to grasp the newspaper; "there, hold your hands, Alexia. I'll hold *him*."

"That's what I call taking advantage of the defenceless," said Pickering, defrauded of his paper. "Ben, you're a nice friend, to turn against me like that."

"Come over here, and I'll let you have part," said Alexia sweetly; and seating herself on a divan, she was soon reading as excitely as Polly.

"Oh! where has she gone?" she cried at last,

jumping up, and dashing the newspaper to the floor. "Where's Polly gone?"

"And Jasper too," said Ben. "Goodness me!" as the door opened, and in came Polly and the two children, Elyot hanging to his father's hand.

"I want these blessed dears to hear it — all about their Uncle Joel now, just as soon as we read it," said Polly with shining eyes. So everybody had to go all over it again, the children hanging on every word.

CHAPTER XXIII.

THE REST OF THE PEPPERS ARE OFF.

"I OUGHT not to say anything," cried Alexia, twisting around a very damp handkerchief in her nervous fingers.

"No," said Mrs. Fargo; "I don't think you had, Alexia."

"But what shall we do when this great place is empty of Peppers?" Alexia rolled her eyes up to the vaulted ceiling. They were in the music-room waiting for Polly, who had gone up-stairs for a list of people to whom notes must be written announcing her sudden departure.

"I don't want to think of it," said Mrs. Fargo helplessly; "but we ought not to say one word to let Polly see how sorry we are they must go."

"Dear me, I haven't said a word!" cried Alexia in a very injured way. "Here I've been just killing myself to keep it all in, Mrs. Fargo. I should think you'd compliment me. But no one ever does. And to think that Grace is going too. Dear me, I shall just rattle around in my old pumpkin-shell too lonely for anything."

"You must come over here, and cheer me up," said Mrs. Fargo, who was to move from the farmer's house over to "The Oaks," with Johnny, to stay till Polly and Jasper's return with the children. "Well, I'm glad for my part that Grace's mother had sense enough to telegraph back 'yes,' and that she is going; she'll see her cousin, Roslyn May, besides being with the Peppers. It will be a good thing for Grace."

"King said he wasn't going without Grace," said Alexia; "he's awfully fond of her — and I don't wonder. Oh, dear me! just think of all those children going away just as my blessed baby had got so he could talk and play with them!"

"Why, they won't be gone more than a month or six weeks probably," said Mrs. Fargo. "They can't be, for it's as much as Mr. Marlowe could do to get Jasper to go anyway."

"Well, oh, dear me!" said Alexia, beginning again on her handkerchief. "I can't do without Polly Pepper a week. We — goodness, here she comes!"

Polly came hurrying in, a long list in her hand.

"Come into the library, please," she said. "Oh, you are both so good to do this!"

Alexia sniffed softly as she followed her, making Mrs. Fargo go between; then she gave a final dab to her eyes, and resolutely stuffed her handkerchief in her pocket. "Gracious me, Polly!" she said, hurrying into a chair, and bending her head so that Polly should not see her red eyes, "that's nothing; we'll do it all — now hunt us up something else to fly at when this is done."

"There's only one thing," said Polly, "that troubles me."

"What is it, Polly?" asked Mrs. Fargo.

And Alexia forgot all about her red eyes, and raced out of her chair, to run around the big table and peer into Polly's brown ones.

"It's Grandma Bascom," said Polly. "I hate to leave her. Mrs. Higby will look after her splendidly; it isn't that; but she wants somebody to go in just as we have every day, and talk to her, and read to her, and cheer her up."

"Oh, dear me!" cried Alexia gustily, and falling back. "I can't take all your old women, Polly Pepper — and they wouldn't like me, either. They'd tell me to go out of the house."

"Oh, no, they wouldn't, Alexia!" said Polly with troubled eyes.

"Yes, they would," contradicted Alexia before she could stop herself; "they'd want to fling things at me. I don't know how to talk to horrible old women, Polly; you know I don't."

"And I'm not much better," said Mrs. Fargo, wrinkling her forehead in perplexity.

Polly stood quite still, her hand on the top of the oaken chair.

"Well, don't look like that," exclaimed Alexia, taking one glance at the troubled face, "and I'll go there every day; I'll sit on the front doorstep from morning to night. I'll do anything, Polly Pepper — Polly, did you hear?" running up to shake her arm.

"You might take Baby in with you," said Polly, turning a brightening face.

"So I could," cried Alexia radiantly. "I never thought of that. Oh! I'll go in every single day. Don't you worry about that, Polly. Promise, now."

She put her two hands on Polly's shoulders, and kissed her till Polly's cheeks were as red as two roses; then she spun her around till they both were quite out of breath.

"There, I feel better now!" said Alexia, releasing her and panting; "we haven't had such a spin since we were girls together. And to think of us two old things. Oh, dear, I've lost all my hairpins!" She put up one hand to her head, while she sank to the floor, and groped with the other under the chairs and the table.

"I think we sha'n't get this list done very quickly," observed Mrs. Fargo, writing away.

"Oh, misery me! Well, what can I do?" wailed Alexia, sitting on the floor, her bright eyes searching the carpet; "here's one — that's good, and that's another," pouncing on them; "there, I'll let the others be, and pick 'em up afterward. Here goes;" and pinning up her hair as best she could, she rushed into her seat, to send her pen scratching wildly over Polly's notes.

"Anybody would know who wrote that," she said, viewing the first one with great disfavor. "Dear me, I wish I could write like you, Mrs. Fargo."

"I write plainly," said Mrs. Fargo, well pleased at the compliment; "and that's all I can say, Alexia."

"Dear, dear! do talk," presently cried Alexia, "or I shall begin again on the old subject. Oh, good! here's Ben," as he came in.

"Writing Polly's notes?" he asked, his eyes lighting up in a pleased way.

"Yes," said Alexia, as usual answering first; "and there are such a lot of them — Mrs. Coyle Campbell's luncheon next week to get out of. I'm just finishing that, and a hundred other engagements, and all sorts of things. Go on and talk, Ben, do, about something. I'm in a bad temper enough, and I want to be amused, or I shall spoil half of these."

"What is the matter?" asked Ben leisurely, and sitting down to laugh at her. "Well, I only wish there was anything I could do to help. But I've been wandering the house over, and there isn't a thing I'm fit for."

"How's Charlotte Chatterton?" asked Alexia suddenly; "seems to me we don't hear much from her lately. I suppose you'll all find her abroad."

Not receiving any answer, she looked up, her sharp eyes resting on Ben's face in surprise.

"She's well, I suppose," he began. Alexia laid down her pen in astonishment, and stared at him. The color was in his cheeks like a girl's, and he began to fumble the little envelopes.

"Well, if I can't help, I won't at least hinder you," he said at last with a short laugh, and getting up, he went out.

Alexia deserted her chair, and ran around to Mrs. Fargo's.

"Did you see? O Mrs. Fargo! did you see?" she cried, shaking that lady's arm.

"Oh, dear me! now I've gone and put a 'g' on Mrs. Crowninshield's name," exclaimed Mrs. Fargo in vexation. "You shook me just then, my dear."

"Never mind your 'g's'," said Alexia coolly; "what's a 'g' in such bliss as this? O Mrs. Fargo, did you see Ben Pepper?" She hung over her now in great excitement.

"No; I'm sure I didn't notice him," said Mrs. Fargo, trying to erase the "g"; and making it worse, she gave up the note entirely. "And

I wish you'd go back to your own seat, Alexia," she added decidedly.

"Oh, I must tell you this!" cried Alexia; "it's my duty to, if you didn't see it for yourself, Mrs. Fargo; Ben Pepper, —don't you see? Oh, how perfectly splendid!" She jumped up, and clapped her hands in glee.

"Alexia Dodge," began Mrs. Fargo. But as well talk to the north wind.

"Don't you see, Ben Pepper is in love with Charlotte— O Mrs. Fargo! we've been blind and stupid as owls not to see it before; but then, she's been gone so long."

"I can't call you a goose, Alexia," observed Mrs. Fargo, laying down her pen in despair; "for you never were a goose, whatever else you are. But this time you've made a mistake, my dear, a very great mistake."

"We'll see!" cried Alexia triumphantly; "I shall just tell Polly to watch Ben as a cat would a mouse."

"You better watch these notes," cried Mrs. Fargo irately, "for they won't be done by the time Polly comes back;" which had the effect of sending Alexia into her chair again, where her pen fairly flew to the tune of the new thought she had gotten into her head.

Ben kept out of her way so successfully, that although she dodged after him at all sorts of times, he always slipped around some angle, or out of a door, leaving Alexia to stare at the bare walls. At last, particularly as there were many little things she found to her great delight that she could do for Polly, she gave it up in despair. And finding David alone for a moment after dinner, she besieged him with questions.

"Tell me, Davie, now like a good boy; isn't Ben going to marry Charlotte Chatterton?"

David drew a long breath; but he wasn't to be caught this way, so he said coolly, "I hope so, Alexia; can't you fix matters up?"

"Oh, you incorrigible boy!" cried Alexia; "you know the secret, I do believe, and you won't tell. I think you might tell *me*," she added wheedlingly.

"Ask Ben."

"I know he is. No need to ask him. Now, David, do you know?"

David assumed a very wise look; then he said, "You can guess at such questions if you like, but I never do. Ask me something easier, Alexia."

"Well, I think you are just dreadful!" cried Alexia in despair. "Oh, dear me, and to-morrow night you'll all be miles and miles away, and me left here without Polly!"

The next morning she turned from the small station after the cars had borne away the little group bound for the steamer. "For I can't ever bid her good-by again on the boat," she had said to Pickering. "I tried that once in the old days you know, and it made me feel a great deal worse. Come, Mrs. Fargo," she said, holding out her hand.

"Where are you going?" asked that lady, pausing with her foot on the step of the King carriage.

"Down to that old Mrs. Bascom's," said Alexia, trying to look pleasant, and hoping no one would look at her, for she was dreadfully afraid she should cry. "I must begin at once, or I never shall get there."

"You go to-day, and I will try it to-morrow," said Mrs. Fargo.

So Alexia jumped desperately into her little dog-cart, and drove furiously down to the cottage just around Primrose Lane, feeling with each revolution of the wheels how those other wheels were bearing Polly on and on, away from her.

"Come in," said Grandma Bascom, to the rap

"'She's gone; and I don't never 'xpect to live to see her again, nor him, nor those pretty creeters,' went on Grandma."

which she gave with her whip-handle on the little old door.

"How do you do to-day?" asked Alexia. Then she saw that the old lady had been crying.

"I'm so sorry for you," she cried, laying her

hand in its neat driving-glove on the poor withered one; while, — "She's gone, and I don't never 'xpect to live to see her again, nor him, nor those pretty creeters," went on Grandma.

"Oh, yes, you will!" said Alexia, gulping down something in her throat. "Well, now, Grandma, I'm coming in to see you every day."

"Hey?" cried Grandma.

So Alexia had to bend her tall figure so that she could scream it all over into Grandma's ear; and this pleased the old lady so much, to think she was going to have company besides Mrs. Higby, that Alexia in great satisfaction pulled up a chair to the bedside, and began to tell all about the getting off, and what Polly said, and how she came running back the last thing after she had bidden her good-by to say over again, "Now, Alexia, remember dear Grandma Bascom."

"Oh, the pretty creeter!" cried the old lady, quite overcome. And then Alexia rattled off what everybody else said, and how the children had each sent a kiss apiece to her, and what Ben and David did, and all about Jasper, till she was quite spent with her efforts.

"Though I don't suppose she heard more than
one word in ten," Alexia told Pickering in re-
lating the events of the day at dinner; "but
her cap bobbed all the while, and she kept saying, 'Yes, deary.' And then, when I got through,
she wanted to know what Joel did, and everything that people said about him, and the whole
thing from beginning to end."

"You better be prepared to tell that story
every day; for depend upon it, Alexia, she'll
ask you for it," said Pickering.

CHAPTER XXIV.

ALL TOGETHER.

" MRS. BENSON," said Joel, regarding her fixedly, "they used to say of me in the old days, that I was perfectly dreadful when I was sick, to make them stand round, you know, and all that. Now, I know you won't say that, will you?" he asked wheedlingly.

"I don't know," said the little old lady, shaking her head at her minister. "You do get your own way somehow or other, sir."

Joel burst into a loud laugh, then he pulled himself up.

"Jim," he said, "I'm dreadfully abused by them all, am I not, my fine fellow?" to a man in the corner.

"Hey, sir?" said Jim, coming forward.

"I say I'm most dreadfully abused," cried Joel. "Now, I'm going to get up out of this bed," giving a smart kick to the clothes.

"And I say you mustn't," cried the little old lady in alarm, and running, both hands full of dishes which she cast on a table on her way. "Hold down the clothes, Jim, that side; oh! what would the doctor say?"

"A fig for the doctor!" cried Joel with another lunge, that brought all the clothes clear away from both sides. "Now, Jim, hand me my toggery, and help me into it."

"Oh, oh!" cried little Mrs. Benson, finding the clothes twitched out of her hands, beginning now to wring them together. "What shall we do? Son Henry has gone to his store, or I'd call him."

"And 'son Henry' couldn't do a bit of good if he were here," observed Joel calmly; and, sitting on the side of the bed, he issued orders for his raiment, to right and to left, to Jim. "No, Mother Benson, I'm not going to be caught by all my family, after they cabled they were to start — why, they may be here to-morrow, and I tucked into bed like a sick baby. No, indeed, ma'am! Why, I'm as well as a fish."

Joel bared a brawny arm, and viewed it with affection, then swung it out for her to see.

"And just think, it was only a week ago yesterday, and you were picked up with a big cut on your head, and we all thought you dead for ever so long," mourned Mrs. Benson.

"Well, I wasn't dead; and is that any reason for being mewed up forever, Mrs. Benson?" asked Joel. "Nonsense! my old head is all ready for another crack."

"Heaven forbid!" cried the little old lady, stopping the wringing, to run around the foot of the bed, and take Joel's black curls in her hands and kiss them over and over.

"Such good nursing as I've had, Mrs. Benson!" exclaimed Joel, who liked immensely all this petting. "Jim, you and I will long remember this, won't we, old fellow?"

"Ay, ay, sir," said Jim heartily.

"There!" said Joel, swinging himself up to his full height at last, and marching across the room. "I'm as good as new, made over, and patched up, and warranted. Now, Jim, get me a barber, and we'll have all this mop off in double quick time." He shook back the black waves over his forehead.

"Oh, sir!" cried the little old lady in the great-

est distress, "don't touch those beautiful curls!
I wouldn't have one of 'em cut for anything."

"They are the bane of my life," cried Joel,
shaking them viciously. "You can't think how

"There!" said Joel, marching across the room. "I'm as good as
new, made over, and patched up, and warranted."

I just detest this poll of mine, Mrs. Benson.
Why that idiot of a doctor didn't shave it all,
I don't see."

"I wouldn't let him, sir," said Mrs. Benson. "And he said the cut on the head wasn't what troubled him; you were exhausted with all you'd done. It's only a wonder that you pulled through at all."

"Nonsense!" exploded Joel. "Well, now, don't you tell my family all this stuff when they come."

"I'm going to tell your family everything and all there is to it," declared little Mrs. Benson obstinately. "I'm a-going to tell them, if 'twas the last word I'd ever speak, how that precious deary took care of the old woman, and got her where she could be saved by you and Jim. And they're going to hear what *you* did, and that nothing would have been of any earthly use if it hadn't been for you. They shall hear it, every blessed word, sir. And after there wasn't so much as a rat left aboard, and you'd seen the captain and Jim off, you jumped for your life, and was struck by a floating spar. There, and there, and there!" she cried.

"Mrs. Benson, dear Mrs. Benson," began Joel.

"You won't get me to say I won't," cried the little old lady, "because I *will* tell them every single thing that you did, and what folks said, and the whole. There again, sir."

"Jim, get the barber!" roared Joel at him in great dismay. So the barber, a thin, dapper little man, soon appeared with all his paraphernalia; and presently Joel's black curls were sprawling all over the floor, little Mrs. Benson on her knees picking them up, and patting them, and doing them up in a clean old handkerchief to lay away in her lavender drawer with the rest of her treasures.

And in the midst of it all, in walked Polly and Jasper, Ben and David, while the three children were here, there, and everywhere.

And on the morrow, the doctor being obliged to say that Joel was perfectly able to go, having recovered in a remarkable manner, all the party bade good-by to little Mrs. Benson and "son Henry" and his family, and off they hurried to Rome; Jim being proud as possible — for wasn't he the Rev. Mr. Pepper's body-servant, to remain so, and go back home with them?

"I like that house," said King, looking back at the ironmonger's red brick dwelling, on the stoop of which was drawn up the little old lady

and her son the ironmonger and all his family,
" a great deal better than I do the hotel. I wish
I could have stayed over night there; it's got lots
of things in the big front room I didn't have a
chance to see."

"And oh, they're so good!" cried Polly, looking back from the carriage with tears in her
eyes. " I can never forget, Joey dear, how good
they've been to you."

" If it had not been for going there, I couldn't
have made Phronsie and Grandpapa go and leave
me," said Joel. " But dear me, Polly, that good
woman just nursed me up; you can't think how
good she was to me," cried Joel affectionately.

"I love her," broke out Barby, and patting
Uncle Joel's knee to attract his attention; " and
she's my very own Mrs. Benson, she is; and when
I go again, I shall say, ' How do you do, my very
own Mrs. Benson, and pretty well I thank you
mostly.' "

So in great glee they kept each other's spirits
up along the way. But as they neared Rome,
Polly's heart sank, and even Joel fidgeted about;
and Jasper and the " Pepper boys " had all they
could do to keep things bright and cheery. Only

now and then had it been possible to hear from
Phronsie and the others, and then but scraps of
information: that Roslyn May was mending, although the fever was not broken up; that Grandpapa was keeping bravely all his anxiety and
distress to himself; and Mamsie wrote how beautiful Phronsie was, till Joel had all he could do to
keep from crying outright. He thought he loved
Phronsie as much as he could before — they all
did; but since that night when they both faced
death, and, worse than anything that threatened
themselves, knew that it hung over dear Grandpapa, Joel's whole soul was bound up in Phronsie,
and it seemed to him as if he could never wait to
see her again. Over and over he beguiled the way
with the story of what Phronsie had said and
done on the ship all through that dreadful night,
till Polly and the boys and the children, hanging
on his words, knew it all by heart. And so on to
Rome. At last they were there.

Little Dr. Fisher, who had received their telegram, met them. He looked worn and tired; but
he mastered a cheery smile for King and for Polly
and her babies, and he wrung Joel's hand as only
he could wring it; and he said. "The fever hasn't

left him, but he's holding his own;" and that was all they could get out of him. And then they all hurried off to the hotel where Roslyn May lay fighting for his young life, and Phronsie, Grandpapa, and Mamsie were watching over him.

"Polly," said Doctor Fisher desperately, and getting a moment with her alone. "I must tell you, I think the chances are slim unless" —

A little cry broke from Polly's lips.

"Hush, Polly, my girl," warned the little doctor disapprovingly, regarding her over his big spectacles, "why, that isn't like you. It all depends on our keeping our heads, you know."

"I won't do it again, Papa Fisher," said poor Polly.

"Unless we can persuade Roslyn that Phronsie and he are not to be separated again, I was going to say," went on Father Fisher calmly. "You see, he has suffered off here alone by himself a long time — I know, because he has told me all about it; and then when he came back after Mr. King, — I don't blame your father," the little doctor made haste to say quickly, "but it was pretty tough on Roslyn, — and then when he came back to plunge into his work again after

Mr. King's send-off, why, he hadn't much strength to fall back on."

"What can we do?" asked Polly eagerly. "O papa-doctor! tell me, what can we do?" and she clasped her hands. "I'll do just anything, if you'll only tell me."

The little doctor beamed on her. "Bless you, Polly," he said, "I depend on you to do it all."

"All?" cried Polly, aghast.

"Yes," Dr. Fisher nodded briskly. "You see, — I must be quick, for that scamp of a Joe is listening with all his ears, — you see, Polly, Roslyn May has got it into his head that as soon as he is well, the old gentleman will spirit Phronsie away again."

"He shouldn't," began Polly indignantly, "when Grandpapa has brought her clear over here just to show that he has given up all opposition."

"Tut, tut, child!" said the little doctor; "you can't reason with a sick man. All I say is, that Roslyn May has got it into his head that Phronsie is to melt away in some sort of fashion as soon as he gets well; and I can't do much for him — I really can't, Polly, as long as that is in his mind." He shook his head, and looked so very dejected and miserable, that Polly's heart ached for him.

"O Father Fisher," she cried, "this is very dreadful! Oh, don't look so!" seizing his hand; "perhaps something will happen," she added, brightening up, "to make him believe that Phronsie is to belong to him."

"There's only one thing," said the little doctor; and he put his mouth to Polly's ear and whispered something. "Oh, no, no!" cried Polly, starting back, "it couldn't ever be in all this world, *here!*"

"Why not?" Doctor Fisher set his spectacles straight, and looked at her.

"Because — because, why, Phronsie should be married at home, and have the biggest wedding, Papa Fisher, you ever saw, and such a beautiful one! Oh, no, no, no, no!" cried Polly, who couldn't stop herself, but felt as if she were racing down hill, and all out of breath.

"Wouldn't it be better than not to have *any* wedding, Polly?" asked the little doctor slowly, and looking at her with his small keen eyes.

"Oh, dear me! yes, of course," cried poor

Polly in horror, and feeling as if the whole world were going awry just then. Not to have a beautiful wedding, such as Phronsie ought to have, just such an one as Polly had planned, oh, so many times in her heart, for the pet of the family! She drew away, and her eyes filled with tears despite all her efforts.

Doctor Fisher paused a moment to give her time to recover herself, and looked very grave. "A big wedding isn't the best of all blessings," he said; "and I don't believe but what Phronsie would prefer the quiet one — your mother thinks so."

"Does Mamsie think Phronsie better be married here?" asked Polly, feeling as if everybody were deserting her.

"She surely does, Polly," said the little doctor. "Well, I looked to you to influence Mr. King — but say no more," as the others crowded around.

Mamsie! oh, when Polly found herself in the dear arms, and felt the dear eyes upon her, she seized Jasper's hand. "O Jasper, we'll never let her go again," she cried, "in all this world!"

But amidst the happiness of all being together

again, Polly carried around with her a heavy heart. She knew that the little doctor was disappointed in her; and somehow, when she saw the dear Mamsie again, she felt that this disap-

"Oh, when Polly found herself in the dear arms, and felt the dear eyes upon her."

proval was shared by the one, whom, next to Jasper, she loved the best in the world. And in amongst all the delight with which the whole bunch of Peppers revolved around Phronsie, there was a little feeling of bitterness creeping up in Polly's heart, that Phronsie herself was pining for something more that they must give her.

Jasper found Polly so. "What is it, dear?"

"O Jasper! I've put it out of my head, but it won't stay out," cried Polly. "Do you think that Phronsie and Roslyn should be married here?"

"I surely do, Polly," said Jasper decidedly.

"What?" cried Polly, aghast, all her fine visions of radiance on Phronsie's wedding morn tumbling at once. "Then, let us go to Mamsie," she said humbly, "and tell her we think so. Don't let us stop to talk about it, Jasper; but we ought to go at once — this very minute."

CHAPTER XXV.

EVERYTHING DEPENDS ON POLLY.

"JASPER," cried Polly, " do let us go to Mamsie;" so hand in hand they hurried off to
Mrs. Fisher's room. But she was not there.

"Oh! now I know that Roslyn is worse,"
mourned Polly, not to be comforted; "and they
would not tell me." But Jasper said cheerfully,
"Oh, no, Polly! probably Father Fisher has taken
her out for an airing."

"Jasper," cried Polly in great remorse, "if I'd
only been willing" — she heaved a sigh even now
at the thought of what might have been Phronsie's marriage-day had all gone well, then she
put it resolutely down — " had I just been glad
to have her married here, perhaps he'd not been
worse — but now, oh, dear me!" and Polly broke
down, and sobbed on her husband's shoulder like
a child.

He patted her head softly. " Polly, hush, dear;

let us go around to Roslyn's room, and see for ourselves."

So Polly mopped her face as best she could with his handkerchief (she had forgotten her own), and away they hurried to the sick-room. There, sure enough, was Mrs. Fisher.

"Come in, Polly and Jasper," she called, as she glanced up, and saw them in the shadow of the doorway.

Polly, with her heart bounding in relief, crept in, hanging to Jasper's hand.

Roslyn looked up from the pile of pillows against which he leaned, and smiled a wan little smile that lighted up his white face.

"Well, Polly," he said, "and Jasper; so you are not out this morning?"

"No," said Jasper, seeing that Polly was past speaking; "but we shall drive to Pincian Hill this afternoon," he added cheerily. "Well, old man," going up to the couch that was drawn to the window, and taking up one of the long, thin fingers, "you'll soon be running around with us, the best one of all."

Roslyn smiled wearily, as if the effort were costing him much; then he shook his head.

"Jasper," he said slowly, "I will tell you now, — as Phronsie is not in the room, — I shall never be well.   Something will happen to separate us again."

"Nonsense, old fellow!" exclaimed Jasper, not knowing what else to say, and taking refuge in those words.   "Why, Grandpapa is willing now, you know, for you to marry Phronsie, else why would he bring her?   You're blue, Roslyn; that's all."

But Roslyn shook his head, and reiterated, "Something will surely happen to separate us again."

Meanwhile Polly was clutching Mother Fisher's gown.   "O Mamsie!" she cried, "do come out of here; I must talk to you."

"'Must' will have to give way now, Polly," said Mrs. Fisher, quietly going on with her work of preparing a gruel by a spirit-lamp over in a corner; "for this ought to be done first."

"Oh, do forgive me, Mamsie!" cried Polly, dreadfully ashamed of her abruptness; "I did not notice what you were doing.   But as soon as ever you get through with that, do, will you, please, then come where I can talk with you."

Mother Fisher gave her a keen look. "Yes, Polly," she said, "I will, unless some other duty comes in between." So Polly was forced to wait as patiently as possible until the gruel was done. Meanwhile she clasped her hands tightly together, while Jasper and Roslyn talked; afraid all the while that she should show her increasing dismay, as certain bits of the conversation fell upon her ears.

At last the gruel was fed to Roslyn, his pillows shaken up, and Dr. Fisher coming in, Mrs. Fisher turned to Polly.

"Jasper," said Polly, holding out her hand.

So the two followed Mother Fisher into a smaller apartment that opened into the sick-room, and Jasper closed the door softly; while Polly threw herself down on the floor, and buried her face in Mamsie's lap in the old way.

"Now, what is it?" asked Mother Fisher, smoothing Polly's hair, as Jasper came and took a chair next to the two.

"O Mamsie!" cried Polly brokenly, "I do want Phronsie not to have the beautiful wedding at home, but to be married here. And do forgive me," went on poor Polly, "for not wanting it before — it's Jasper now who has shown me how wrong I've been."

"O Mamsie!" cried Jasper, who held Polly's hand in both of his; "indeed, she decided this herself. This is all Polly's own idea."

"He said he thought Phronsie ought to be allowed to have the wedding here, when I asked him," said Polly; "then I knew at once how selfish I'd been."

"Don't say selfish, Polly," begged Jasper.

"Polly," said Mother Fisher, and her face lightened, "I do think you have saved Phronsie from terrible sorrow; for if you can persuade Mr. King to let her be married here, — and no other person can do it I'm very sure, as Phronsie won't speak, — you'll see Roslyn well again. And nothing else will bring him up, the doctor and I both think."

"I persuade Father King!" exclaimed Polly, raising her head in dismay to look first at Mother Fisher and then at Jasper. "Oh, I never could in all this world!"

"I imagine you could for Phronsie," said Mrs. Fisher slowly.

"But he has just brought her clear over here

at a dreadful sacrifice to his feelings," went on
Polly in greater dismay; "and then to be teased
and urged to let her be married, and in a plain
little way, here — oh, I can't do it!"

" 'Can't' is a word that you ought not to spell,
Polly," said Mother Fisher gravely.

Polly shivered, and shrank down again into
Mamsie's lap. "Oh! I know you've been disappointed in me, Mamsie," she cried, "because I
didn't want Phronsie to lose the beautiful marriage-day we all want to give her at home."

"Yes," said Mrs. Fisher slowly, "I was disappointed, Polly."

"But Polly has come to see it all right now,"
cried Jasper eagerly, and pressing Polly's hand
comfortingly.

"I am glad of that," said Mrs. Fisher, still
smoothing Polly's bright brown hair.

"I'll do it," said Polly at last, with a gasp, and
getting up to her feet. Jasper put his arm around
her, his eyes saying, "I wish I could help you,
Polly."

"Polly better do it alone," said Mother Fisher,
"and at once; for Mr. King is in his room
reading."

So Polly, feeling scarcely less miserable than she was before, since now she must inflict a great blow on dear Grandpapa, went slowly out into the hall, and on her errand.

Old Mr. King, as usual, was in a terrible state over the newspapers. A little pile of them lay before him on the table waiting to be scanned, while he fumed and fretted over the one he held in his hand. Polly felt, as she obeyed his "Come in" to the timid rap she bestowed on his door, as if the worst time in all the day were chosen to proffer such a dreadful request. And for a moment her heart stood still, and she did not attempt to enter.

"Come in," commanded the old gentleman in such a dreadful roar that Polly trembled in every limb, while he marched across the long apartment and threw the door wide open. "Why in the name of all that's sensible, don't you — oh, my goodness me, Polly child!" and he drew her in.

He trembled inwardly as much as she, but with difficulty controlled himself to lead her to a seat. "Now, then, Polly, my child, what is the matter? Tell your old daddy." Then, his fears getting the better of him, he broke out, —

"You've brought bad news. Roslyn is worse;" and started for the door.

"Grandpapa — father dear," cried Polly, flying after him.

"Oh, it isn't that! It's — it's — I've come — to — to ask you —"

Old Mr. King stood in front of Polly waiting for her to proceed.

The old gentleman led her back to her seat with a puzzled air, and stood in front of her waiting for her to proceed; then, seeing that she made no headway, he exclaimed in displeasure, "Why, Polly, am I so very dreadful that you cannot come to make a simple request of me without all this fear?"

"Oh! it isn't a simple request, dear Grandpapa," said Polly, clasping her fingers nervously as she realized that all this was only making matters much worse for Phronsie and for Roslyn; yet for her life she could get no farther than "it's — it's " —

Old Mr. King took a turn or two down the apartment, then came back to her with such a displeased countenance as she had never seen him wear before; at sight of which Polly forgot all the attempts at a proper introduction to her plea, and crying out, "O father, dear! do let Phronsie and Roslyn be married here; for Dr. Fisher thinks he won't get well unless you do," she threw herself into his arms, and sobbed like a child.

"Is that all!" exclaimed Mr. King, patting her brown hair.

"All!" cried Polly, taking up her head suddenly to look at him; "all, Grandpapa! *Are* you willing?" she gasped.

The old gentleman smiled down at her. "Child,

I'm not only willing, I'm glad," he said. "Did you think I'd no more sense, Polly, than to make my little girl any further trouble? They shall be married to-morrow if they want to be. Now send Phronsie here to me, just as quickly as you can fly for her," he commanded, in such a merry tone that Polly laughed in glee. Seeing which, as it was what he had aimed at, he got so very cheery as he escorted her to the door and saw her down the hall, that she ran off on light feet. "Tell her to hurry," called old Mr. King as a last word before she disappeared.

"Why, man alive!" said little Dr. Fisher, left alone with his patient, "I tell you, you are in a fair way to recovery, if you only think so." He set his big spectacles straight on his nose, and glared at the white face on the pile of pillows in what he meant to be a reassuring way.

Roslyn May shook his head, and clasped his long, thin fingers together.

"Dear me!" exclaimed Dr. Fisher, as he felt something coming in his eyes that caused him to pull out his big handkerchief, and blow his nose violently. "You are the last man I should expect to preach pluck to. You've had a double

allowance of backbone all your life, I take it,"
he added with a short laugh.

"I used to think that I was the possessor of
one," said Roslyn, weakly smiling.

"Land alive!" cried the little man, delighted
at the smile, and getting cheerier than ever.
"You've set us all an example in grit and en-
durance. Now, don't be like a cow that gives a
good pail of milk and then kicks it all over,"
and he laughed again. "That's New England
advice; you know I was raised on a farm," he
added.

"I've had my death-blow in this fever," said
Roslyn, the smile dying all out, and turning his
face on the pillow. "We shall only be separated
again; for Mr. King will never" —

The little doctor sprang to his side. He had
fainted. And in the next few days, when the
fever came back again, each one looked into the
other's face with despair. All except Phronsie
herself.

"Oh, I can*not* endure it!" It was Charlotte
Chatterton who said this. Charlotte, who had
just come, walking in suddenly, with no word of
greeting, or expecting any. She just went up to

Mother Fisher, and put her two hands into the firm ones extended.

"Hush!" said Mother Fisher through white lips. "You will say something you will be sorry for afterward, maybe, Charlotte."

Charlotte bit her lip. "Let me help; give me something to do," she begged. "No, I don't want to go to Phronsie yet; it would kill me to see her suffer. I can*not* bear it, dear Mrs. Fisher."

"Charlotte, could you leave your lessons?" asked Mother Fisher suddenly.

"Yes," said Charlotte, "it was no use for me to stay away; I got so nervous I couldn't sing; and even Herr Mericke said I best take a little time off, and come and see for myself how you were getting on. And then Ben's last letter told me that things were worse than you had reported. And so here I am;" and she drew a long sigh.

"Charlotte, you don't know how I have wanted you," said Mrs. Fisher, drawing her to her side.

"Have you?" cried Charlotte delightedly. "Oh! if I had only known how badly things were going, I should have dropped everything and come before."

"That is precisely the reason," said Mother

Fisher, "why I wouldn't let you be told, Charlotte."

"Where's Charlotte?" asked Phronsie, hearing some one call her name in Mamsie's room.

"You needn't see her, dear; Charlotte will wait. Do, Phronsie, try and get some rest," said Polly.

Phronsie, in her soft white wrapper on the sofa, got up and went to the door. "Is she in Mamsie's room?" she asked.

"I'll call her," said Polly, "if you'll only let me tuck you up on the sofa again, Phronsie."

"Yes, I will, Polly," said Phronsie, obediently going back, "if you will only call Charlotte in."

So Polly tucked her up, and then ran into Mother Fisher's room. "Charlotte, you're to come," she said, picking her by the sleeve.

"Oh, I can't!" cried Charlotte, edging off toward Mother Fisher.

"But you must," said Polly imperatively, "for Phronsie has sent for you."

"Charlotte," said Mrs. Fisher, with a smile at the tall girl, "I'll trust you."

So Charlotte went off, with her heart warmed, into Phronsie's room; and Polly left them together,

and ran away to comfort old Mr. King, who nowadays would hardly let her out of his sight.

"O Charlotte, how good of you to come!"
cried Phronsie, putting up her lips to be kissed,
as Charlotte went unsteadily over to the sofa.

Charlotte kneeled down by the sofa, and got
tight hold of Phronsie's hands, mumbling something, she couldn't have told what, determined
she wouldn't break down.

"Charlotte," said Phronsie very earnestly, "you
are not to feel badly for me, because I almost
know that Roslyn will get well. I almost know
it, Charlotte."

Charlotte gave a deep groan, and slid down to
the floor, where she sat, hanging to Phronsie's
hands.

"God has kept him for me," Phronsie went on;
"and he has brought us through just everything,
Charlotte, and he is going to let Roslyn get well,
I know. And now I want you to help to make
the others feel so too. Will you, Charlotte?"

But Charlotte couldn't speak. So Phronsie
said, "I am so glad you have come, Charlotte;
for you can help Mamsie to see it—that Roslyn
will get well. Poor Mamsie is so tired too."

Charlotte buried her face in Phronsie's soft wrapper, and her shoulders shook with her efforts not to say anything that she "was to be sorry for afterward."

"And Polly is worrying," said Phronsie as a matter of deep confidence, and a troubled look came over her face.   "O Charlotte! if you can only help Polly not to worry, it will be just beautiful in you.   Will you, Charlotte?"

Again Charlotte could not speak.   "Charlotte," said Phronsie gently, "I wish you would let me see your face."

Charlotte brought her head up suddenly.   Both cheeks were very red, and her lips were pressed tightly together.

"Charlotte!" exclaimed Phronsie with a sudden fear; "are you sick?"

"No," said Charlotte explosively; "but I am afraid I shall say something I ought not.   O Phronsie, if I only *could* help you!"

"You can," said Phronsie quietly.   "And O Charlotte! I am so glad you are not sick;" and she gave a relieved sigh.

"I can't be any help to anybody," declared Charlotte, "except to work.   I can work, if there's

anything to do, Phronsie; but as for influencing
any one, or helping them to believe anything, I'm
good for nothing."

"Charlotte," said Phronsie affectionately, "you
help me ever and ever so much. And so you do
help every one of us. And I will tell you what
you can do for me now. Will you sing to me,
Charlotte, just those soft little things you used to,
and hold my hand; and I shall go to sleep."

So Charlotte grasped the edge of the sofa
tightly with one hand while Phronsie held the
other; and sitting there on the floor, she sang over
and over the things that she knew Phronsie
wanted.

"Charlotte is singing to Phronsie," cried David,
rushing into Grandpapa's room, where Polly and
Jasper sat with old Mr. King. "Mamsie said I
was to tell you, Polly, so you needn't worry, for
now she will go to sleep."

CHAPTER XXVI.

DESTRUCTION THREATENS THE LITTLE BROWN HOUSE.

"NOW," said Mr. Tisbett, "see here, young man, ef you're a-goin' to ride along with me, you've jest got to set still. My senses, that ma of yourn would give me fits ef anythin' was to happen to you; though why she should, I don't see."

"Let me have the whip," cried Johnny, wriggling for the possession of that article.

"No, you don't!" declared Mr. Tisbett. "Whoa, there!" this to his horses. "Now, that Mis' Lambert wants to go to th' deepo, I'll be bound," pulling up to a big white house a little back from the road. "Yis'm," as a handkerchief waved frantically out of one of the small-paned windows.

"I want to go to Hubbardville, Mr. Tisbett," said the woman who held it.

"Well, if you're a-goin' to Hubbardville," observed the stage-driver, whipping out a big silver watch, "I take it you better be steppin' lively, Mis' Lambert. I'm on my way to th' deepo now, an' I don't come back this way."

"Mercy me!" exclaimed Mrs. Lambert, darting away from the window; and in a minute or two she came out, catching her paisley shawl by its two ends to tuck them under her arm, while she endeavored to pin her bonnet-strings.

"Susan," she called over her shoulder to some one in the entry, "I've forgot my bag." Then she took out one of the pins which she had hastily put into her mouth for just such emergencies, and pinned up the long ribbons that might be said to have seen better days.

"I wish folks would be ready when they hail th' stage," observed Mr. Tisbett to Johnny, not careful in the least to lower his voice from his ordinary tone. Then he roared out, "Come, Mis' Lambert, I shall have to go without you."

"I'm coming!" said Mrs. Lambert quickly.

"Your bonnet ain't on straight, ma," said Susan, coming with the bag to the doorstone.

Mrs. Lambert put up both hands, and twitched

it the wrong way, thereby letting the paisley shawl slip to the ground.

"That's worse than 'twas before!" exclaimed Susan, giving the bonnet a pull that carried up one set of her mother's puffs as neatly as if she had been scalped, and sent a side-comb flying to the ground.

"Never mind," said Mrs. Lambert, putting out her hand for the comb, and beginning to look around for the shawl. "There, fling it on my arm; I c'n put it on in th' stage."

Mr. Tisbett rattling his whip against the dashboard, she stepped off the stone at the same minute that Susan twitched the puff into place. "You tell your pa he'll find his clean shirt an' stock on th' bedroom bureau," she called, looking back, "this aft'noon."

"Yes," said Susan.

"An' don't forgit th' meat bilin' in th' pot."

"No," said Susan.

"Air you goin' to git in?" asked Mr. Tisbett sarcastically, by this time holding the stage-door open, "or air ye goin' to hold conversations only? Please let me know, ma'am, for I'm goin' to start this ere stage."

Here was Johnny's opportunity. He seized the whip, and brought it smartly down on the off horse, with the result that Mr. Tisbett was laid flat on his back on the roadside, — round went the wheels, up flew the horses' heels, and, in a cloud of dust, Johnny was driving down the turnpike.

"Th' stage is goin'!" exclaimed Mrs. Lambert, starting in dismay, and huddling up her bag and shawl in a small heap together on her arm; "now I sha'n't get to Hubbardville. Oh, be you hurt?" as Mr. Tisbett picked himself up, and plunged down the road after his vehicle.

He roared to some farmers at work in a field to help in the chase, pointing frantically to the lumbering stage ahead; but they had already stared at it, and now stopped to listen to him without stirring a muscle, as he dashed on. The only thing he could think of by way of possible comfort, was that the horses, through force of habit, might take it into their heads to go straight to the depot, which proved to be the case; Johnny being so paralyzed with the grandeur of driving, that he held the reins steadily all the way.

The only passenger in the stage, a woman with

a big bandbox, got out more dead than alive, as
the horses swung up to the little station; and
the men collected there waiting for the train
to come, wrenched Johnny, notwithstanding his
howls, from his seat and down to the platform.

"Who is that boy?" demanded the passenger
when she could get her breath.

"He b'longs to Mrs. Fargo, one o' th' rich folks
that's stayin' here this summer," said one man,
rolling his quid over to the other cheek.

"Rich, is he?" the woman set down her bandbox, and advanced to Johnny. "Well, I'm goin'
to shake that boy, 'cause I know his folks won't;
an' I want to see it done." And before any one
could put up a hand, she seized Johnny's sailor-
collar, and shook him smartly. Then she picked
up her bandbox, patted out her dress in satisfaction, and sat down to wait for the train.

Mr. Tisbett, running along quite blown, came
up just then, as Johnny ran to the woman.

"You shook me," said Johnny, with blazing
cheeks.

"I know it," said the woman grimly; "an' if
I had time before the train comes, an' wasn't so
beat out with th' shock, I'd do it again."

Johnny clinched his small hands, and beat the air fruitlessly. "I'll tell Mr. King," he howled.

"Hey? What's that you say?" cried the woman.

"I'll tell Mr. King," screamed Johnny, quite red in the face.

"What's that boy got to do with the Kings?" said the woman to Mr. Tisbett; "hurry up and and tell me, 'cause the train's comin'. Mercy! I wouldn't 'a' shook anybody they know, for nothin'."

But there was no time to explain; and she was helped on the train, with her bandbox, saying the last thing, "I wouldn't have shook him for nothin', if I'd known" —

There was only one passenger for Mr. Tisbett's stage, — an old colored woman with a big-figured lace veil over her face and a variety of bundles. The stage-driver settled her and her belongings within the vehicle, then he turned off for Johnny.

"Yes, sir-ee!" dragging him along by his big collar; "you're goin' to set inside, after that 'xploit. Now, marm," as they reached the stage, "will you have the goodness to keep an eye on that boy," hoisting Johnny in; "an' where do you want to stop?"

"To Mr. Jasper King's," answered the woman. "Land! but ef here ain't Johnny Fargo! I done am s'prised" —

"O Candace!" screamed Johnny, tumbling all over her, "did you bring some red-and-white drops?"

"Yes," said Candace, "I did; but they's fer" —

"Look out for him!" screamed Mr. Tisbett, clapping to the door to fly to his seat. Then he gave the horses their heads, and presently swung up to "The Oaks" in his usual fine style; for nothing but the best flourish would satisfy him there.

Candace got out of the stage as leisurely as she could, with Johnny hauling at her, and insisting that he must carry all the bundles; and Mr. Tisbett drove off toward Hubbardville.

The big mansion was very still as Candace waddled up the carriage drive, with Johnny spilling portions of his armful as he went along, and then hurrying back to pick them up. "Land!" exclaimed Candace, toiling on, "if I ain't glad to get here to see my bressed folks an' s'prise dem. I hain't slept a week o' nights sence dey done lef dere ole home. Whew! Ise all out o' bref."

"We don't want to buy anything," said one of the maids coming out to the side porch, and looking at the big bag on the old colored woman's arm, Johnny being back of the evergreens around one of the curves, picking up the last article dropped.

"Who's asked yer to buy anyting?" demanded Candace in scorn, and seating herself on one of the steps, utterly unable to go farther. "Yer speak to Mrs. Jasper King as quick as you kin, or to him."

"Mrs. Jasper King isn't home. They aren't any of them home; they've gone abroad," said the maid.

"Whar's abroad?" screamed Candace, letting her bag roll out of her hands to the ground.

"Oh! over to England; and then they were going to Rome," said the maid coolly.

"O my bressed chilluns!" mourned Candace, swinging her heavy body back and forth on the step, while she wrung her black hands. Johnny staggered up with all the parcels.

"It's Candace," screamed Johnny. "Hannah, don't you know, she lives where I do when I'm home, and where Mr. King used to live before he came here. Now will you give me some red-and-white drops?" He deposited all the bundles on the floor of the porch, and hugged up to the big black figure.

Hannah ran to call Mrs. Higby, who sent her

"'O my bressed chilluns!' mourned Candace."

for Mrs. Fargo; but she had gone over to Grandma Bascom's, it being her morning for that duty, so the maid hurried down the lane to the little cottage. "O Mrs. Fargo!" she exclaimed, hurriedly entering. "Oh! where is she?" as the old lady sat up against her pillows, the only occupant of the room.

"Hey?" said Grandma.

"Where is Mrs. Fargo?" called Hannah excitedly.

"I can't hear what you say," replied old Mrs. Bascom, putting one hand behind her ear.

"I say I want to know where" —

"No, I don't want anythin'," said Grandma, dropping her hand, and settling back into a good position again. "I'm pretty comf'able this morning, Hannah."

"Do you know where Mrs. Fargo went to?" cried Hannah in a loud, excited key, and running everything together. "When did she leave here?"

"Hey?" cried Grandma.

So Hannah had to shout it all over again, till she was quite exhausted; then she began to content herself with one word, "Fargo," which she said over and over.

"She's just gone," at last said old Mrs. Bascom.

"Where?" cried the maid, her mouth close to the old lady's cap-frills.

"Down to th' village to get me some med'-

cine," said Grandma. So Hannah flew out and over home, and Mrs. Higby sent one of the men in a pony-cart for Mrs. Fargo. By this time Candace was in a truly dreadful state with longing to see the face of this old friend. As that lady used to go with members of the King household to the little shop on Temple Place, the poor old black woman thought if she could only catch a sight of Mrs. Fargo, she would somehow get nearer to her "bressed chilluns."

"How she does act, doesn't she, Mrs. Higby?" cried Johnny, who now gave up all thoughts of the red-and-white drops, and crowding up to compass as much of this new excitement as possible.

"Hum! I don't know as she's any worse actin' than some other folks not a thousand miles away," said Mrs. Higby. "Well, I wish to goodness your ma would come;" and she hurried to crane her neck out of the window. "Now, thank fortune," she cried joyfully, "here she is! Now, Johnny, you run off an' play, that's a good boy," as Mrs. Fargo hurried in.

Johnny, thus dismissed, ran down the terraces, and over in the direction of the little brown house. He was never allowed to go in it without a maid, but this morning he determined to peep in one of the windows, "Just to see if everything's there," he said; and then, after that performance was over to his satisfaction, he began to play that he was really going in, and that he lived there, just as the little Peppers had told about so many times. And then he tried every door; and at last, to his astonishment, found the one in the "Provision Room" unlocked, as a careless maid who had been cleaning there that very morning, under Mrs. Higby's direction, had left it.

"Oh, goody!" cried Johnny gleefully, racing in; "now I'm a little Pepper. I'm Joel — no, I don't want to be Joel. I'm David — no, I don't want to be David, either. I'll be Ben — I'll be Ben and Joel and David and all of 'em," he declared, hurrying around. "Now, what shall I play first? I'll — I'll " —

His eyes fell on the stove. "I'm going to have a baking-day all to myself!" he cried in joyful tones, and capering in the middle of the kitchen. "Oh, won't that be fine! And when they see what splendid cakes I can bake, they won't care. Phooh! I can make better things than any of 'em, I b'lieve. And I know how to make the fire too."

He was now so busy that the old kitchen presented the appearance of being the scene of the
most active operations of a dozen small boys, as
he brought flour, trailing it all over the neat floor,
and sugar and molasses from the buttery, leaving
a chain of sticky drops everywhere he stepped, to
run and get the rolling-pin and handsful of dishes.

"I better make my fire first," he said in the
midst of this, and dropping everything where he
stood. "Now I must get the paper and the
wood;" and he scuttled off to the "Provision
Room" to bring them in. Then, stuffing them
into the stove as tightly as he could cram them,
Johnny backed off, and surveyed his work in great
pride.

"Now, I know where the matches are kept," he
cried in a jubilant voice — "in the little blue dish
on the shelf;" so pulling up a chair, he soon had
them in his hand, and drawing one as he ran back,
he had a merry little light that made him crow
gleefully.

"There, now, sir-ee!" he cried, holding this to
a bunch of paper that stuck up one end out of the
stove; "you'll burn, I guess, when *I* get hold of
you. Yes, sir-ee!" but the fire running down the

match-end and nipping his fingers, he twitched them off, to wipe them hastily on his blouse; what there was left of the match tumbling down back of him, in a small heap of paper and shavings that wouldn't go into the stove.

Johnny rubbed his hands together joyfully, and hopped up and down before the stove. "Oh, what cakes I will bake!" he cried. "And perhaps I'll put white on top of some of 'em; I haven't decided yet. And I'll make a gingerbread boy — I'll make a dozen gingerbread boys — I'll —

Just here his little legs felt warm; and he backed off from the stove and whirled around to cool off a bit, to see the heap of papers and shavings on the floor, in the merriest little blaze imaginable, while one small tongue of flame reached out and licked his blouse.

Johnny gave one scream and rushed out; the little tongue of flame persisting in staying on his blouse, while the other little flames left behind in the old kitchen, every second growing big and strong, were having a jolly time of it.

"*Fire!*" screamed Johnny, leaving wide the "Provision Room" door as he bounded off across the lane.

Johnny whirled around to see the heap of papers and shavings on the floor in the merriest little blaze imaginable.

"Hillo!" cried Patsy, who came around the palings to look at him, but not hearing what he said as he rushed madly off for the terraces. "Oh, murther — murther!"

He cleared everything between Johnny and himself by one or two bounds, and soon had him rolling over and over on the grass. "Now, to make *absolutely* sure," said Patsy at last, "I'm going to turn the hose on ye. Been building a bonfire somewheres, I s'pose."

"There's more of it in there," said Johnny, and finding his voice to point a shaking finger in the direction of the little brown house.

"Where?"

"There."

No need to ask now. Smoke was coming out of the little brown house "Provision Room" door. Patsy yelled "*Fire!*" as loud as he could scream, and dashed down to it. In less time than it takes to tell it, every man on the place was busy, working with a will to save the little brown house. The big mansion was deserted of all. Even Candace forgot her misery and desolation, to waddle as fast as she could to the scene, wringing her hands and crying as she went.

CHAPTER XXVII.

PHRONSIE'S MARRIAGE BELLS!

OH, the dear, precious little brown house! How they worked — every man, woman, and child on the place — to save it! There was no time for the fire-department down in the village to get there, although the private alarm from "The Oaks" was sounded. What was to be done, must be done quickly; and everybody took hold and did the thing that seemed nearest and best.

Mrs. Higby passed pails of water as rapidly as if her hands and feet were young; preferring the old-fashioned ways of putting out a fire to the long lines of hose that the stable-men soon had in and around the little brown house. Candace, who immediately found that when she could work for her "bressed folks" she wasn't lonely, waddled in and out, carrying everything she could lay her hands on, out to the grass

in safety, despite the fact that she was invited
several times by the workers who didn't know
her, to "get out of the way."

"Git out ob de way, you'd tell me, pore w'ite
trash, you!" Candace would mutter to herself
at such times, smothering her wrath as best she
could till she was sure the little brown house
was safe; then she would teach these servants,
one and all, that she was "a relict," and had
lived with Mr. King's folks long before they
were born. "Tink dey kin teach *me*," fumed
Candace under her turban, waddling on fiercely.

And after the last vestige of the dreadful
flame was out, and the smoke cleared away, it
was found that nothing was burned that would
bring sorrow to one of the "Five Little Peppers."

Mamsie's rocking-chair, in which she used to
sit in the old days, sewing the coats and sacks
to keep the wolf from the door, was carried out,
the little old cushion blazing at one end; but
quick hands had beaten out the fire, so this was
saved. And though the fire had run along
the trail of shavings and paper dropped from
Johnny's armful, as he carried it in from the
"Provision Room," strange to say, beyond mak-

ing dreadful black marks on the old kitchen floor to show its progress, and the scorching of the cupboard door, no damage was done. And then everybody drew a long breath, and stopped working, to gaze into each other's faces; for the little brown house was safe!

And just then up clattered the village fire-department, and right back of them appeared Alexia, who, coming out of the post-office to drive to "The Oaks," when told the news, made her pony run at top speed, so that she reached the scene almost at the same moment.

Patsy, who always ran to Mrs. Dodge's aid, saw her first, and tore across the lawn, to catch the reins as she flung them to him.

"Is it the little brown house?" gasped Alexia, not daring to look in that direction, as she jumped out.

"Yes, ma'am," said Patsy.

"Is it gone? all gone?" she screamed. Then she sat right down on the bank, and burst into tears.

"No, ma'am!" cried Patsy; "sure it's not."

"Not out? Oh, dear, dear, dear!" cried Alexia, waving back and forth in distress: "it will kill

them all. We might as well all be dead as to
have the little brown house burnt up. Oh, dear
— dear — dear!"

"'We might as well all be dead, as to have the little brown house
burnt up,' said Alexia."

"It's there!" cried Patsy, extending all the fingers of one hand to point at it; "a-standing just
as nice and"—

Alexia sprang to her feet, and seized his arm. "Patsy!" she cried, "do you mean to tell me that if I turn around I shall see the little brown house the same as ever?"

"Yis'm," said Patsy; "if you opens your eyes you will."

Mrs. Dodge whirled around and took one look; then she sped on light feet over the terraces and across the lawn.

"She rins like a birud would fly," said Patsy, watching her; "dishdainin' the ground like"— then he hopped into her cart, and drove it around to the stables. "If ye could turn yere hose onto that boy as did it, it ud be a blessing," he said to the firemen.

"Don't say a word," said Mrs. Higby, flushed and anxious, "Johnny's badly burned; and you must run for Dr. Porter, Patsy."

"Burned is he?" cried Patsy, and his face fell; for Johnny was a great favorite of his, despite his words; and he rushed off in Mrs. Dodge's pony-cart.

Alexia, after first satisfying herself by investigation that the little brown house was really safe, and that the precious things huddled out on the grass were not all burnt up, rushed off to find some one who could tell her all about it. The first person she ran against was Candace.

"Oh, my goodness me!" cried Alexia gustily; "how did you get here, Candace?"

"It's a mercy I did come," said Candace, not stopping to answer the question; "for I don' know wot dey'd done widout me. Wy, *I* brung out mos' o' dem tings," sweeping her black arm over toward the household treasures on the lawn. "I brung de little cheer, an' de "—

"Yes yes," said Alexia. "Well, how *did* it ever happen?"

"An' I brung de tea-kettle an' de plates an'"—

"Yes, well, never mind those now!" exclaimed Alexia impatiently; "do tell me, how did it ever happen?"

"Chile," said Candace, "nebber min' how it done happen — de ting now is, who had sense enough to 'tend to gettin' out de tings. Wot dey'd done ef I hadn't a-come I d'no eber in all dis worl'"—

"Hannah!" cried Mrs. Dodge in despair to the maid hurrying by, "do you know? Tell me, how came the little brown house to be on fire?"

"Johnny Fargo went in and played making a fire," said Hannah.

"Johnny Fargo! Oh, the little scamp!" cried Alexia; "now that boy ought to have a good drubbing," she cried, quite beside herself.

"There can't anybody give it to him," said Hannah, hurrying on, "because he's burnt, and the doctor's coming."

"Oh, the pore leetle lamb!" exclaimed Candace, raising her black hands; "now I must nuss him. He was so good to bring up my passels, an' to wait on me in — well, well, I d'no know wot dey'd have done ef I hadn't 'a' come;" and she waddled off, Mrs. Dodge closely following, remorsefully determining to do everything in the world now for Johnny instead of the drubbing.

And so it turned out that the two letters in her pocket she had just taken out of the post-office when she heard of the fire, remained there forgotten until the doctor had dressed Johnny's burns and gone, and she had Mrs. Fargo on the sofa in Polly's room, where they had fled for refuge.

"There, now, you ought not to cry, you know, Mrs. Fargo," she said. "Oh, dear me! what would

Polly Pepper say to you if she were here ?   I'm good for nothing; but you really ought not."

"Oh, I cannot help it!" cried Mrs. Fargo, deep in her handkerchief. "My poor little boy ! and then to think of that precious house — why, if he'd set this one on fire, it wouldn't have been one-half as bad."

"Well, it didn't burn up," cried Alexia, twitching her sleeve, "so what's the use of crying now. Oh, dear me — why, here are the letters !" and she tore them out of her pocket.   "One for you, and one for me — from Polly !" and in a minute she was deep in hers.

Mrs. Fargo, just commencing to read the heading of her own letter, heard a funny little sound ; and glancing up, saw Alexia making every effort to speak, her face working dreadfully.   The letter had fallen from her hands to the floor.

"Oh ! what is it ?" cried poor Mrs. Fargo, feeling that this day must be bewitched, and dreading she knew not what; and she jumped up, too frightened now to cry, and ran to Polly's toilet-table for salts.

"Read — read — your letter !" gasped Alexia.

"Oh, I can't, if it's bad news!" cried Mrs. Fargo,

shrinking and trembling. "Where are they—oh, here!" She brought the bottle of salts, and held it to Alexia's nose.

"Phronsie Pepper is married!" cried Alexia, twitching away her head.

"*Phronsie Pepper is married?*" repeated Mrs. Fargo blankly.

"The very day that Polly wrote," declared Alexia tragically; then she made a dive for her letter on the floor.

"Read it, Alexia," begged Mrs. Fargo, "for I can't;" and she sank down on the sofa, and wound her arms around Mrs. Dodge.

"And I'm sure I want to hold on to somebody too," declared Alexia. "Oh, dear me, Mrs. Fargo, to think you and I won't ever see Phronsie married! Oh, dear, dear!" and the tears of vexation sprang to her eyes. "And it will almost kill Polly not to have the wedding here—and all the hosts and hosts of friends Phronsie Pepper has, and—what shall we do?"

"We can't do anything," breathed Mrs. Fargo; "it's already done—do read it all," she added faintly.

So Alexia dashed ahead,—

"'HOTEL COSTANZI, ROME, *July*, 18—.

"'DEAR ALEXIA, —

"'You are to be very glad to begin with, at the piece of news I shall tell you right away. And that is, that Phronsie was married this morning to Roslyn May.' —

"Glad! Indeed I'm not!" cried Alexia; "to go and steal such a march on you and me and all her piles of friends, Mrs Fargo — and *such* a wedding as we'd have given her."

"The precious dear," murmured Mrs. Fargo. "Go on, Alexia."

Alexia sniffed off two or three disappointed tears, and rushed on, —

"'It was just this way. You see, Roslyn, poor boy, got it into his head that Grandpapa would separate them again, though of course that was the fever, and because he had suffered so much since he had last seen Phronsie; and although he got better, and it seemed as if he were coming up finely, he brooded so over that idea that Papa-Doctor got quite in despair. And then Father King' —

"Can't you see Polly's face when she is going to tell something splendid about Mr. King," cried

Alexia, glancing down the page. " Oh, dear me!
— where was I," going back again, "oh, — 'and
then Father King was just royal! He told
Phronsie that all he cared for was to make her
happy, and that nothing would make him so
happy as to have the marriage take place here;
and they were just going to tell Roslyn, when
Papa-Doctor sent them word that Roslyn was
worse. And then those were just dreadful days;
for the fever came back, and Phronsie smiled
when we looked troubled at her; but she was
just like a shadow — so thin and so white. O
Alexia, I can't bear to think of those days!
Charlotte Chatterton came from Germany, and
she was such a comfort; but we all just clung
to each other in despair. Only Phronsie kept
saying she knew Roslyn would get well.'

"This is very dreadful," sniffed Alexia, wiping
away the tears furtively. At last she just let
them rain down. "I'm a miserable, selfish little
pig," she said, "not to be glad to have her married there."

" O poor Phronsie!" sighed Mrs. Fargo, "and
poor Polly, and all."

" ' And — and ' " went on Alexia recovering

her place in her letter, "'and one day when everything seemed the blackest, and as if we couldn't bear it another minute longer, Roslyn came up again. And then Grandpapa told him how everything was to be as he wished. Well, from that moment, Alexia, the world was bright again, and the sun shone, and we all were as glad as glad could be: and Roslyn just adores Grandpapa. You can't think how devoted they are to each other. And so everything was quickly arranged — for who do you think should drop down suddenly but Roslyn's father, General May! Now, wasn't that perfectly lovely! I always suspect that Father King sent for him, though he doesn't say so.'

"Just think how all those people had Phronsie to themselves," mourned Alexia, who, now that Roslyn was mending, returned to her own grievances. "And Grace Tupper too — she was at that wedding; and Pickering and you and I, Mrs. Fargo, left out in the cold."

"I know it," sighed Mrs. Fargo; "well, go on, Alexia."

"Oh, dear me! well, where was I? Oh — 'and so this morning Phronsie and Roslyn were mar-

ried. Roslyn was very weak; but he was lifted
out of his chair, and insisted on standing dur-
ing a part of the ceremony. And Joel married
them beautifully. And Grandpapa gave Phronsie away.'

"Oh dear, dear!" screamed Alexia, quite carried out of herself, "why *couldn't* we have been
there!

"'And Roslyn's just as beautiful and splendid,
and he's my brother now,'" Polly's letter went on;
"'and I'm so happy, Alexia, about it, you can't
think. And Phronsie wore one of her white
muslin dresses, and carried the white prayer-book
that Roslyn gave her; and she was married with
his mother's ring he had worn all these years.
And Roslyn looked like one of the pictures of the
young gods, he was so handsome; and Phronsie
— well, she was our Phronsie! Oh! and Roslyn's
work, begun in his studio, is considered most remarkable. He is surely, so we are told on all
sides, to be one of the foremost sculptors of
the age. And you can't think how proud Grandpapa is of him!'

"'And now, you poor dear! I know how badly
you feel not to have Phronsie married at home.'"

Alexia gave a deep groan, as if words were beyond her.

"'And that you couldn't even see her married. Well, now, Alexia, Phronsie wants me to tell you a piece of news, a secret just yet, only for you and Pickering and dear Mrs. Fargo to know. Roslyn and she are to live in the little brown house; and he is to build a studio in the meadow back of it, and not go to Rome only once in a while, when they want to travel. Did you ever hear of anything so splendid!'"

Alexia squealed in delight; then her sallow cheek turned quite white. "Mrs. Fargo," and she clutched that lady's arm, "suppose, only suppose for an instant, that it had burned down this morning!

"'And we are to give her and Roslyn the most beautiful marriage reception. Oh, you can't think how beautiful it will all be at "The Oaks" when they come home'—

"Oh!" squealed Alexia, again seizing Mrs. Fargo by the arm; "now, you and I will have our good time, won't we, for being cheated out of all the rest? It's too splendid for anything! Mrs. Fargo, I never thought of the welcome-home party we could give them! Why, that will be almost as good as having Phronsie married here;" and she jumped off the sofa, and began to pirouette around the room. "But how can we ever plan it with Polly away?" and she came to a sudden stop, her brow wrinkling in perplexity.

"You better finish your letter," advised Mrs. Fargo. "Polly probably has something to say on that point. Then you can jump, Alexia, all you want to."

So Alexia flew back to her letter. "Where was I? Oh — at ' "The Oaks" when they come home. We are coming first, Jasper and I, with the children and Grace, who has been the dearest little comfort in all this world. Joel and David, of course, must get back as soon as possible, so they are coming with us. Ben will stay with Mamsie and Dr. Fisher, and Grandpapa and Phronsie and Roslyn, a few weeks longer; and then they will all come home together, and bring Charlotte Chatterton with them.'

"Oh, goody, goody!" exclaimed Alexia, beating her palms together in joy. "And I'll venture to say that then you'll see I'm right, my dear Mrs. Fargo, about Charlotte Chatterton and Ben."

"Maybe so," said Mrs. Fargo wisely. "Well, is that all?"

"Um — um — let me see," said Alexia, whirling the letter again; "yes, except — 'I have written a letter with all these details to dear Mrs. Fargo — and I know you go to see dear Grandma Bascom every day, Alexia; and do tell her all this that I have told you, and that, please God, we shall be home, the first party of us, very soon now. And then, dear, won't you and I plan for Phronsie's home-coming!'

"Won't we, though!" cried Alexia with shining eyes. "Well," drawing a long breath, "I must hurry off and tell Grandma Bascom all the news; and then, says I, I must let that blessed baby know all about it."

CHAPTER XXVIII.

HOME TO THE LITTLE BROWN HOUSE.

POLLY and Jasper and the children were home once more, and everything was back in the old ways, with Joel in his parish, and David in his instructor's chair at the college. And now an intense excitement filled all the minds of the "Peppers" and their friends over the approaching "Welcome Home" they were to give Phronsie.

"It shall be just as splendid as the wedding would have been!" declared Alexia positively. "Just as bride-y and stunning as it can possibly be!" she would cry, on one of her rushing-in-and-out visits to "The Oaks."

"Do tell me, *are* the Dunraven Home children surely to be here?" she asked one day, bursting into Polly's room, to find her surrounded by a cloud of white muslin, and clashing her scissors in and out of little skirt breadths. "Oh, my goodness me! what *are* you doing, Polly Pepper?"

"Yes," cried Polly happily, and sending her scissors down another breadth; "and these are their dresses, Alexia. Don't you want to get another pair of scissors, and help cut off the skirts? Miss Bangs down in the village is going to make them."

"Yes, indeed!" cried Alexia, plunging over to Polly's neat work-basket. "Oh, dear!" as she rummaged it; "I can't find another pair, Polly!"

"In the sewing-room," said Polly, fluttering the cloud busily, to measure another breadth.

"I'll set that basket to rights when I come back, for I've messed it up dreadfully," cried Alexia, flying off, to return with a pair which she brandished high. "Oh, dear me, Polly Pepper, will you ever in this world get through with all you've on your hands, I wonder! How many Dunraven youngsters are coming?"

"Twenty," said Polly, her head on one side, calculating; "that is, Mrs. Henderson thinks that it is safe to plan to bring as many. And Susan is really to sing a Welcome-Home song, as they march around Phronsie and Roslyn."

"Oh, how perfectly sweet!" breathed Alexia, already deep in the cutting-off process. "Dear

me, how do you keep yours straight ? Mine all
skews up."

"You better draw a thread, then," advised
Polly; "unless you can follow your eye."

"My eye is as crooked as can be," declared
Alexia; "I'm in such a twitter. Well, isn't it
just too lovely that Susan is really to sing.
Phronsie will be delighted. Dear me, don't you
remember how Susan roared that first day she
came, and how she looked — little black image, I
can see her now, sitting up there on a cricket on
the platform. I was frightened to death, and expected she'd break the whole thing up; and now
how good she is, and quite the pride of Phronsie's
heart."

"Oh! it will be a perfect surprise, I think,"
hummed Polly ecstatically. "Oh! and the village
children are going to be at the station when the
trains gets in, with baskets of flowers, and throw
blossoms in Phronsie's path."

"Are they?" cried Alexia in delight; "oh,
my!"

"Yes, they've begged to," said Polly; "and we
are going to let them do whatever they wish.
Phronsie belongs to them too, Alexia, you know."

"Yes, I know," said Alexia.

"Polly!" called Jasper, over the stairs.

So Polly threw down the muslin cloud, and ran to meet him.

"Here's Mr. Tisbett wants to say something," said Jasper with a smile. "Now, then," to the stage-driver, "say just what is on your mind, Mr. Tisbett."

"I want to know," began Mr. Tisbett, shuffling uneasily from one foot to the other, "'hem — if you'll let me drive Miss Phronsie an' her husband home here from the deepo?"

"I don't understand," began Polly.

"In the stage, ye know," said Mr. Tisbett. "If ye could now let me, I'd be 'bleeged to ye. Seems if 'twould set me up fer th' rest o' my life. I want to do somethin' fer that blessed child I've seen grow up from a baby;" and he covered his face with his big hand.

"And so you shall!" cried Polly, seizing his other horny palm, and ashamed of herself for the dismay that swept over her at this plan, that would deprive Jasper and her from driving Phronsie and Roslyn up to "The Oaks." "Indeed, it is lovely of you, Mr. Tisbett, to think of it;"

which thrilled the honest stage-driver with delight to his finger-tips.

"An' I want to hev the priv'lege to drive yer par up too," said Mr. Tisbett, turning to Jasper a face covered with confusion. "Land, but when I think how I shook him up that fust time he ever come here, — an' I can't never forget it, — I want to do somethin' fer him too."

"Father forgot all about that a long time ago, Mr. Tisbett," said Jasper simply, "and so must you."

"Land, but you can fergit a thing teetotally when you're the one it's done to," said Mr. Tisbett, scratching his head awkwardly. "Well, if he'll only fergive me enough to let me drive him up too, I'll be mortally obleeged." He peered anxiously into Jasper's face.

"I can answer for father," cried Jasper heartily; "that he'll be glad to have you drive him up here, and it's very kind of you to think of it;" and he shook the honest stage-driver's hand so cordially that Mr. Tisbett shambled off delightedly.

And the old church where Phronsie had gone since babyhood, and Mr. Henderson had preached so long, was to peal its new chimes for the first

time when she came back to Badgertown again.
This the people had begged.   The meeting-house

"' An' I want to hev the priv'lege to drive yer par up too,' said
Mr. Tisbett."

was still standing it is true; but it had been
Mr. King's work, when he gave up his old home

to be with Polly and Jasper, to make it just such a church as Badgertown had longed for.

Oh, and Grandma Bascom was to be brought over in a chair, and have the seat of honor on the lawn; for this was to be an out-of-door *fête* for Phronsie, when the day after the arrival the wedding-party at "The Oaks" would take place, to which all Badgertown was invited, in addition to the hosts and hosts of other friends.

And the Beebes and Mr. and Mrs. Babbidge and the "Scrannage girls," all had very especial invitations; Miss Sally composing a neat little piece that would tell Mr. King how thankful they were for the old home saved to them, and that would supplement nicely Miss Belinda's stiff note, written after the first shock of finding the check was over. For the old Scrannage pride had somehow melted away, in a fashion that probably would have surprised the old squire, who had not much else to hand down to them but his crotchety disposition and the mortgage. And Bella Drysdale was invited to stay a few days with Grace, who was in the seventh heaven of delight that Phronsie Pepper was now really her cousin.

And dear Mrs. Beebe had a pretty new cap that had a great deal of pink ribbon about it, that Phronsie had bought abroad for her, and sent home by Polly.   Barby and Elyot begged so hard to carry the box containing it down to the little shoe-shop, that they were bundled into the pony-cart one fine morning, and Johnson took them down, each holding fast to the box between them. And old Mr. Beebe protested, at the trying on that began at once, that he never had seen a cap in all his life that was so beautiful nor so becoming — oh! and the shops in the village were all to be closed on the day of the *fête*, so that everybody, old as well as young, could be at "The Oaks." And the long supper-tables were to be set on the upper lawn, and the lower as well, where the terraces ended; and the little brown house, filled like a very bower of flowers, would be open from morning till night to guests — for was not this to be Phronsie's own dear, sweet home?

Oh! and the ground was broken a little distance off in the beautiful old meadow, where the "Five Little Peppers" used to play when any moments in their busy childhood allowed; and there, near the old apple-tree, was to be laid the corner-stone — a beautiful block of marble from Roslyn's Roman studio — of the new studio that was to rise very soon. And this was to be put in place on the *fête* day.

Was there anything that was beautiful and bright and joyful that was not to be crowded into that blessed day?

And Johnny Fargo, his burns all well, after many repentant talks cuddled up in Polly's lap, was comforted. And one day he tugged in a poor, lean cat, found nobody knew where. "She'll like it," he said stoutly, "when she comes home; and I shall give it to her."

And every farmhouse dotted here and there around the hill that overtopped Badgertown Centre had letters from city folk for the next two weeks, to know if they would take boarders about that time, and there wasn't a farmer's wife who said "No." And the hotel in Hingham had all it could do to get ready for the friends who were going there. And the steamer was hurrying over the sea, that was bringing Phronsie and her husband, Grandpapa, Mamsie, little Doctor Fisher, Charlotte Chatterton, and Ben.

At last the day arrived, one of September's most golden ones, when Mr. Marlowe telegraphed, "Steamer in. Take the 12.10 train for Badgertown." And all the good old town, in waiting for this same beautiful message, hurried to the little station, at the signal from the church chimes.

The schoolma'am down at the little schoolhouse on the road to Spot Pond dismissed her scholars instantly on the first note, and tied on her bonnet, locked her door, and put the key in her pocket, to hurry off with the rest.

Over the roads to the little station they came by twos and threes, and in wagons and carryalls, and everything that could be drawn by a horse. And down around the hill wound an ox-team or two; and every child held a little nosegay — and then there were the flower maidens, gay with their baskets of blooms. Oh, old Badgertown was in its gala dress! While as for the small station, when they arrived it looked like a flower-garden indeed!

"How can we ever wait, Jasper?" cried Polly, the color flying in and out of her cheeks, as they found their way out, from among the groups of waiting people, to the end of the platform; "isn't it almost time they should be here?"

"Almost," said Jasper with shining eyes, and looking at his watch for the fiftieth time; "only ten more minutes, Polly, and the train will be due."

"Ten horrible minutes!" cried Polly, wrinkling her brows. "O Jasper! keep me off here, or I shall disgrace myself before Barby and Elyot. They are so patient," with a glance in their direction.

"Good reason why," said Jasper with a laugh; "they've all those flower-girls and nosegay children to supervise. See! they are in the very thickest of the crowd, Polly."

"Well, they must come with us," said Polly in a tremor, "or they'll lose the first sight. Oh, do bring them, Jasper!"

"And Johnny and King," cried Jasper, flying off. "Here, you children, the whole bunch of you, this way!"

But Barby and Elyot, deep in the charms of the Badgertown children, were so excited that they did not hear. "I'll get 'em," said Johnny running up; and immediately he dashed off and

flushed and triumphant, brought the two little
Kings.

"Children," said Polly with a happy ring in
her voice, "you'll lose seeing Aunt Phronsie and
Uncle Roslyn come in if you do not stand close
by papa and me. Thank you, Johnny," with a
bright smile to him "for telling them."

"And I'll get King now," cried Johnny, his
little heart bumping with pleasure that he had
helped Mrs. King. "Hooray, here, King!" and
he flashed off at a sight of him in one of the
groups, while Barby and Elyot, aghast at what
they might have missed, clung close to Polly's
hand.

Just then up stepped the first selectman, and
touched his hat, "We've arranged a place for you,
Mr. King and Mrs. King and family," he said,
"if you'll come this way." And he led off im-
portantly through the groups of townspeople, to
whom Polly nodded happily and Jasper raised
his hat, to the other end of the platform. And
there, on a staging a little higher than the platform, and trimmed about with evergreens and
flowers, was a little waiting-place reserved for
them.

"Oh, how perfectly lovely, Mr. Bunce," cried Polly, "for you to do all this for us!"

"It is so good of you," said Jasper heartily.

"Ye can see the train come in around the curve," said Mr. Bunce straightening up, with conscious pride in every feature of his face. "And the conductor's goin' to stop it right at this pint. Glad you like it all, Mr. King," he said; "th' s'lectmen'll be pleased."

"Indeed, how could we help it!" cried Jasper with feeling. "We shall never forget all that you have done this day, Mr. Bunce."

"When'll the train come!" begged Barby, pulling the first selectman by the arm; "say, when will it? I want it very much, I do."

"Oh, you'll see her a-comin' around that curve pretty soon," said Mr. Bunce, taking her soft little palm in his stubby one. "Look sharp, now!"

So Barby stood on tiptoe, and Elyot and the other boys did the same.

"I'll get you a chair to stand on," said Mr. Bunce, hurrying into the station to bring one out; then he put Barby on it. "And now I'll get Rev. Mr. Pepper and Mr. David, for you want to be all together;" and he shambled off, Elyot and

King and Johnny swarming upon the chair to look over Barby's fat little shoulders.

"I don't believe it will ever come," began Barby, as Joel rushed up and swung her to his broad shoulder with Elyot on the other, and David hoisted King. Johnny stuck to the chair, when — "Here it comes! *Here it comes!*" and all the white handkerchiefs came fluttering out, as the country folk hurried up; the children with the flower-baskets, drawn up in two lines, gathered their hands full of pretty blossoms; the old stage, decked with garlands and festoons, with Mr. Tisbett resplendent in his Sunday clothes on the box, drove up around a waiting corner with a flourish, to the platform front. And there was Phronsie and Roslyn! and old Mr. King, his handsome white head bared to the sun, was bowing to right and to left, while Mamsie and little Doctor Fisher, with Ben and Charlotte Chatterton brought up the rear.

And then arose a mighty cheer from the throats of the village people! And the flowers were strewn, and the little nosegays were thrown, and the whole bunch of Peppers, big and little, passed up through the blossom-covered path. And Phron-

sie was helped into the old flower-decked stage
right gallantly by Grandpapa, who turned, and
bowed low to the Badgertown people. "I thank
you, my dear friends," he said, "for this tribute
to the one whom we all love." And then Jasper
said something to him in a low voice. "And
thank you, Mr. Tisbett," said old Mr. King, his
hat still in his hand, and he put up his other
palm to grasp that of the stage-driver's, "for asking me to drive up too."

Mr. Tisbett thought he should fall off from the
driver's box with pride and delight after that.

And then away — Phronsie smiling into the
faces of the village people, and Roslyn, tall and
handsome beside her, bowing his thanks for this
tribute to her. Was there ever such a home-coming before?

"Now, if it won't rain," gasped Alexia, on the
edge of it all, "to-morrow, O Pickering!" as they
ran for their dog-cart, and drove off to "The
Oaks," by a short cut.

"Never you fear, Alexia," said Pickering; "and
if it does, nothing can spoil this Badgertown welcome. It was the finest thing possible."

"That may be," said Alexia; "but 'The Oaks'"

fête to-morrow — that will be *absolutely* perfect.
Do hurry, Pickering; we must get there to see
them drive up."

And it not only did *not* rain on the morrow,
but was another golden day for Phronsie. The
arches were all up on the lawns at an early hour,
and so was the marriage-bell of white orchids;
while the Dunraven children were in readiness
to march, to be followed by Susan's "Welcome-
Home" song. The rose-trimmed tables couldn't
take on another blossom; while as for the little
brown house — well, it was a bower of roses, from
the old front door clear through to the "Provision
Room."

And Phronsie, in her soft white gown trimmed
with white orchids, and her tall young husband,
destined to be so soon famous, moved around with
old Mr. King to all the groups, welcoming and
making happy every one — for it was to be an
all-day *fête*, with music and games for the little
ones, and flowers, collation, supper, and wedding-
cake for everybody.

And Jasper was toast-master when everybody
was seated at the long rose-trimmed tables, and
right royally did he manage that ceremony. And

Mr. Bunce, the first selectman, responded for the town of Badgertown, covering himself with glory; and Grandpapa responded for Phronsie right gallantly. And then she rose in her place by her husband, in the centre of the table, and Roslyn stood by her side. "I thank you all very much," said Phronsie in a clear voice, "for all you have done for us. We shall never forget it. And we love you very much indeed, and we are glad to make our home here with you in dear old Badgertown."

And then everybody got out of their chairs, and waved their handkerchiefs, — a white, fluttering cloud, — and tears of joy were on many cheeks; and then Roslyn May was called on for a speech, and a splendid one it was too, that all the village folk cheered mightily. And Mr. Mason Whitney and Mr. Marlowe spoke, and Ben and David, and there were many calls for Joel. And Pickering Dodge had a word or two to say; and Rev. Mr. Henderson, oh! — "it was a goodly wedding-breakfast, and," as Alexia said, "just *absolutely* perfect."

"Oh, dear, dear, dear!" she gasped to Mrs. Fargo, after the feast was over, "it seems as if I couldn't

"The little children from the Dunraven Home marched around Phronsie and her husband, each giving her a white rose as they passed."

bear any more bliss. But do look at Charlotte
Chatterton and Ben. Now will you tell me there
is nothing in it?"

"I didn't say there was nothing in it," said
Mrs. Fargo with a keen glance at the two.

"But you were cool as an oyster when I tried
to tell you about it long ago," retorted Alexia.
"Oh, dear me! — well, we mustn't stand here talking; they are going to dedicate the studio now,
and lay the corner-stone."

And when this was over, and the block of
marble from Roslyn's studio from across the sea
was laid in place on the old Badgertown meadow,
to be made famous over two continents, then, at
a signal from Rev. Mr. Henderson, the little children from the Dunraven Home marched around
Phronsie and her husband, each giving her a
white rose as they passed. And Susan sent all
her young heart into her "Welcome-Home" song;
and everybody applauded her, but she saw only
Phronsie's smile.

"Whoever would have thought that little black
creature, that terrorized us all so that Christmas
Day at Dunraven, would turn out such a beautiful singer?" said David.

"A good many things turn out differently from what we expect," said Mamsie with a smile, "and that's the best of it."

Joel looked into Amy Loughead's blue eyes, "Yes, that's the best of it," he said.

Well, the best of all this beautiful *fête* was yet to come. It was at sundown, when some of the people, those who had far to drive, were beginning to talk of going home, and were gathering up their little children and saying "good-by." Jasper called "Attention!" and announced that his brother, Mr. Roslyn May, had something to say to them all. So they turned back where he stood with Phronsie by his side in the centre of the lawn; and when the large circle was formed, and all was quite still, he said in a strong, clear voice, —

"My wife wishes me to tell you that she desires to mark this beautiful day by a gift to the people of Badgertown, to show her love for you all. She has therefore asked her brother Jasper to buy for her the Peters homestead, and all the land belonging to it, and to keep this purchase a secret until to-day. Added to this, she presents to the town this check," he held it aloft, —

those who were nearest could see that there were several figures upon its face, — "that a free library may be built and maintained, imposing only one condition, and that is, that the name of the library shall be the 'Horatio King Library of Badgertown.' Mr. Bunce, as first selectman, will you take charge of this bit of paper?"

Didn't the people cheer then! The echo of it seemed to reach to Badgertown's very centre. And some one ran down and set the church-bell to ringing again, a merry peal. And with those joyful notes in their ears, the country folk drove home to their farmhouses, casting many a backward glance at the "Five Little Peppers," and the little brown house, over which the golden gleams of the setting sun were falling.